ALSO BY CANDICE

THE INHERITANCE SERIES

Rewriting Yesterday

https://books2read.com/u/3JVj6v

In this Moment

https://books2read.com/u/bxvnJd

The Promise of Tomorrow

https://books2read.com/u/bowEy1

THE FOUR HORSEWOMEN OF THE APOCALYPSE SERIES

The Pures

https://books2read.com/u/mdGl1y

For my Son
You will always be the hero of my story.

CONTENTS

Chapter 1	1
Chapter 2	9
Chapter 3	21
Chapter 4	31
Chapter 5	43
Chapter 6	69
Chapter 7	87
Chapter 8	107
Chapter 9	117
Chapter 10	137
Chapter 11	159
Chapter 12	173
Chapter 13	191
Chapter 14	209
Chapter 15	241
Chapter 16	249
Chapter 17	265
Chapter 18	287
Acknowledgments	313
About the Author	315

CHAPTER ONE

My grandpa always told me there were times in our lives where we should stand and fight and there were times when we should run and hide. Running when you knew the odds were stacked against you didn't make you a coward, it makes you smart. This is one of those times.

I'm wearing little silver ballet flats and a knee-length navy blue sundress with spaghetti straps. Although the dress does amazing things for my legs, it doesn't give off a particularly intimidating vibe. Not that a five-foot woman with white-blonde hair in crazy ringlets and blue eyes that are a touch too big for her face could ever really be described as intimidating. Badass maybe, but not intimidating. The hulking biker chasing after me certainly doesn't seem to find me intimidating in any way.

The gorgeous huskie beside me is keeping pace despite

the pain he must be feeling from the swift kick to the ribs he received earlier. A kick which ultimately led to my current predicament.

LET ME BACK UP A BIT. My name is Luna Cartwright. I'm twenty-eight years old and I was born to two awesome parents, James and Kate, who were the very definition of hippies. Now, before you laugh at my name, you should know I have two older brothers named Ziggy and Cosmic. Yep, you read that right, Ziggy and Cosmic. I happen to love my name, largely because I know it could have been so much worse.

The five of us lived in a tiny town in Ireland, just outside Dublin, up until the summer I turned eight. That's when both of my parents were killed in a car accident, leaving my brothers and myself in the custody of my wonderful, yet slightly insane, grandpa.

Gramps was a retired Vietnam War vet who lived on a farm deep in the wilderness of Tennessee. My mother had left home as soon as she could get her student visa and study abroad, which is how she met my father. But me? Well, I loved it here. We were taught to hunt and shoot and tend the farm and I was treated just like one of the boys. In fact, the only girly thing I owned until I was about seventeen was a box of tampons. When I was eighteen, my brothers enlisted, so I decided to move closer to the city. That's where my love of all things girly came from. Seeing shop windows filled with everything from beautiful dresses and intricately designed underwear to soft fluffy throws and pretty trinkets meant my little studio apartment had looked like the center page of a women's magazine. But it was also how my business got started. I began to make custom gift baskets as presents for my friends and family—baskets full of goodies for moms-to-be or bottles, blankets, and bibs for baby showers.

When Gramps got sick, I moved back in with him, staying by his side until his frail body eventually gave out. By then I had my own website and, although I still deliver the odd thing personally, most of my stuff is shipped online. There are even a couple of shops in the neighboring towns that have started stocking my goodies.

This is how I accidentally met my furry friend beside me. I have, as a general rule, no sense of direction and without the use of GPS, I'm pretty sure I would have ended up in the wrong state a time or two. I was making a delivery to a cute little shop that had opened in Neavsham, which is a twenty-minute drive from where I used to live, when I got turned around and my GPS decided to have a meltdown on me. Even with my lack of direction, I still managed to figure out pretty quickly that four lefts had me turning in a circle. After a fair bit of cursing, I had pulled over next to a large industrial building that was partially hidden by trees, to text Megan, the shop's owner, when I became aware of a dog whining. I got out of my truck and followed the noise until I came upon a huge white and gray huskie on the other side of a six-foot chain-link fence. He heard my approach and growled at me a little, not in an I'm-going-to-rip-your-arm-off kind of way, more in a back-off-and-leave-me alone-I'm-having-a-shitty-day kind of way. I sat on the grass on my side of the fence, pulled some beef jerky out of my pocket (don't judge) and poked a piece through the fence for him. He whined a little but wandered over, scooped up the jerky, and lay down right in front of me. In a moment of bravery or stupidity, I stuck my fingers through the fence and started stroking his beautiful coat until his tongue lolled out and he was panting. That day I fell a little bit in love with him and anytime I was in the area making deliveries, I came to visit.

That's how I happened to witness a tall wiry man with a pockmarked face and long greasy black hair kick the shit out of the poor dog when he hadn't respond fast enough to the asshole's commands. I felt my blood boil beneath my skin. No way was I going to leave him there to be subjected to that kind of treatment. I made my delivery to Megan's and then asked her if I could leave my truck there for a little while. She kindly agreed, so I pulled wire cutters and old gloves from the toolkit in the cargo bed, courtesy of my brothers, and retraced my steps on foot to save my furry friend. It was getting late by the time I got there but he was waiting by the fence, sitting in the humid evening heat when I returned, like he knew I was coming for him, and my heart melted a little more. Using the cutters, I made an opening in the fence big enough for him to get through without scraping himself on any sharp edges, when I heard a shout from the side of the building. I dropped the cutters, urged the dog through the fence, and then I took off like a shot through the woods with my escaped prisoner.

Which brings me to now—huffing, puffing, and stumbling over the uneven terrain as I run blindly through the woods in ballet flats. Not my finest hour, for sure. Out of nowhere, I find myself wrapped up in leather-encased arms and pulled back hard against someone's chest. The dog snarls ferociously at my captor but calms when the voice behind me, with a Texas drawl, tells him to settle.

I wiggle and kick my legs, trying to gain some leverage, but with my arms pinned to my sides, my movements are limited.

"Settle down, sugar," the deep voice rasps out.

His arms are firm, his grip strong, but he isn't hurting me. He isn't using more force than necessary and he isn't trying to grope me in the process, so I calm myself down and take stock of the situation. I have always been able to read people, ever since I was a kid, and something is telling me this guy isn't going to hurt me. He loosens his grip as he feels me relax and leans down to speak softly into my ear.

"Want to tell me why you're stealing our dog?"

I'm about to answer him when the pockmarked asshole who started this whole thing by kicking the dog comes running toward us. He must have circled around and come from the other direction.

"You fucking cunt," he shouts. He surprises the shit out of me and the biker at my back by swinging his arm out and slapping me across the face with the back of his hand.

Now, let me tell you, that shit hurts like a bitch. Before I can even get my bearings, I find myself facing the burning deck of cards logo on the back of biker man's jacket as he places me behind him. Before either of us can say or do anything else, though, my furry friend is on the pockmarked biker, dragging him to the ground, pinning him with his teeth in his shoulder and growling a warning that if he moves, he's dead.

I smile as my face throbs, taking a small amount of satisfaction from the fact that the dog now has the upper hand. The biker that grabbed me calls him off, unfortunately.

"King, heal," he commands.

King, huh? Great name. It suits him. Oh, right, focus.

King obeys immediately, clearly trained and familiar with my pseudo protector.

Biker dude steps forward, then bends down and, I kid you not, he picks up the pockmarked asshole around the throat like he weighs nothing. If I wasn't so busy looking for a way out of this mess, I would be totally impressed. Okay, so I'm still a little bit impressed.

"Do you want to tell me what the fuck you think you're doing?" he growls—the biker, not the dog.

"That bitch stole our dog," the idiot with the hand wrapped around his throat manages to reply, which is actually quite impressive as his face is turning an alarming shade of purple.

"You never put your hands on a woman in anger, you

piece of shit," my biker tells him. He pulls back his right arm while still holding with his left and sucker punches the guy in the face. The pockmarked ass drops to the ground like a sack of bricks and doesn't get back up.

Biker man then turns to me and, holy shitting hell, this man is pretty, although I probably wouldn't say that to his face. He looks a little like Chris Hemsworth with his blond hair in a man bun, his faded denim eyes, and chiseled jaw covered in day-old stubble. He's taller than me, but then, everyone is, but at around six feet two he towers over me and he's built in a way that screams "I work out." I didn't even know men this gorgeous existed in real life. I'm tempted to pinch him just to make sure I'm not dreaming. He ignores me checking him out and gently runs his thumb over my cheekbone, causing me to wince and him to frown.

"Come on, let's get you to the compound and get you cleaned up." He grabs my hand and starts pulling me back through the woods with King following behind us. I'm so busy marveling at how hands that size could be so gentle, it takes a while for his words to penetrate my thick skull.

"Hey, um, yeah, I'm not going anywhere with you. Thanks for sticking up for me back there, but I'm going to just go now." I pull my hand free and manage to take a couple of steps away from him before I find myself upside down and over his shoulder.

"Hey, put me down."

He slaps my ass, hard enough to make it sting, effectively stilling my movements. "Settle down. I don't want to drop you and cause any more damage to that pretty face of yours. You stole our dog, sugar, I can't just let you go. Besides, you need to tell my president what just went down."

We walk, well, he walks, I bounce, for what seems like forever but is probably closer to five minutes, while I mentally berate myself for getting trapped in this situation to begin with. We end up at a huge gated entrance to what I'm assuming is their compound. It's hard to see much from my upside down angle. He slides me down his body and shouts over my shoulder to the guards, I'm guessing, to open the gates. I'm thinking this is a very bad idea and I can tell he has noticed my train of thought because he places both hands gently on either side of my face.

"Nobody is going to hurt you in here, sugar. Your punishment will more than likely be a favor of some sort."

My eyes must be the size of my head as I guess what kind of favors they could ask of me. He takes one of my hands in his and tugs us toward the door.

"Not what you're thinking, sugar. Nobody here would ever put their hands on you without your permission, okay?"

I nod because what else can I say? Despite my small stature, I'm quite good at defending myself but unarmed and in a compound filled with god knows how many bikers, I'd be screwed. I just hope that doesn't mean literally.

CHAPTER TWO

We push through two heavy oak doors and find ourselves in a large room that has a bar running almost the length of the far wall, as well as tables and chairs scattered everywhere. In the far corner, there are a couple of worn brown leather sofas. It reminds me of an Irish-themed pub my brothers took me to a few years ago. It's cooler in here than it is outside, making me wish I had a cardigan or something to slip on. I look around. Although a few of the tables are occupied, the room itself is quite quiet. I let out a relieved breath. Maybe I'll survive the evening after all.

"Rebel!" pretty boy shouts across the room to a table of four men. "Can you find King for me?"

I look down at King, who is sitting at my feet, then up again at my biker and give a little tug on my hand that is firmly encased in his to get his attention.

"Dude, he's sitting on my feet." I nod my head in King's direction.

Mr. Pretty just smiles and shakes his head before the guy named Rebel returns from wherever he went with another man in tow. The new guy, a handsome man in a silver fox kind of way scowls in my direction. Crap, this must be the president. He takes me in, his eyes pausing on our linked hands, and quirks an eyebrow.

"Pres, this is our local dog thief." Pretty boy looks down at me, waiting for me to fill in the blank with my name.

With a grumble, I answer, "It's Luna and I am not a dog thief. I'm a dog liberator." I huff, trying to snatch my hand away, but he just laughs at me and holds on tighter.

"I don't really care what you call yourself, little lady. You can't come onto Kings of Carnage property and take something of ours and not expect there to be repercussions."

Pretty boy tries to interject. "Listen, King, she didn't know."

But that's when I interrupt because something else dawns on me.

"Your name is King?" I ask for clarification but don't wait for an answer. "And you named your dog after yourself? Isn't that a little"—I wave my free hand around for dramatic effect—"narcissistic?" The entire room goes silent, except for the stupid chuckling biker attached to me.

I lean into his shoulder and whisper, "I probably shouldn't have said that out loud, huh?"

"Probably not, sugar, and besides, the pres didn't name him," he tells me, finally letting go of my hand.

I look up at him when he doesn't continue. A deep voice vibrates from behind me. "I did."

I spin around and nearly fall on my ass before I'm pulled forward, making me face plant against another hard chest.

I suck in a sharp breath as the side of my face connects with a wall of leather, reminding me of pockmark's handiwork.

I wince. "Ouch." Strong fingers lift my chin and I find myself face-to-face with what can only be described as an Adonis. Whereas Pretty Boy, and I really must stop referring to him as that in my head, is gorgeous and fair, this man is breathtaking and dark. Taller than my biker friend at about six four with inky black hair and cerulean blue eyes that are currently checking out the mark on my face. He has a slightly crooked nose that looks as if it's been broken a time or two and full lips he slowly starts to lick when he notices me looking. I feel myself flush. Jesus, what is in the food around here?

I try to take a step back to compose myself but he refuses to let go.

"What happened to your face?" he asks me.

There is a loud boom but when I look around nobody else seems to have heard my ovaries exploding, so I sigh in relief.

"Erm, that would be the pockmarked biker asshole."

He looks up and over my shoulder to my friend for a clearer explanation.

"That would be Weasel's handiwork. I'd caught up to her and had her restrained when he runs up and smacks her in the face, calling her a cunt." The room goes wired at this and I can feel the animosity pouring off Adonis in waves.

"What the fuck? Where is he? That little fucker's dead! He's already had his last warning."

"Out cold, still in the woods at the back of the compound if the fucker's lucky," Pretty Boy answers, sounding pleased with himself.

Adonis looks down at me again. I don't know if he wants me to confirm the pretty biker's story or what, so I shrug and tell him.

"It's true, Pretty Boy knocked him out with one punch. It was kind of awesome."

Adonis looks at me in question. "Pretty Boy?" he growls at me. What is with bikers and growling?

"Well, I didn't mean to say that out loud, but that's what I've been calling him in my head. I couldn't just call you biker one and two, could I?"

Pretty Boy is laughing so hard he looks as if he might fall over.

"Shut it, Halo," Adonis barks at him.

I look back at Pretty Boy. He has the face of an angel for sure. "Halo, huh? It suits you." He winks at me, making me blush before Adonis is turning my head to face him again.

He leans down until he is so close I can feel his breath upon my face.

"And what have you been calling me in your head?" he asks in a seductive tone.

"Adonis." My voice is breathy like a phone sex operator's. It isn't until his face turns smug that I realize what I've said.

"Goddamnit, why won't the words just stay inside my mouth? No more questions. Apparently, my filter is broken." This makes Adonis smile and, oh my god, he should do that more often.

"The name is Orion but Adonis works for me too."

A loud whistle has us turning to face the president. "All right, boys, focus." He looks behind to the table of bikers and shouts, "Rebel, Agro, find Weasel and bring him to me."

Turning back to face us, he points at me, making me gulp. I try to keep my face neutral, not wanting to give him the satisfaction of knowing he has me rattled. "As I was saying, you can't come on Carnage property, steal something that belongs to us, and just expect to walk away."

Orion steps closer to my back and slides a hand onto my hip, which is both an odd thing to do to a stranger and rather comforting. I guess I'm not hiding my apprehension as well as I thought I was. Halo takes my hand again, looking down at me with a reassuring smile. The president looks to Orion and then to Halo. Whatever he sees helps him make up his mind.

"You can consider yourself our guest until I've decided what to do with you."

"What?" Is he joking? From the grim-set line of his jaw, it doesn't look like it but he can't be serious. I look up at Halo in shock. He promised me everything would be okay. He must see the hurt in my eyes, as he tries to tug me toward him, but the hand on my hip refuses to let me go. Orion snakes an arm around my stomach and pulls me tight against his chest. Halo sighs and laces his fingers behind his head.

I'm not a stupid person and, although I have never encountered a real-life biker before, I have indulged in many biker stories. If this guy is implying that I'm to be a sweet butt or a club whore or whatever the hell they call them here, then president or not, he's in for a rude awakening.

"Dude, I'm not sleeping with you. If you touch me, you're going to experience firsthand what it's like to become a eunuch." I might not have much experience with bikers but I do have experience with overbearing male assholes. I straighten my shoulders and glare at him, refusing to cower.

The arm around my waist spasms but I refuse to back down. The president's lips twitch a little in response to my outburst.

"That's not what I was implying. Besides, I like my women with a bit more up top," he tells me straight-faced.

"Hey, there's is nothing wrong with my boobies. I grew them myself." I sniff with indignation. I mean, how dare he? Orion is shaking behind me and it takes me a second to realize he's laughing. What is so freaking funny? I rub my fingers on my temples because I can feel a headache coming on. I am beyond ready for this day to be over.

"You'll be expected to pull your weight in other areas, like cooking and cleaning, until you can prove to us you are trustworthy. I need to know you won't pull that kind of shit again. You were lucky it was us and not another club. They might not have been so lenient."

I stare into his eyes, knowing I should keep my mouth shut but I can gradually feel myself getting angrier and angrier.

"He was hurting him, and I couldn't just let him get away with it." I sniff and blink back the tears I can feel approaching at the thought of leaving King to suffer because I refuse to cry in front of everyone.

"Who was hurting who?" Orion asks from behind me. I look around and realize nobody knows what I'm talking about. Even Halo looks as confused as everyone else.

"The pockmark dickface—I mean Weasel—was kicking King in the ribs and I couldn't just leave him behind."

"What? That fucking fucker. Wait until I get my hands on that prick," Orion spits out behind me. He's so angry, he's literally vibrating. I rub my hand backward and forward across the arm still wrapped around me to offer some comfort.

"Orion, calm down. You'll get your turn. That little prick is done. He's blown through all the chances Joker gave him. Gecko, get today's security feed and bring it to my office. I want to see just what this little fucker is up to," the president orders, yelling to the bikers drinking in the corner.

He turns his attention back to me, a gleam of respect present in his eye.

"Your punishment still stands." He holds his hand up as I start to object. "However, in light of the circumstances, I'm willing to give you some leeway. You will stay here for thirty days and help out like I said, however, you are free to come and go as you please. If, after thirty days, you want to leave, you can. But who knows, you might just decide to stay." He's looking directly at Orion and Halo as he says that last part and I feel as if I'm missing something but I'm too stressed out to think about it right now. Why on earth wouldn't I want to leave? I contemplate his words, pissed for putting myself in this fucked-up position to begin with, and nod. I'm not stupid. This is their world and they follow their own set of rules. Putting up a fight now would be reckless and I doubt very much I would come out the victor. Maybe later the fear will come but at the moment all I feel is angry and disappointed with myself.

"Okay, fine, but I need my truck. I've left it in town. Plus I'll need to go shopping to grab some clothes and shit."

He considers this and nods his head in acknowledgment. "One of the guys can drive you home to collect some things."

I shake my head, not keen on the idea of these guys knowing where I live. I might not be scared but I'm not stupid either. "It's too far away. It will take about three hours to get there and another three to get back. It's not worth it for the sake of some clothes."

"You don't have a man waiting for you at home?" Halo asks from beside me.

"No, I don't, which is a good thing, really, because you guys are a bunch of touchy feelers. If I did have a man, I'm pretty sure he wouldn't like that." Halo's eyes spark with something I'm unfamiliar with, but before I can figure it out he looks at Orion and nods. Men are so weird.

"Give Halo your keys. He can fetch your truck for you," King says, drawing my attention back to him. "The guys will take you to get some clothes tomorrow. Happy?"

Ecstatic. I bite back the sarcastic retort and nod, not trusting myself to speak. The events of the day are catching up to me and I'm going to crash soon. I fish my key from a little hidden zippered pocket inside my dress and toss it to Halo.

He gives me a panty-dropping smile before shocking the shit out of me and placing a soft kiss on my lips and heading out. I stand there gaping like a fish for a second before I'm being led by Orion through the corridor King first emerged from and up some stairs to another corridor that has half a dozen rooms on each side. Walking to the one closest to us, Orion opens the door to a bedroom bigger than my whole studio apartment was. A queen-size bed dominates most of the room with a dresser and a wardrobe on the left and a large screen TV on the wall facing the foot of the bed. On the right, through a half-open door, I spy a bathroom, and farther down is a large window overlooking the woods I was running in earlier. Underneath the window are an armchair and a floor-standing reading lamp. The room is decorated in blues and grays, a far cry from the baby-pink walls of my old apartment or even the lemon-yellow walls of my bedroom now, but it's clean and cozy and smells like the man behind me. He walks to the dresser and comes back with a T-shirt which he hands to me.

"Bathroom's through there. Get cleaned up and get some rest. You look exhausted. I'm going down to sort out this business with Weasel, okay?"

I nod but I'm feeling all kinds of off-kilter. He places his hands on my face, much like Halo did earlier, and kisses my forehead. "Relax, you're safe here. Nothing is going to happen that you don't want, okay?"

"Yeah, okay, and thank you for the T-shirt and the use of the room."

He turns to leave but he turns back and there is something in his eye I can't quite get a read on. "No worries. It's your room as long as you're here. Goodnight."

"Night." He leaves, closing the door behind him. I throw myself back on the bed and close my eyes.

How I get myself into these messes, I don't know. Taking stock of everything, I realize I'm not scared, which is fucking ridiculous but not surprising. I always have been wired a little differently than other women my age. Most of my friends are looking for a good man to treat her right. I'm more interested in finding someone with a big dick who'll pull my hair when he fucks me from behind.

I never was one for white picket fences, despite the fact

that my look screams wholesome girl-next-door. I guess these guys will just have to find out what kind of girl I am for themselves. I smile to myself thinking the men around here are too damn hot for their own good.

I'm in so much trouble.

CHAPTER THREE

It has been brought to my attention on numerous occasions that I sleep like the dead. However, finding someone's morning wood pressed up against your ass when you know damn fine you went to bed alone... yeah, that will wake a girl up real quick. There are no gentle morning stirrings followed by lazy stretches; my eyes pop open and I'm out of bed a nanosecond later yelling out curses at the top of my voice. But what really tells me how shitty my day is going to be is the gun I find pointed at my face.

It's when the bathroom door flies open that I snap out of my stupor and remember where I am. Halo is standing in the doorway looking sleepy, yet alert, with his gun aimed at me too. My eyes drift back to the bed, knowing who I'm going to find now that my brain is starting to function. Which, let's be honest, doesn't usually start until after at least two cups of coffee. What I didn't prepare myself for was the naked chest, the six—no, make that eight—pack on display because the sheet has dropped to his waist, and the thick, strong arms covered in full sleeve tattoos. Adonis may not be pointing his gun at me anymore but the smirk he's aiming my way is just as deadly.

"Want to tell me what the noise is all about, sugar? I'm pretty sure you could teach us bikers a thing or two with that dirty mouth of yours," Halo says while lowering his gun and making his way over to the side of the bed. His Texas twang sounds stronger this morning.

Shit, Halo is half-naked too. That is a lot of abs on show first thing in the morning. He's covered in tattoos and has that sexy V that guys have—the one that makes me want to reach down and slip my panties off and throw them at him. And if that isn't enough, he has a little trail of fine hair that disappears into his tented boxers. Fuck, I snap my head up, discreetly wiping my mouth in case I've drooled. I point my finger at Orion.

"He was pointing his gun at me and it took me by surprise." I manage to get that out while edging backward toward the bathroom. I need to get out of here before my panties spontaneously combust.

"I only pointed my gun at you after you started screaming profanities like a drunken sailor in a bar. I thought something was wrong." Orion rubs his hand through his hair, looking slightly baffled.

I sigh because it's too early for this.

"It was the other gun you had pointed at me that woke me up." I drag my eyes down his chest to his sheet-covered groin before quickly looking away. When they both start laughing their asses off, I realize I wasn't discreet enough. I spin on my heel and stomp the rest of the way to the bathroom before slamming the door and locking it. It dawns on me that I never questioned why Halo was coming out of Orion's bathroom clad only in a pair of boxers. Which begs the question, did he sleep in here too? How the fucking hell did I manage to sleep next to what might possibly be an angel and the devil without realizing?

You know what? Never mind. I need coffee before I can process anything else. I take a quick shower to wake myself up and cool my raging libido, only then realizing I didn't bring any clothes with me into the bathroom. I wrap a towel tightly around my body, grateful for once for my lack of height and slight figure, and swipe my hand across the steamed-up mirror. There is puffiness around my eye and my cheekbone is red and tender but I'm grateful it was a slap instead of a punch or I would have been looking a lot worse this morning. I finger comb my hair and then braid it and pull it over my shoulder, freeing some tendrils to help hide my cheek. I check the cabinet above the sink and the cupboard below but can't find any spare toothbrushes, so I decide to just use Orion's. Hey, if he can rub his dick on my ass, I can put his toothbrush in my mouth. Not brushing is not an option. I gaze around as I brush. It's a basic bathroom made up of a shower, sink, and toilet. There's a cupboard under the sink with toiletries and toilet rolls and a cabinet above with razors and Tylenol. Nothing exciting, not that I snooped, much. All the fixtures are white, as well as the towels, and the walls are a dark gray. Classic, clean but all man. I tidy up my mess and figure I've procrastinated enough. If I stay in here any longer it's going to look weird.

Orion is alone when I walk out, which is a relief as I might not be flashing the goods but I'm still only wearing a towel. He's dressed now in a pair of dark blue jeans and a black T-shirt and sitting on the end of the bed fastening his black work boots. When he hears me enter, he looks up. Whatever he was going to say looks like it died on his tongue. His hot gaze scorches me as he takes me in. His eyes slowly glide up my body from my feet to my face. So much for having a cold shower. He stands and prowls toward me like a panther, graceful and deadly.

"You're so fucking gorgeous that if I don't leave this room right now, I'm going to do something I don't think you're ready for." He kisses my forehead before heading toward the door. "I'll meet you downstairs. Halo brought up the duffle bag that was in your truck in case you needed it. It's in the chair by the window. If you need anything else, just help yourself. Got it?"

"Got it. Thanks, Orion."

When he leaves, I place the bag on the bed and search through the contents. I always keep what my brothers call a bug-out bag in the truck just in case. Their reasoning is that if I ever need to get a hotel room or leave somewhere quickly for whatever reason, I have the essentials to keep me going. I'll never admit to them the reason I go along with it is because I'm forever dropping food down myself so having spare clothes is a bonus. I select a pair of gray skinny jeans and a pale lemon-colored fitted V-neck T-shirt. For underneath, I have a white padded bra and matching lace panties. Once I'm dressed, I slip on the ballet flats from yesterday and shove the bag under the bed. I don't really want anyone going through my stuff even if there isn't anything exciting in there to see. My jacket and over the shoulder bag with my phone, purse, and keys to my house must still be in the truck. I take a deep breath and then one more, just to be sure, and head down to see what fun awaits me.

Making my way through the compound, I realize it's still quiet. I guess the biker lifestyle doesn't fit with early mornings. I find Orion in the same room I met him last night. He's sitting next to Halo, a couple of guys I don't recognize, and Rebel. Checking them out as I head toward their table, the first thing I notice is that Rebel is a lot younger than I initially guessed, at maybe twenty-one or twenty-two. He's a good-looking guy. It must be a requirement here because they all are but he has a soft, almost baby-ness to him. His cropped strawberry-blonde hair and dusting of freckles only adds to his youthfulness. He kind of reminds me of myself in that way. I bet people underestimate him too. I glance around the table. Skipping over Orion and Halo for a second, I focus on the others.

There is an older guy with a short gray beard and gray hair but it suits him in the same silver fox kind of way that King's does. His laughter lines tell me he's quick to joke but I bet he can be intimidating when he wants to be. I would put him at late forties, early fifties. The guy next to him is probably closer to thirty but he gives off an I-don't-give-a-shit vibe. It goes quite well with his dark green hair and multiple facial piercings. The guy on the end is the shortest by far, closer to my height than theirs, at around five feet five but what he lacks in height he makes up for in bulk. If I stood behind this guy, you wouldn't see me at all. With his bald head and resting bitch face, he reminds me of a henchman from my brother's comics when we were younger.

Which reminds me... I lift my arm and pretend I'm checking the time but I activate my GPS. I might, for some unknown reason, trust Orion and Halo, but I don't know the rest of these guys in the slightest and if there are any more like Weasel, I want my brothers to know exactly where to find me. The thought makes me smile. They would burn this place to the ground if anything happened to their baby sister.

"What's got you smiling?" questions Halo as he reaches out and pulls me onto his lap. Orion lifts his hand and places it on my thigh. What the fuck is going on with these guys?

"Erm... Just thinking of my brothers," I answer, acting like sitting on a hot guy's lap is an everyday occurrence for me.

Halo leans back a little, pulling me with him, making Orion's hand drift a little higher. They are trying to kill me; I just know it.

"You guys close?" Orion asks. Huh? Oh, right, my brothers.

"Yeah, but it's been a while since I've seen them and I miss them."

"I'm sure they miss you too. Here, let me introduce you to a few of my club brothers. Guys this is Luna. Luna," he gestures to his right, "this is Rebel, the guy with the green hair is Gecko, baldy on the end is Half-pint (I might have had to bite my lip at that one) and this," he points to the silver fox, "is Inigo."

"I'm sorry, did he just say your name is Inigo?" The silver fox nods his head at me, a smile playing on his lips like he knows exactly what I'm going to say. "As in 'My name is Inigo Montoya. You killed my father, prepare to die?'"

That gets me a full-blown Colgate-worthy smile.

"That's awesome," I whisper, and it's true. My brothers and I were obsessed with eighties movies when we were younger and *The Princess Bride* is one of my favorites.

I turn to Gecko. "I like your hair. I tried to dye mine pink once but it turned out orange. It was not a good look for me."

"Thanks, sweets. What about piercings, you have any?"

"I like them but I don't think I could pull them off on my face like you. I don't look tough enough." He chuckles at that. "I have my ears done, my belly button, and both nipples, though." I feel Halo's sharp intake of breath behind me and the unmistakable bulge in his lap. I also have the undivided attention of every male at the table and none of them are looking at my eyes. Typical.

"I'm joking, well, about the nipples. I really do have my belly button pierced." I lean back into Halo, who grips both my hips to stop me from falling, and raise the hem of my T-shirt to show them the pink gem just inside my belly button.

"Nice, sweets. I know a great guy that does all my piercings, so if you ever do decide to get those nipples done, let me know," Gecko offers. It's not something I've really thought about but if Halo's rapidly growing dick is any indication, he loves the idea.

A shudder runs through me as Orion leans over and traces his finger around my piercing. I yank my top back down and sit forward again, trying to ignore the flush of heat rushing through my body from his touch. "Very sexy," Orion whispers so only Halo and I can hear him. "I wonder how much you would squirm if I traced it with my tongue?" Halo groans softly at his words, making my pulse speed up, but I decide to ignore them both and focus on Half-pint.

"I can't reach the top shelf but I'm awesome at hide-and-seek," I deadpan.

He counters with, "Punching someone in the face who is over six foot is awkward as fuck but I can rip someone's balls off with one hand."

I nod in understanding. "Good chat."

That makes all the guys laugh. I look at Rebel and study him closely. His eyes are guarded. It's hard to see someone so young looking so jaded.

"I miss my brothers so I'm adopting you, okay?" He looks

completely taken aback, as if that was the last thing he was expecting, which I'm sure it was.

"It comes with the perks of borrowing my awesome truck from time to time, although if you get blood in it, please wash it, and I will be your wing chick when you want something other than sweet butt, okay?"

He considers it for a second before he nods his head. "Works for me."

Orion grabs my hand, pulling me up and leading me toward the door.

"Come on, gorgeous. Let's go pick up the things you need before you adopt anyone else. We can get coffee on the way."

"Now you're speaking my language, Adonis."

"Hold up." Halo stands and snags me from Orion. Before I can even speak, his lips are on mine and his hand is burrowed into my hair. The guys at the table whistle but all I care about is the feel of Halo's tongue against mine. When he pulls away, I moan in protest but he just laughs, the fucker, and kisses the tip of my nose.

"I have to go out for a job. I'm going to be gone for a few days, so try to stay out of trouble, okay?" My brain freezes from shock, and before I can say anything he kisses me one last time, says his goodbyes, and heads off. I just stare at his retreating back, still feeling the weight of his lips on mine.

"Come on," Orion tells me laughing, before flinging his arm around my shoulder and leading us out into the bright morning sunshine.

"He just kissed me." I point out something Orion is very much aware of.

"He sure did. Feel good?" he asks. I look at him to see if this is some kind of trick but his expression doesn't show any anger or jealousy.

"I... it was good," I reply, not sure what the fuck is going on.

"Good?" He laughs before leaning in and whispering against my ear. "I bet if I slipped my fingers inside your panties, I would find them wet. I'd say that was better than good." Cocky, stupid, arrogant bikers.

"Well, you'd be wrong," I tell him.

"Is that so? Care to prove it?" His voice has taken on a husky quality.

I reach up and tug his T-shirt so he bends down a little. I place my lips against his ear and whisper, "I'm afraid that won't be possible. You see, I'm not wearing any." And with my lie scoring a direct hit, judging by Orion's groan, I strut to the truck feeling pretty fucking proud of myself.

CHAPTER FOUR

It was after we had shopped for a bunch of stuff, half of which I wouldn't need and all of which Orion insisted on paying for, I realized these guys, or at least Orion, might be interested in me for more than just sex. How did I come to this conclusion? Watching him interact with Laura, our glamorous assistant today.

I like boys, always have, always will, but if I were ever going to take a dip in the girl-on-girl pool, it would be with a girl like Laura. She was freaking gorgeous. We're talking six feet of bronze skin, long tousled waves of brunette hair and a body that would, and probably has, stopped traffic. You could tell she was smart but also super sweet and she never once made googly eyes over Orion. While I dragged him around the store, she followed along, asking questions about my size, style and what kind of pieces I was looking for and not once did he check her out. In fact, he hardly seemed to take his eyes off me. I've got to be honest, it's quite an intoxicating feeling, having the undivided attention of a man like that. It isn't until we're back in the truck heading toward the compound once again—with Orion driving because, apparently, if you have a penis, it gives you driving rights over us poor vagina-wearing females—that I say what I've realized.

"You like me," I say quietly.

Orion takes his hand off the gear stick and slides it over one of my thighs.

"Just figured that out, huh?" He chuckles.

"It's just that Laura was gorgeous and you barely even glanced at her."

"She was a looker, that's true, but Luna, you are fucking beautiful. Besides, what kind of dick checks out another woman when he's standing next to his own?

"I'm your woman?" I blink in surprise. Say what now?

"I'm working on it," he answers.

When I try to speak, he gives me a look which shuts me up and carries on. "I get that this whole situation is a little fucked-up but I'm not one to look a gift horse in the mouth. You aren't exactly a prisoner, you must know that. It's just to save face with other clubs and, well, it gives us all a chance to get to know you better and, Luna, I would really like the chance to get to know you better."

He's right. I know I'm not really a prisoner. If I were, I

certainly wouldn't have been allowed the freedom to leave the clubhouse.

"Well, we have a month to get to know each other, right? Hmm... What do I need to know? What's your favorite color?" Seriously? That's the best I could come up with?

He full on belly laughs and I'm slightly worried we might crash if he's not careful. "Of all the questions you could have asked, you went with 'what's my favorite color?'" He carries on laughing for a few minutes before he manages to get himself under control.

"I guess black is my favorite color," he finally answers me. Why am I not surprised? "Okay, my turn. What do you do when you aren't rescuing dogs?"

"Funny." I stick out my tongue at him before answering. "I make custom gift baskets for everything from baby showers to retirement gifts. That's what I was doing yesterday before running into you, making deliveries. There's a shop in town that sells them."

"That's pretty cool."

I beam a big smile his way. "What about you, what do you do?"

"I'm a sort of bounty hunter. That's how I got the nickname Orion."

Orion is a badass name for a badass, hot-as-hell man. "Orion suits you, or Adonis."

He smiles at that. "Baby, you can call me whatever you like." He lifts my hand and kisses the back of it, making me blush. That was cheesy as hell but it still does things to my insides.

"What about Halo? What does he do?"

When he doesn't answer straight away, I turn to face him, worried that I've overstepped. He finally speaks. "He's a facilitator."

Huh? A facilitator of what? I'm about to ask when he changes the subject. "It's my father's birthday on Friday, go with me?"

"Is mister biker man asking me on a date?"

"I don't date, babe, but make no mistake, I want you, I'm all in, so I'm going to fight tooth and nail to get you to give this thing a shot. Bikers play by different rules, Luna. Our world can be dark and fucked-up, so when you see something that shines brightly, that radiates light and banishes those shadows for a while, well, you grab on to it and you hold on tight. This is me, Luna, holding on tight."

"How can you say that? You know nothing about me," I whisper, shocked to my core by his declaration.

"I know you saved a dog that was being hurt regardless of the risk to yourself. I know you were marched into a compound full of dangerous as fuck bikers and held your own. I know you have brothers and miss them and you wear your heart on your sleeve. People are drawn to you, my men included, because you ooze sunshine. I know on a subconscious level you want me because you don't shy away from my touch and, lastly, I know you are the most beautiful goddamn woman I have ever seen in my life."

"Yes," I blurt out. He looks at me, puzzled for a second, before I put him out of his misery.

"Yes, I'll go to your dad's party with you." What I don't add is that, with his words, he's already on his way to making me his and it's only been twenty-four hours since we met. How am I supposed to survive a month? And how does Halo fit into all this?

We drive in comfortable silence before Orion pulls over and turns into the parking lot of a quaint diner.

"I promised you coffee and I'm a man of my word," he explains, climbing out of my truck and walking around to my side. He opens the door and offers me his hand. I look up at him in shock for a second. Who knew Mr. Big Bad Biker was such a gentleman? I don't think any guy has ever held the door open for me before. Silently, he leans in and unclips my belt before gripping my hips and lifting me out. He slides me down his body, far slower than necessary, making my mind flash back to visions of his naked torso. Instead of stepping back, he pushes me up against the truck, his hard body flush with mine, leaving me no other choice but to grip his arms and breathe him in. I look up at him, startled by the intensity I see in his gaze. I lick my lips and my eyes widen as I feel him harden against my stomach.

"Tell me you feel it too," his deep voice rumbles out, making goosebumps break out all over my skin.

My mind is still stuck on the ever-growing bulge in his pants. "Oh, I feel it," I mutter.

It takes him a beat to understand what I'm referring to,

but when he does, he throws his head back and laughs. I kid you not, I have a mini orgasm right there and then in the middle of the dusty parking lot.

"I have no control over my own goddamn body when you're around. You make me feel like a fifteen-year-old boy again."

Rubbing against him a little, I have to disagree. "You don't feel like a fifteen-year-old boy to me," I tell him a little breathlessly.

"Jesus, you're going to be the death of me. Let's get you some coffee." He slides me a little farther along the truck so he can slam the door and lock it. I wait for him to pocket the keys before making my move.

"Orion?" I say his name softly, making him turn back toward me. With only pure need fueling my next move, I grab him by the neck of his T-shirt and yank his head down to meet mine before slamming my mouth on his. It takes him about three seconds to overcome his shock and take control. He hoists me up with his hands under my ass, letting me wrap my legs around his waist. He pushes me against the side of the truck as he devours me, thrusting his tongue inside my mouth and frying my senses until all I can think about is him. I have never been kissed like this before and if I live another ten lifetimes, this would still be, hands down, the kiss all other kisses will be measured by. When he reluctantly pulls away, resting his forehead against mine as we both struggle to catch our breath, it dawns on me that I might just be in way over my head.

"Coffee?" My breath caresses his lips, causing a shudder to ripple through him.

"Coffee," he agrees, sliding me back to my feet before snagging my hand and pulling me toward the diner.

We walk through the doors and find all eyes trained on us, and I flush when I realize everyone could see us through the large plate glass window. Orion ignores everyone, heading for a booth in the back where a few other members of the Kings of Carnage MC are eating. I spot King watching me so I make sure to avoid eye contact with him and check out the other members instead. There are four of them, not counting King. There is a guy about the same age as him on his left with short blond hair and the kind of tan you can only get from spending the bulk of your time outside. Next to him is an older guy, at maybe sixty, with shoulder-length gray hair and slight build. On the opposite side of King is a beast of a man who looks like he might be part machine, reminding me of a bodybuilder in size and shape. Height-wise, he easily towers over everyone else at the table. Heck, he towers over everyone in the diner. He too has shoulder-length hair but his is a rich dark coffee color that matches his eyes. Lastly, on King's right is a handsome man with dark hair like Orion's and the same cerulean blue eyes—wait. I look up at Orion in question.

"The guy on the left of King is Joker, our vice president. The guy next to Joker is Chewy. This monster of a man here," he points at the huge bodybuilder, "is called Conan, and the asshole next to my father is my brother Diesel."

"Father? King is your father?" I ask, death staring him. Seems he failed to mention that nugget of information earlier.

"I thought you knew." He shrugs and the smirk on his face makes me want to punch him.

"Gotta problem with me, missy?" King barks out, causing the other diners to turn our way. If he thinks he's going to intimidate me, he has another thing coming. I stand tall, all five feet of me, and scowl at him.

"You mean aside from the whole me being a guest of yours?" I spit the word guest out, and the men surrounding us tense. I sigh, knowing I need to back down.

"I just got invited to your birthday party and now I have to get a gift ready for the president of a freaking motorcycle club. I give great gifts," I explain to him, sitting down next to Diesel and snagging a piece of bacon off his plate and devouring it before I continue, ignoring the incredulous faces looking back at me.

"It's kind of my thing, but what the heck do you buy someone like you? Maybe I could get vouchers for a strip club or something." I ponder the last part to myself. I reach over and steal the last piece of bacon off Diesel's plate as Orion sits down beside me and wraps his arm around my shoulder. I look up at his smiling face as I finish chewing.

"Do you know where I could hire a hooker maybe? A classy one though, because, well, it's your dad and I need to make a good impression." Then maybe he will forget I stole his dog.

"I never forget anything, missy." I whip around to find King laughing at me.

"Shit. I said that out loud again, didn't I?" All of the guys crack up laughing while I bury my head against Orion's chest.

"I think I'm going to steal your girl, bro," Diesel says from beside me, chuckling.

"Fuck you. Why would she want you when she's got this right here?" He waves his hand up and down his body, making me smile.

"So modest," I tease before facing Diesel. "Hi. I'm sure you're awesome and you're really hot but what can I say? Cocky conceited assholes do it for me."

"Watch it, Luna, or I'll bend you over this table and show you just how cocky I can be," Orion whispers in my ear, making my nipples perk up with interest. Thank god for padded bras.

"Well, if you ever change your mind," Diesel tells me wistfully.

"I'm good but thanks." I look back up at King who is watching me without his usual hostile stare.

"So, about those hookers?"

He shakes his head, a smile covering his face that he just can't fight.

"I think I can manage to get my own pussy for the evening, darlin', but thanks for the offer."

"Damn, back to the drawing board," I mumble to myself. I'll think of something to give him.

"I'll take a hooker or two if you're offering?" the guy called Chewy shouts across the table, not giving a single fuck what the other patrons think.

"I'll see what I can do." I look up to ask Orion again to see if he knows where I can find one but shut up when he kisses me stupid in front of everyone. By the time he pulls away, I'm not even sure what my own name is, let alone what I was talking about before.

When the waitress arrives, we order coffee and pancakes, which I wolf down, not realizing just how hungry I was until it was placed in front of me. The guys talk quietly around me but I can tell they are being careful about watching what they say. Part of me gets it but the other part of me just feels uncomfortable and ready to leave. Orion must notice, as he places some money down on the table and tugs me from my seat. I wave goodbye to everyone as he ushers me out the door and back into my truck. He sits beside me, squeezing his hands around the steering wheel.

"Do you have a problem with my brothers or my father?" He turns to look at me with disappointment on his face.

"What? No, I like them just fine. I just feel like an interloper. I could tell they were watching what they were saying like they were waiting for me to leave." He sighs but loosens his grip on the wheel and reaches over with one hand and squeezes my knee.

"It's not like that, Luna. It's just that we don't discuss club business around women, period. It's not you personally, it's just the way it is, the way it's always been." I look out the side window as he starts up the truck and stare at the bikers through the diner's window. See, this is why I'm not sure about staying when the month is up, no matter how I feel about Orion or Halo at the end of it. I've spent too long proving to men over and over just how capable I am and I don't want to be cast back into a role I fought so hard to break away from.

"Give it some time, Luna, you'll get used to it. We don't treat our women badly. We treat the woman we love like queens, but the MC is a man's world and that won't change any time soon."

I don't answer. What's there to say? I offer him a small smile, vowing to enjoy every single moment with him, just in case I end up having to say goodbye.

CHAPTER FIVE

We make our way back to the compound in relative silence. When we pull up outside, I spot the row of bikes I failed to notice on our way out.

"Is one of those yours?" I turn and ask Orion as he parks and turns the engine off.

"Sure is. Come on, I'll show you." He hops out and helps me down before leading me over to a jet black and chrome Harley.

"Wow. She's pretty."

"That she is. Have you ever been on a bike before, Luna?"

I nod my head.

"Your brothers ride?" he guesses.

"They do. My grandfather used to ride too. I think it's in our blood." I smile, remembering how much I love to feel the wind in my hair as the world whips by at dizzying speeds.

"I'll take you for a ride tomorrow, how's that sound?" He slides his hands around my hips and pulls me in for a quick kiss.

"Sounds perfect."

We grab my bags from the truck and head inside. It's bright outside, so it takes a minute for my eyes to adjust but when they do, I notice there are more people here than yesterday and a few more scantily-clad women mingling about. I spot one of them making a beeline for Orion the second she sees him. She's pretty in an overly-made-up kind of way. I suspect she is younger than she looks with her heavy makeup, bright red lips, and over-teased bleach blonde hair aging her slightly. She's wearing a red sequin bra and tiny denim miniskirt that would no doubt flash what she had for breakfast if she bent over.

She ignores me completely as she stops in front of Orion and trails a red-tipped finger across his chest. I look around and see most people have stopped what they were doing to see how the scene unfolds. I snort out a laugh and head for the bedroom. If they're after a smackdown catfight, they will be sorely disappointed. It's not that I can't hold my own, that couldn't be further from the truth, but I don't react to petty shit. If Orion wants me, then he needs to prove it. I'm just at the door that leads to the bedrooms when Orion calls my name.

"Yo, Luna!" I turn to face him, one of my bags thrown over my shoulder, and notice he isn't paying the girl any attention but he hasn't removed her hand from his chest.

"Yes, Orion?" I answer him in a bored tone, checking out my pink nails, noticing that some of the paint is chipped and remind myself to pick up some nail polish next time.

"Aren't you going to protect my virtue?" The guys around him laugh but he keeps his eyes on me. Is he trying to get a rise out of me or is this some kind of arbitrary test I was unaware of?

"Orion, if I thought you had some virtue worth saving, I would kick her scrawny ass. But we both know you're big enough and ugly enough to look after yourself. I don't play games, Adonis. If you want her, have her. She's offering herself up to you on a silver platter. Enjoy." I turn toward the door when he calls out my name again. I ignore him and push the door open but I'm stopped by the woman's voice this time, making my anger spike.

"Round here we fight for our men, sweetheart."

I turn and face her, ignoring her smug smile. "Where I'm from, real men fight for their women and don't use them as toys in a game they never agreed to play. Besides, he's not my man. If he were, he would have removed your hand the second you touched him and he would be standing by my side instead of yours. Have fun." I finally walk through the door and pull it closed behind me. Fuck him and fuck her too.

I make my way up to his room, dump my bag in the corner, and let out a frustrated breath as I throw myself down on the bed. To think the morning had started out so well. The door slams open and bounces off the wall behind it. Orion stands in the doorway looking like a pissed off bull.

"What the fuck was that?" he shouts at me before stomping inside and slamming the door closed behind him.

I just roll my eyes at the overdramatic fucktard.

"What was what, Orion?" I reply sarcastically.

"Telling me to fuck Stacey. Is that what you want? For me to climb into bed with you smelling like some club whore?" I grimace at the word whore. So much for treating women like queens.

"Are you kidding me with this, Orion? What, you're pissed because I refused to play your little game?"

"No," he growls, stomping toward me. He climbs on top of me and grips my wrists, pinning them above my head.

"What I want is for you to fucking stay," he says between gritted teeth.

"Then stop giving me reasons to leave," I tell him softly. His anger drains out of him as his body relaxes into mine. He presses his forehead against mine and breathes me in.

"Shit. I fucked up," he admits.

"Yup," I agree, not giving him an inch. He buries his head against my shoulder, placing a feather-soft kiss against my neck.

"Luna," he implores.

"What would you do if I pulled that kind of stunt?" His body locks rock-solid as he lifts his head, his fiery gaze blazing into mine. "Yeah, exactly. Not nice, huh?"

"Shit." He rolls off me but when I start to get up, he pulls me back toward him and wraps his arms around me so my head is on his chest and my leg is hooked over his.

"I'm a dick. I knew when we left the diner you were going to leave me as soon as the month was up. I didn't know what to say or do to change that, so when Stacey approached me, the idiot part of my brain thought making you jealous might work. I don't know." He sighs, turning so he's face-to-face with me.

"I've never really thought about wanting anyone longer than to get myself off and I know that makes me sound like an even bigger dick, but it's true. When I saw you facing off against my father yesterday, I knew it was because I was just waiting for you to show up."

I soften at his words. Damn him.

"It's not that I don't want to take a chance on you, Orion, I do, but staying here means giving up a piece of myself in the process. I'm not going to make you any false promises. We literally only met yesterday and by the time this month is up, we could be sick to death of each other. So I propose we just do what comes naturally and let it run its course. Forget about time limits and expectations and let's just see how it all plays out. If it's meant to be, Orion, it will be.

"Sounds good to me. I promise you now, though, while you're here and we're figuring out what's going on between us, there won't be anybody else. I don't want you worrying that every time you turn your back, I'm taking someone else to the bedroom. I'm not that guy, Luna."

"So prove it." I lean forward and nip his bottom lip then

soothe it with my tongue. He opens his mouth, granting me entrance, and fights his natural instinct to take control and lets me explore. I slide my tongue against his and grip his hair hard, pulling him close to me, feeling like a goddess when he groans in surrender. I pull away panting and look up at him through my lashes.

"I need to ask you something," I tell him as I bite my lip.

"If I can answer, I will."

"What's the deal with you and Halo? I don't want to get caught up in some game of tug-of-war between you."

He sighs and looks at me like he's expecting me to flip out at his answer. Oh boy, hello red flag. "You haven't had a chance to see much of the club yet but you will at my father's party. We do things a little differently here."

"Differently how?"

"It's hard to explain."

"I'm far from dumb. Try me."

"Fuck, okay. Most MCs work as a whole right? One solid unit that works to protect its president always, to keep each other safe, and for everything to keep running smoothly. Well, this MC is pretty big so it's hard to always know where everyone is. If you don't know, then you can't protect them."

I nod. I get that. Still not answering my question though, big guy.

"So, we have smaller groups, or teams if you like, within the group. They only have to focus on each other's safety. This way everyone has at least one person to watch their back when they need it."

I glare at him, wondering if he is ever going to get to the point.

"As a result, they get pretty close as they do most things together..." He trails off, leaving me to fill in the—*Oh*.

"Women? You share women?" My eyes widen at the thought and a rush of warmth has me squirming in my seat. "Wow!" I don't know what to say to that.

He watches me before nodding. "You going to run now?" He looks like he expects me to.

"I'm not sure you understand the buzz us shoppers get when we come face-to-face with a two-for-one special," I whisper.

"What?" It's his turn to look shocked. Oh, and now he looks horny. Nope. I jump from the bed and grab the door handle.

"Come on, hot stuff. I have a present to get ready for your father."

He groans but gets up. "We are not getting my father a hooker for his birthday."

"I know. It's too short notice anyway. But I do have an idea. I need to nip into town and collect a couple of things but the rest I have in my truck. Want to come with me?"

"Will it make you happy?" he asks, clearly looking to earn himself some brownie points.

"Well, yeah."

"Then let's do this." He snags my hips and ushers me out the door with him. "The things I do for you, Luna. I fucking hate shopping."

"I appreciate your sacrifice, Adonis," I reply, laughing and pulling the door closed. I'll be gentle with him.

* * * * *

"Never again, Luna. The next time you want to go shopping, take a prospect with you."

I can't help but laugh. The guy catches assholes for a living, but he can't handle a little shopping.

"Stop your whining. There." I finish tying the ribbon on the gift basket I've just put together.

"What do you think?" I ask him as he peers over my shoulder at the finished project.

"I think he'll love it. You going to be okay up here for a bit? I've got church in ten minutes."

I wave him off. Lucky for him, I had my laptop in the truck with me, so I'm good.

"No worries." When he doesn't answer me, I look up to see him studying me.

"What?"

"You don't want to know what church is and you're not bothered about being up here when there will be sweet butts downstairs?"

"I've read a biker book or two. I might not be an expert but I think I get the gist of what church is all about. As for the sweet butts, what's that got to do with anything? You said while you were with me you wouldn't touch anyone else, so what's there to worry about?"

"Just like that?" he asks.

"Just like that."

"Fuck, what did I do to deserve you?" He presses a hard kiss to my mouth before dragging himself away.

"Just luck, I guess," I tell him, admiring my handiwork.

"Damn straight. I won't be long." He's gone before I can answer.

I take a quick shower and slip on some clean underwear and one of Orion's Harley T-shirts before grabbing my laptop and crawling into bed. Time to make some real money. When Gramps passed, he left his business to me. A lot of it I can take care of online. It fits perfectly around my gift basket making, and I have to admit, I enjoy it. I spend the next hour doing what I do best, taking hard-earned money from men who think girls don't know what they're doing. It's a lesson I'm all too happy to teach them. By the time I'm finished, I'm struggling to keep my eyes open. I wipe my history and shut the laptop down, popping it on the chair by the window. I snuggle under the covers, breathing in the scent that is all Orion and drift off to the sounds of laughter and music below.

The next few days pass far more quietly than I would have expected given where I am. But then again, I've spent most of it up here either working or being lazy. I'm starting to go a little stir-crazy but with it being King`s party tonight, I'm looking forward to letting my hair down.

Every morning since the first, I wake up knowing exactly where I am and just who's morning wood is pressed against me. Today, as much as I would like to stay here wrapped in Orion's arms, I need to pee even more. I manage to climb off the bed without disturbing him and head to the bathroom to take care of business. A glance at my watch reveals that it's seven o'clock. The trouble is, once I'm awake, I can never fall back to sleep again. I slide my jeans on, slip the T-shirt off to put a bra, and pull the shirt back on again. I tug on the tennis shoes I picked up yesterday and head downstairs to scrounge up some food.

The compound is eerily quiet at this time of morning. I notice a couple of sleeping bodies sprawled out on the beat-up old sofas in the sitting area but pay them no attention as I head into the industrial-sized kitchen. I find the fridge well-stocked and remembering what King said about pulling my weight, decide to cook breakfast for everyone. I keep breakfast simple, not knowing what time people get up to eat around here, and make a huge batch of pancakes I can keep warm in the oven. I fry up a whole pig`s worth of bacon, scramble two dozen eggs, and call it good. I'm just downing my second cup of coffee when a sleepy-looking Joker walks in with a somewhat more alert canine King in tow. I drop to my knees and rub the dog behind his ears, slipping him a piece of bacon. I stand up and face the vice president I haven't spoken to yet.

"Morning, Joker. Coffee?" He ignores me and walks over to the pot, pouring himself a cup and sitting down at the end of the counter. Guess he's not a morning person. I make him up a plate of food and slide it in front of him before sitting down with a plate for myself. We sit in silence as we eat, both in our own little worlds. I'm halfway through when he finally speaks.

"You shouldn't be wandering around here without one of your men."

I sigh. I thought he was just the silent type. I guess not. "Neither Orion or Halo can be with me twenty-four-seven, Joker." We both know this.

"Then you need to stay in your room. You can't be gallivanting around here if you aren't an old lady. People will think you're a sweet butt or a hanger-on."

"Locking me up in Orion's room makes me a prisoner and I was told I was free to come and go as I wanted. Are you saying if I said no to one of your men, it wouldn't mean anything?"

"The women that come here who aren't old ladies come here for one thing and one thing only—a good time. They know the score." He sips his coffee without looking at me.

"And if they change their minds and say no?"

"Like I said, they know the score," he repeats. What a load of utter horseshit. Rape is rape. It doesn't matter how you dress it up. Losing my appetite and knowing I won't win against this particular boss man, I decide to leave him to it.

"Don't make those boys any promises you can't keep. You and I both know you're too soft to deal with all the shit that goes along with being a member of an MC. What you three get up to is down to you but if you mess them up, you'll have me to deal with." He has no idea what kind of woman I am and with an attitude like that, it's doubtful he ever will.

"Pretty judgmental for a biker, aren't you?" I walk around the counter and bend down to give King one last fuss before I stroll out of the kitchen and head back upstairs. There's a part of me that understands the appeal of the MC—the comradery between the brothers, knowing there is always someone there to have your back. It's the archaic views toward women that I can't get past.

It doesn't change anything. I know the best thing for me will be to walk away. So why, when I walk into the room and see a sleeping Orion, does my chest twinge at the thought? Fuck. I said I would give this month my all and I meant it. It will either be the start of something or a wonderful memory to look back on. With that thought in mind, I strip out of my jeans and shoes and crawl back in beside Orion. He wraps his arms around me tightly, breathing in deeply when my hair falls on his face.

"Mmmm... You smell like pancakes," he mumbles without opening his eyes.

"That's because I just made breakfast."

"What?" He opens one eye to look at me. "Next time wake me up and I'll come with you, okay?"

I lower my head and rest it against his chest. I'm not going to have the same argument I just had with Joker. There's no point.

"Okay," I whisper, hating myself a little bit for giving in so easily.

"Is there any left?" He's perked up somewhat at the thought of breakfast. I snort. All men are the same when it comes to food.

"There was plenty but I could hear people waking up as I was coming back here."

He throws himself out of bed and yanks on his jeans, pulling the door open before disappearing, all without saying a word. He comes back five minutes later with a plate piled high. I can't help the smile that spreads across my face as he tucks in.

"Good?"

"Hmmm... So good," he mutters around a mouthful. "I got there just in time. The vultures had started to descend."

I shrug. "Just pulling my weight."

"Well, you can cook for me anytime you want," he offers, shoveling the last of it into his mouth.

I smile at him, my eyes roving over his bare chest.

"If you keep looking at me like that, these pancakes won't be the only thing I eat this morning."

I snort out a laugh and smack him over the head with his pillow.

"Calm down, Casanova, I was just thinking this was the first time I can remember you leaving this room without your jacket on."

"Cut," he replies, dipping his chin and touching his lips to mine.

"Cut?" I ask in confusion.

"My jacket. It's called a cut. It's a symbol of the brotherhood. I'm lucky neither King or Joker was around to see I forgot it or they would have handed me my ass."

A loud banging at the door prevents me from saying anything else.

"Orion!" I hear shout through the door. Orion pops his plate on the dresser and swings the door open.

"Morning, sweets." Gecko dips his head to me before turning to Orion. "King wants to see you downstairs."

"Tell him I'll be down in five."

Gecko's eyes linger over me for a beat before he turns and walks away. Orion heads to the bathroom and turns on the shower. Looks like I'm going to be stuck up here again for a while. Actually, no, fuck that. I throw my legs off the side of the bed and rummage through my bags for some clothes. I have a few orders that need filling and King said I was free to come and go as I please, so that's what I'm going to do. I can't spend my day cooped up in this room, so if that means spending it away from the compound, then so be it.

Orion strolls out of the bathroom, hair dripping and completely naked. I freeze on the spot and take him in. Hard corded muscles, that sexy V line, that—holy mother of god, he has a third arm.

"See something you like, Luna?" the sneaky bastard asks with a devastating smile.

"It's the first time I've been rendered speechless by a cock that I wasn't choking on," I sputter out.

He pauses as he's putting his boxers on and looks up at me with a glare. "We are just going to pretend, for argument's sake, that you're a virgin. I can't think about anyone who came before me putting their hands on you without wanting to kill someone."

I'm sure if my eyes weren't comically wide and staring at the one-eyed monster between his legs, I would have rolled them. "Orion, if I were a virgin, I'm pretty sure you would end up serving time for murder because there is no way that thing will fit inside me without killing me."

He groans as he pulls his boxers over his cock, gripping it to try and get it to lie flat. "Now she has me thinking about how tight she is," he mutters, pulling on a pair of black jeans and finally breaking me out of my dick stupor.

"I'm five foot nothing, Orion. Aside from the fact that it's going to be like squeezing a salami inside a straw, it's also entirely possible you'll be able to fuck me and get a blow job at the same time, as I suspect that thing is going to end up coming out of my mouth," I grumble, ignoring his stupid shaking shoulders as he laughs at me.

"It'll fit," he tells me, pulling on a black T-shirt and shoving his wallet into his pocket and grabbing his gun.

"That's easy for you to say. It's not your hoo-ha I can feel pulling down the shutters and popping up a sign saying 'out of order' on it."

His deep sexy laugh rings out as he bends down to put his boots on. He finishes tying his laces and stalks toward me. He grips my hips and pulls me against him so I can feel just how hard he is. "It'll fit. Now I have to go and meet my dad with a raging hard-on, thanks to you."

"Oh, no. You don't get to blame me. You were the one that came strolling out here waving it around—" He kisses me, cutting me off. Despite my reservations, I'm so fucking turned on right now that if he threw me down on the bed, I wouldn't stop him. Unfortunately, he pulls away with a groan.

"I've got to go. Stay out of trouble." He turns and with one last glance back, he's gone.

My plan was to jump in the shower and get out of here but as soon as I step into the shower stall, I'm surrounded by Orion's scent. Closing my eyes, I picture him watching me undress as he strokes his cock up and down. Fuck it. I slide my fingers down between my legs, not surprised in the slightest to find myself slick already. I dip a finger inside and slide it back out, swirling the moisture around my aching clit. I use my other hand to cup my breast and tweak my hardened nipple between my fingers. I speed up my movements, dipping inside again briefly, enjoying the slickness as I coat myself with it. I put a little more force into my movements as I feel myself getting closer to the edge. Finally, when I feel I'm about to peak, I pinch my nipple hard and explode all over my hand with a groan of satisfaction. I clean myself up and climb out, toweling off and running some product through my hair so when it dries the curls will be smooth and glossy. I slip on a baby-pink thong and a floor-length red and white striped maxi dress that ties around my neck, leaving my shoulders bare. I forego a bra, thankful that as a B-cup I can get away with it. I brush my teeth, apply a little lip gloss, and head for the door. I swing it open and find Orion leaning against the doorframe, breathing short shallow breaths that remind me of a bull getting ready to charge.

"The next time you come, it will be around my cock, understood?" he barks at me.

I nod as my cheeks flush with embarrassment at having been caught.

"I have something to do but there is a prospect outside your door if you need anything." He snatches his keys from the dresser and walks off, slamming the door behind him without saying goodbye. I'm not sure if I'm meant to be feeling aroused, pissed off, or a mixture of both.

"Fuck you, biker boy," I mutter to myself as I stomp like a petulant teen into the bedroom and snag some silver bangles from my bag. I slide a bunch of them up my arm and throw on a pair of red flip flops. I grab my laptop bag and shove everything in it I might need before grabbing my truck keys off the bedside table and heading for the door. I look to the left and find a man a few years younger than me that looks like he could be the star in a teen movie. Classic good looks with his floppy brown hair, dimpled smile, and straight white teeth, he reminds me of the actor who played the sparkly vampire but with just enough of a bad boy vibe going to make little girls cream their panties.

"Hey, I need to get out of here for a bit. Are you the

prospect Orion said was going to hang with me today?" He turns his head at my voice. His dark brown eyes take me in, trailing from my pink painted toenails all the way up to my crazy blonde ringlets.

"Fucking Orion, always gets the best ones," he mumbles. I think that's meant to be a compliment. "Name's Kibble and my job is to stick to you like glue today. So what do you need?"

"I have some errands to run and some bits to pick up for work. Nothing exciting, I'm afraid."

"Well, lead the way, lady. I'm all yours to do with as you please." His smile is deadly. Oh yes, I just bet he's popular with the girls. Trouble is, all he does is remind me of my brothers. Oh, shit that reminds me. I press the key on my watch which is the code we use to let them know I'm safe. They know where I am thanks to me activating the GPS but they won't send in the cavalry as long as I'm all right. They found out the hard way when they busted in on me with guns blazing while I was going down on my ex. They couldn't look at me for a month after that. There are just some things that can't be unseen.

There are a few people milling about but most don't pay us any attention until I walk into Rebel. He steadies me before I can fall flat on my ass and glares at the prospect behind me like it's his fault I wasn't paying attention.

"Where you off to?" he asks me

"I have shit to do today for work so I need to pick a few things up."

He looks at the prospect behind me again before turning back to me. "Want some company?" I'm a little taken aback by his offer but smile big in thanks.

"I would love some company, thank you." We walk out into the bright morning sunshine and head toward my truck.

"Prospect, follow behind on your bike. I'll ride with Luna in her truck."

"I thought we were going to just take the bikes. Luna, you're more than welcome to ride with me," Kibble says with a smirk. I might not be up on all things biker but I'm pretty sure riding on someone's bike other than Orion's or, given the situation, I guess Halo's, is a big no-no. He must know that, so I wonder if he's trying to get me in trouble or if he likes getting into trouble himself.

"I'm good, thanks, Kibble. I have supplies I need that won't fit on the back of a bike. It's why I have a truck in the first place." He shrugs like it's no big deal but I spot the tic in the side of his jaw as he walks away.

I offer Rebel the keys but he waves me off, climbs into the passenger seat, and leans his head back against the headrest with his eyes closed.

"What was that back there?" I ask him as I climb in and adjust the seat and mirrors after Orion drove it yesterday.

"What was what?" he asks without opening his eyes.

"You and Kibble."

"I don't know what you're talking about, Luna."

"Rebel... Is there something I should know about him?"

He looks over at me and sighs. "Kibble and I were

prospecting at the same time. I proved myself faster and got patched in a little over two months ago. He's been a dick since."

"Ah, so it's nothing to do with me? Just an old-fashioned case of the green-eyed monster?"

"For the most part, yeah, but don't underestimate him. He's called Kibble for a reason," he explains before looking in the side-view mirrors.

"What's that supposed to mean?" Damn it, I need a biker handbook or something.

"It means he got his name because pussy flocks to him. They eat up all the shit that spews from his mouth regardless of the consequences."

"Rebel, I love that you're looking out for me, but I'm twenty-eight years old. It's been a long time since I let my vagina make my decisions." I think back to earlier and Orion's super dick. "Okay, I will amend that by saying I'm into Orion and possibly Halo but that's it. I don't care if Kibble's dick is made of solid gold, I'm not interested."

He offers me a small smile but I can see he's not convinced.

"He's really good at twisting the situation to fit his needs. Just don't underestimate him, okay?"

I look away from the road briefly so he can see my face. "I won't, I promise." He closes his eyes again and naps the rest of the way to Megan's shop.

I find a space and maneuver my truck in before nudging Rebel awake.

"You didn't have to come, sleepy."

"Nah, it's fine. I needed to get out for a bit." Kibble pulls up behind us, so Rebel barks at him to watch the truck as we head inside the shop I love so much.

Megan's boutique opened about four years ago, right at the edge of Nevesham town. Megan had bought a few of my gift baskets online before opening her store. When her doors opened for business, she contacted me and asked if I would be interested in selling a few items out of her store. I immediately agreed and the rest is history. The little bell above the door and a flash of light signal our arrival and straight away I'm hit with the soothing scent of jasmine and lavender. The shop is decorated in various shades of purple and the floor to ceiling chrome shelves are filled with an assortment of trinkets and knick-knacks.

The woman I'm after is behind a high glass-topped black counter with her back to us, her sleek dark hair obscuring most of her face. I don't bother shouting for her, knowing she won't hear me. She obviously wasn't facing the door to see the entrance light go off when we entered. I lift the partition on one side of the counter and walk through, gently placing my hand on her shoulder before stepping back. Megan has quite a startle response so I don't want to be in hitting distance when she spins around. Sure enough, she whips around, swinging her arm out in a fist. Rebel takes a step forward but I hold up my hand for him to stay where he is. She flushes with embarrassment when she realizes it's just me and signs that she's sorry, blushing down to her roots when she sees Rebel glaring at her.

"Chill, Rebel, it's not Megan's fault I snuck up on her." I glare at him while I sign so that Megan can understand me too. She's pretty fucking amazing at reading lips but obviously, that only works if she can see them fully and the person she's reading doesn't look away.

"You need to face the front when you're here on your own. I could have been anyone coming in," I scold her, my fingers flying as I reprimand her but she knows I'm right.

"I'm sorry," I translate for Rebel as she signs back. "I'm having a shit morning and my brain isn't firing on all cylinders. My coffee machine died, my car wouldn't start, and then a shipment of goods got delayed."

"Damn, girl, you're not kidding about having a shitty morning, are you?" I turn to Rebel. "Do you think we could get Kibble to make a coffee run for us? There's a coffee shop just across the street." He glances at me then back at Megan and nods, heading toward the front of the store. Megan takes in his cut with wide eyes.

"A latte for me with three sugars and a black coffee without the added yumminess for Megan, please." He lifts his hand to let me know he heard me before opening the door and yelling for Kibble.

I turn back to Megan and see she's as white as a sheet.

"*Hey, what's wrong?*" I sign without speaking now that Rebel isn't here.

A motorcycle club, Luna? Are you nuts? She is signing so fast I can barely keep up.

Relax, Megan, you make it sound like I'm joining the circus.

Don't be ridiculous. The circus has less freaks.

And you would know this how, Megan? Been to many circuses? My sarcasm is lost on her. She doesn't answer but looks down at her feet. I walk forward and lift her chin so I can see into her pretty blue eyes. I let go so I can sign.

Or have you got experience with motorcycle clubs? She looks away again and I know I've hit the nail on its head. What the fuck? She's saved from me asking more when Rebel reappears beside us.

"Coffee will be here in a sec. Grab what you need, Luna, Orion is blowing up my phone."

"Why? I've been gone for thirty minutes, max."

"Because he didn't know where you were." Oh, give me a break.

"So what? It took him all of two seconds to call Kibble who I'm guessing mentioned you and boom, what do you know, he found me. I have shit to do and it doesn't involve sitting around in that fucking room all damn day while he's off doing whatever he needs to."

Rebel raises his hands in surrender. "Not my fight, Luna. That's between you and Orion."

I know he's right so I stomp over to the shelves and pick up the items I want and pop them on the counter with more force than necessary. Megan rings the stuff up, looking at me with worry clear on her face. I need to get back here without the leather army and find out what that's all about. Kibble strolls in with our coffees and places them on the counter before offering Megan a flirty smile. She just glares at him before picking up her coffee and taking a sip.

"Bit off your game there, huh?" Rebel laughs, making Kibble flip him off before walking back outside. I give Megan a quick squeeze, noticing how she holds me a little tighter than usual. Something is definitely off with her. I sign that I'll text her tomorrow and she nods as we turn and head back out to the truck. I throw the keys to Rebel so I can drink my coffee and try to get my anger in check at being summoned before getting back to the compound. Rebel wisely stays quiet as I sip my coffee and listen to the faint twang of some country song playing on the stereo. We pull up outside the gates. The same prospect that let us out, lets us back in again but this time Orion, with a face of thunder, is ripping my door open.

"Hey, Adonis. What's up?" I ask, casually placing my empty coffee cup back into the cupholder.

"What's up?" he asks me, his voice deceptively low.

"Yes, Orion. What. Is. Up? Because I know there's no way you would have ordered me back here like a fucking dog when I already had a prospect and a fully patched member with me. Especially after I was told I was free to come and go as I pleased." My chest is heaving by the time I've finished spitting out my words. I can hear Rebel choking on a laugh beside me but I don't take my eyes off the asshole in front of me.

Before I can blink, I find myself up and over his shoulder as he practically sprints toward his room.

"Hey, you big bastard, put me down." I slap his ass which makes him slap mine in response and his slap fucking hurts. He opens his door and tosses me down on the bed before he slams the door closed and pounces on me. Ignoring my sharp intake of breath, he kisses his way down my neck to my chest, licking the slope of my breast exposed by my dress. He scoops my breast out and sucks my nipple into his mouth, hard. When I buck underneath him, he bites down, making me scream.

"You drive me fucking crazy. Now, stay still." He uses his tongue to soothe the sting from his bite before he switches to my other breast. He's reaching up to loosen the strap around my neck, when there's a pounding at the door.

"Fuck!" he shouts before jumping off the bed. I squeal and rush to cover myself as he swings the door open, ready to rip someone's head off.

"Joker's looking for you," a voice I'm not familiar with tells him and his shoulders slump.

"I've got to go," he tells me with regret clear in his voice. He doesn't give me time to reply before he walks out, closing the door behind him. I roll over and scream into the pillow in frustration. How did my life become so fucking complicated in such a short length of time?

A glance at my watch lets me know King's party will be starting in a few hours. I could go downstairs and help out, ignore the questioning stares from the other MC members and the downright hostile ones from the women, or I could just stay here and psych myself up for later. I think about it for two seconds and decide an even better idea is to have a nap. I snuggle up to Orion's pillow as my heartbeat slowly returns to normal and drift off wondering if blue ovaries syndrome is a real thing.

CHAPTER SIX

Standing in front of the mirror, I put the finishing touches to my biker-chic outfit consisting of skin-tight black jeans that have rips across the legs from just below my crotch down to my calf, a white tank with a black rose printed on the front, and my trusted leather jacket always kept in my truck. Black rose earrings and matching choker finish the look. I leave my hair to dry naturally after my shower and run a little more product through it. I now have a mass of sexy waves falling down my back and over my shoulders. I went darker with my makeup—smoky eyes and dark red lips. I look a far cry from the wholesome girl who arrived a week ago. After this afternoon's impromptu make-out session with Orion, I'm hoping tonight's look will entice him to take things a little further. And if someone interrupts us, I will kill them myself.

I'm just finishing zipping up the black studded I'm-going-to-regret-these-later super high ankle boots that Orion insisted on buying, when the man himself walks through the door. I stand and watch as he looks up from his phone and freezes on the spot. He takes me in from head to toe and back again. The heat of his gaze scorches me through my clothes as he mentally undresses me.

"We need to go now," he snaps at me.

Disappointment replaces the heat in my veins from moments before. Would it kill him to say I look nice?

"Don't look at me like that, baby. If we don't leave right this second, I'm going to say forget the party, opting instead to bend you over the dresser and fuck you until your legs give out. Then I'm going to spread you out on the bed and start all over again. I'm so hard, I'm surprised I haven't burst out of my pants."

See, now that's what I was aiming for. I fight my grin, aiming for something a bit more seductive as I walk over to him. I trail my fingertips over his chest and down toward his waist. Snagging my fingers in his belt, I pull my body flush against his. Peeking up at him with wide eyes, I chew on my lip. I see the exact moment his control snaps and in the blink of an eye, I find myself in his arms with my legs around his waist. He has one hand under my ass keeping me up and the other in my hair, which he uses to hold me in place while he devours my mouth with a hard demanding kiss.

Reluctantly, he pulls away, lifting his head away from me.

"I have plans for you later," he tells me as he takes one last swipe of his tongue against my lips before lowering me back to my feet. He grabs my hand and hauls us out the door while I'm still trying to recover from that mind-blowing kiss.

"Stay by my side tonight, okay? We have guys in from another Kings of Carnage chapter." I nod in agreement before taking a deep breath to center myself. We head to the main room in the compound which is crowded tonight. I easily spot Gecko behind the bar, thanks to his hair, but he is the only familiar face I can see in the ocean of leather and Old Spice. Orion keeps a tight grip on my hand as he maneuvers us through the crowd toward the other side of the room. Spotting a woman on her knees giving head, I do a double-take. She is oblivious to my perusal but the guy with his dick in her mouth spots me and licks his lips, gripping her hair and forcing himself farther into her mouth until she gags, all while he smiles at me.

Ew, that's just nasty.

I take back everything I said before about all of these guys being hot. That man is in desperate need of a shower and a clean change of clothes. I look away from him as I make my way past, holding tight to Orion so I don't get lost in the crowd. This is the first time since I got here, despite everything that's happened, that I've felt wary. Finally, the crowd breaks and I find myself standing in front of a table surrounded by a few more familiar faces. King is there—the president, not the dog—with Inigo, Half-pint, and Joker on his left and two others who I haven't met yet to the right. One looks to be in his late thirties with chestnut brown hair and matching eyes, the other is built like Half-pint but much taller. In fact, the tall one seems to tower over everyone at the table, although that's only because Conan isn't around. Orion gestures to the big guy first.

"This is Tink and this is Hose. Guys, this is Luna." I give a little wave and promise myself I won't ask. Okay, that's a lie. I'm totally going to ask.

"Tink? As in Tinkerbell?" I smile so he knows I'm not trying to offend him but he still frowns, although the guys around us chuckle.

"I'm good at fixing things," he mumbles before taking a swig of his beer.

I focus on the guy with the chestnut hair.

"Hose? As in garden hose?" Okay, that one makes me scrunch up my face in confusion. Who wants to be compared to a garden hose?

"More like fire hose. It's because of the size of his dick. Apparently, he has to roll that thing up to put it away," Orion whispers in my ear.

"Really?" I shout, letting my excitement show. Who cares, I'm a freak for all things odd.

"Can I see?" Oops, maybe I shouldn't have asked that while he had a mouth full of beer.

A growl from behind me reveals Orion isn't happy with my question, which makes me sigh. Why are men so damn territorial? It isn't like I want to touch it, much. Okay, maybe I would poke it like a snake or something but come on, wouldn't everyone?

The table is deadly quiet as everyone watches me.

"Why is everyone staring at me?" I whisper to Orion.

"I don't know, maybe it has something to do with you wanting to poke the snake."

"Huh?... Shit, I said that out loud again, didn't I?" Instead of answering me, he crowds me until I'm pinned between his body and the table.

"The only dick you'll be touching tonight is mine," he tells me before crashing his mouth down on mine. Consuming me, completely unconcerned about the roomful of people around us. Every time he kisses me, I swear its better than the last, but this is more than kissing, this is him branding me, marking me as his in front of all his brothers. He pulls away from me to a round of catcalls and whistles but I ignore them and run the tip of my finger over my swollen lips. He watches my tongue flick out over my fingertip. His eyes dilate with lust and something in him snaps. I find myself tossed over his shoulder for the second time today, making the catcalls reach a fever pitch before we disappear back upstairs to the room we haven't long departed from. Being dropped to my feet jars me out of my stupor in time to watch him lock the door, turn, and prowl toward me. Gripping me and pulling me flush against him, he levers me to him with one hand on my hip and one wound tightly into my hair.

"I can't wait anymore, cherub, tell me you want this."

"Cherub?" I question as he pulls my hair tighter, tilting my head back so he can look into my eyes.

"It's all the golden curls and big blue eyes. It makes you look all sweet and innocent but I have a feeling you have a bit of bad girl in you just waiting to get out."

"More like I have a bad boy wanting to come inside me."

"Damn fucking straight."

He spins me so my back is pressed to his front and grips my throat with one hand, not enough to hurt but with just enough pressure to show me who's in control. He bites my neck, then relieves the sting with his lips, trailing them down to my shoulder before biting down again. I arch my back into him. Helpless with need, I grind against him.

"I wanted to spend hours torturing you the first time we were together but it's you who has been torturing me. I'm about to come in my pants. This time is going to be hard and fast but I swear, I will spend the rest of the night worshiping you."

I try to reply but the sound that comes out of my mouth is nothing more than an animalistic groan of consent. He slides my jacket off my shoulders before pushing me toward the bed.

"On your knees, cherub, head down, ass up." I do his bidding despite the fact I'm still fully clothed.

I feel his hands slip around my waist, popping open the button on my fly and lowering the zipper. Holding the waistband of my jeans, he peels them down over my ass taking my underwear with them. They only go as far as my thighs but when I try to lift up so I can get them off, Orion's hand stops me.

"Stay down," he growls at me.

A warm breath of air against my folds is the only warning I receive before I feel Orion's hot mouth against me, swiping through my wetness. Gasping, my hands fist the sheets as he flicks my clit with his tongue before sucking hard. The sensation is so intense, I have to bite my lip to keep myself from screaming. He dips his tongue inside me before he starts fucking me with it. I push back against his face, relishing the sensations rushing through me. I can feel myself dripping and my legs start to tremble, threatening to collapse beneath me.

"Fucking delicious," he says as he climbs up behind me. I hear him ripping open a condom wrapper before I feel him nudging his cockhead against my folds. He rubs against me, up and down, gathering my wetness and lathing it on his dick. I'm just about to lose my ever-loving mind when he surges inside, not stopping until he bottoms out inside me. I scream into the bedsheets at the intrusion, part in pleasure, part in pain.

"Holy fucking shit. Does your dick have to be so fucking big?" I manage to gasp out, surprised that I even remembered how to speak the English language.

He laughs, making me groan as he twitches inside me. Drawing back out slowly until just the tip remains, he's surging back in again, making me scream as I spasm around him.

"I'm a big guy, cherub. Think I would have cried like a little bitch if God decided to play a joke and gave me a small dick," he tells me as he powers inside me again and again.

"Guess the joke's on me. It feels like you're rearranging my insides."

He pauses for a second.

"Want me to stop?"

"If you stop, I'm going to chop it off."

He laughs again before slamming back into me. This position and the fact that I can't open my legs to accommodate him any more than I am already, makes him feel gigantic. I can feel my orgasm rapidly approaching; the vulnerability of this position as he takes what he wants from me adds to my arousal, leaving me a hot panting mess. Faster and faster he fucks me until I know I can't hold on any longer.

"Orion..." I warn him. He thrusts hard, seating himself fully inside me, gripping my hips firmly.

"Come, now," he orders and that's all it takes for me to detonate around him.

A haziness descends as I feel him pulse inside me before he collapses on the bed.

"You're going to have to carry me everywhere from now on," I manage to get out as I flop down onto his chest.

"Is that right?" I can hear the smugness in his voice

"Asshole," I mutter into his shoulder before I'm flipped onto my back with Orion looming over me.

"I'm up for a challenge but we might need to warm you up a bit first."

I frown at him for all of two seconds as my mind connects the dots. "Oh, hell, no! That is an exit only, I repeat, exit only. Jesus, you must think I have a death wish."

"Is it just my size or is it something you're generally not into?" he asks curiously.

"Do we have to have this conversation with my jeans around my thighs and your dick still jammed inside its cock sock?" He laughs but pushes himself up off me and removes the condom before heading into the bathroom to dispose of it. I attempt to sit up and peel my legs out of the jeans that took me ten minutes to squeeze into but I need to get off the bed to do that and I'm not sure my legs are willing to cooperate just yet.

"Need a little help there, cherub?" Orion asks with a smile on his face.

"I need to get cleaned up," I tell him, flopping back down with a dramatic sigh.

"Well, why didn't you say so?" He grabs the hem of my jeans and yanks my feet out, making it look ridiculously easy. I wait for him to move away but instead, he spreads my legs wide and buries his face between them.

"Ohmygod" comes out on one long breath as Orion licks up my arousal from before, making me wet all over again in the process.

"I'm not sure this is helping—fuck!" He flicks his tongue

over my clit, then sucks it. He laps at my juices before pulling away and wiping his mouth with the back of his hand.

"All done. Now let's get back down to this party." I just lie there gaping at him. Surely he isn't planning on leaving me like this, is he?

When he climbs off the bed, I realize that's exactly what he intends to do.

"What the—" He yanks me up off the bed and carries me into the bathroom, popping me on the edge of the counter as he rummages in the cupboard beneath it. Snagging a washcloth, he gently cleans between my thighs and over my sensitive folds, making me grind shamelessly against him, looking for friction.

"Behave," he scolds.

"But... but..." I can't believe he would get me this worked up and then leave me hanging. He leans over me and places his lips against the shell of my ear and whispers.

"That's for earlier. Listening to you get yourself off in the shower has been playing on a loop over and over in my mind all day. If you're a good girl, I'll make you come so hard later, you'll see stars. But for now, you need to get your cute ass dressed and downstairs.

"You are the one that's going to see stars because I'm going to smack you upside the head." I jump down off the counter and stomp back into the bedroom. I get dressed and yank my boots back on, all while muttering under my breath about the things I'm going to do to him later and none of it is going to be pleasant. I'm just touching up my makeup when he wraps his arms around me from behind.

"Just a little advice. If your attitude is meant to be turning me off, you've fucked up, cherub. I'm going to tie you to this bed later and fuck you until you can't breathe." He steps back, so I turn and drop the mascara wand and watch with a smile as it bounces off his chest. Okay, fine, I threw the mascara wand at him. Semantics.

"Why, you little—" He lunges for me, making me squeal. I run for the door and manage to make it out into the corridor before I collide with a wall.

"Ow, fuck." Thankfully the wall grabs me before I can fall—wait, what? I look up and see a dark chocolate-haired handsome—naturally, because aren't they all fucking handsome around here?—man scowling down at me with black eyes. I'm not even kidding. Who has black eyes? Demons, that's who.

I step back as Orion steps up behind me and slings his arm over my shoulder.

"Gage, I didn't realize you guys were back yet," Orion says to the demon who hasn't stopped staring at me. I wonder if he's trying to steal my soul. Bad demon.

"Seriously?" The demon—er—Gage asks, looking me up and down and finding me lacking.

"Not now, Gage," Orion warns, a threat evident in his voice.

"She'll break in a heartbeat. Then what, Orion? Pick someone else." What the actual fuck?

"If you're talking about his monster cock, I think I managed quite well, actually. I mean, sure, my uterus is now up behind my ribs somewhere but you don't hear me complaining, do you?" Asshole.

Orion chokes behind me as a look passes over Gage's face that has the hairs on my arms stand up. He steps up to me, invading my space without touching me.

"Little girl, you have no idea how much that mouth of yours is going to get you into trouble."

"Gage!" Orion barks at him before Gage slowly turns and walks away from us.

"What the hell was that all about?"

"Nothing you need to worry about right now, Luna, but you need to be careful how you speak to these guys. You can't show the brothers any disrespect."

"They can disrespect me, though, right?" I feel my high from earlier fading away.

"It's not that simple, cherub. There's stuff going on that you don't know about and tensions are running high."

"So tell me then."

"It's club business." End of conversation.

"Right." I give up.

I head toward the party with Orion hot on my heels and weave my way through the crowd to the bar. I find an empty stool and claim it before anyone else can, all while ignoring Orion's hulking presence behind me. Gecko spots us and heads over, nodding his head toward Orion before offering me a cheeky smile.

"What can I get you, sweetheart?" he asks me as he grabs a bottle of beer for Orion.

"Can I get a Jack and Coke please?" I need something to take the edge off.

"You got it."

"Luna, you can't ignore me all night. So unless you want me to bend you over the bar and spank the shit out of you in front of everyone, I suggest you knock it off."

My shoulders slump in defeat. I'm being a bitch and I know it. Plus, I know he really would do it. Now, I like a good spanking as much as the next girl but in front of a room full of bikers? No, thanks.

"Fine. But I reserve the right to get mad at you again later," I tell him, looking up at him and catching him trying to fight back a grin.

"Duly noted."

"There you go, sweetheart." Gecko places my drink in front of me. I pick it up and drink it down in one. Ahh, reminds me of home.

"Easy, tiger. I don't want you getting too drunk. I have plans for you later, remember?"

"Trust me, I can handle my whiskey. It's a requirement where I'm from."

In the mirror behind the bar, I see Halo and Gage approach us and I tense up. A small glint in Gecko's eyebrow catches my attention for a second, drawing my eye to the pretty little peridot stone. On anyone else, it would look utterly ridiculous but I have a feeling Gecko can make anything look badass.

"I like your new bling, Gecko. It brings out the color of your hair," I tease, making him laugh.

"Just like a woman to spot the jewelry," Gage mutters as Gecko slides him a glass with what I'm guessing is vodka. Shame, he looks like he would benefit from a little arsenic.

I spin around and glare at him but before I can say anything else, I find myself wrapped up in Halo's arms. I watch Orion as he takes a sip of beer, expecting him to rip Halo's arms out of their sockets despite everything he's said about sharing. But he really doesn't seem to have a problem with it.

"Well, hey now, sugar. What's a man gotta do to get a little lovin' around here?" Halo asks, flashing me twin dimples that I want to fill with milk and eat cereal out of.

"Have a monster cock and a bad attitude," I deadpan, making Orion spray his beer all over the bar.

Orion glares at me while the guys laugh around us. I keep my eyes on him and offer my sweetest smile while Halo bends down and whispers into my ear.

"Well, one out of two ain't bad, right?"

I crack up beside him. "I've seen you in your boxers, Halo. I never knew you had such a bad attitude." He looks at me, then to Orion who is still watching us with a grin.

"Wait, did she just imply that I have a small dick?" he asks Orion. I can't help it, I burst out laughing in his face. When he grabs my hand and places it on his hard and, might

I add, large cock, I freeze. This is one of those times when my mouth has gotten me into trouble yet again. My eyes fly back up to Orion's to find him not looking like he wants to kill me but like he wants to fuck my brains out. Holy shit, it's true, Orion is turned on because I'm holding his friend's dick. Which reminds me, I'm still holding on to his fucking dick. Let go, Luna. Let go of the dick. I give it a squeeze, which is definitely not letting go of his dick. When Halo groans in my ear, it finally snaps me out of my grope-fest. I slide off the stool and head for the front door, face aflame with embarrassment, needing to get some air before I climb him like a tree. I'm just about to head outside when I'm grabbed from behind and shoved against the wall face first.

"Well, hello, gorgeous. Let's go and have a little fun." Whoever it is grunts as he grinds against me.

"I would rather masturbate with a cheese grater. Now take your fucking hands off me or I'll break your fingers."

He licks the side of my face, bathing me with his rancid whiskey-fueled breath. "I like them feisty," he tells me as he slips his hand around to the button of my jeans.

"Yeah? Well, you're going to love this then." I lift my leg and slam the heel of my stiletto boot down onto his foot, making him bellow and loosen his grip before I swing my hand back and grab him by the balls. I turn around, briefly registering this is the guy who was getting a blow job earlier, and twist his balls hard until he makes a high-pitched noise.

"What the fuck?" I hear Orion's voice like thunder before the asshole in my grip is ripped away from me and thrown to the floor. The music cuts out for a second as people turn to see what's going on. I see Orion and Halo standing over the prone body of Mr. Grabby Hands, both of them giving him a kick for good measure before King whistles loudly.

"That's enough! Orion, Halo, walk it off. Now!" He looks at Half-pint beside him and nods his head. Half-pint makes his way through the crowd, which has parted for him, and pulls the groper up to his feet before half walking, half dragging him away.

Gage walks up to Orion and says something to him quietly, then he nods. Orion looks at me for a beat before turning and walking away with Halo right behind him.

Well, don't I just feel like utter shit now? I rub my hands up and down my arms, suddenly wanting to be anywhere but here, when Gage snags my hand and pulls me outside into the cool evening air. I could resist but wherever he's taking me has to be better than here, so I follow along without a word. When he leads me over to a bike, I hesitate. I look around. I don't see anyone I recognize and certainly not Orion. He left me. Well, fuck him.

"I just need to grab my bag from my truck," I tell him, not waiting for an answer as I hurry over to it. I open it up and find my laptop bag in the footwell where I left it earlier and slide it over my head and across my body. I head back over to Gage, who is waiting for me on his bike, holding his hand out for me to climb on behind him. I stand for a second and stare at his outstretched hand, knowing that climbing on the back of a bike that doesn't belong to Orion or Halo is asking for trouble. I remind myself those fuckers left me behind and grip him with my cold fingers. Once I'm on, he offers me his helmet which, stupidly, given all the things that have happened tonight brings a tear to my eye. I slip it on and adjust the chin strap before wrapping my arms around Gage's waist. I rest my head against his jacket, close my eyes, and hold on tight.

CHAPTER SEVEN

I keep my eyes closed the whole ride, letting the wind on my face soothe the frazzled edges of my mind. I only open them when the bike comes to a stop. The darkness has descended, casting shadows around us, making me realize I'm out in the middle of fuck knows where, with a man who clearly dislikes me. The ranch-style house before us is the only thing I can see in the fading light. Everything else seems to be trees as far as the eye can see.

"Where are we?" My voice seems overly loud in the quiet of the night.

He doesn't answer me. He just helps me off the bike and grabs my hand again, pulling me toward the house. He opens the door and flicks on the lights, revealing an open plan sitting room to my left and a kitchen to my right. The sitting room is decorated in creams and browns with a large brown leather sofa and a huge television on the wall in front of it. There is a dark wood coffee table scattered with bike magazines and empty beer bottles and an old-fashioned rocking chair in the corner.

I tear my eyes away and follow Gage into the kitchen. It's cream and perhaps a little dated but it looks like it serves its purpose. There is a small round table and chairs, big enough to seat four people, littered with more magazines and mail but aside from that, the kitchen is clean and tidy.

"Drink?" I jump in surprise when Gage opens his mouth to speak the first words he has said since he brought me here.

"Um... water?" It comes out more of a question than an answer. I look up at the big man with the chip on his shoulder.

"What's going on, Gage? Why did you bring me here?"

He grabs two glasses and slams the cupboard doors in his quest to get us both a drink and I think for a second he isn't going to answer me.

"I brought you here so that cooler heads could prevail. The Kings of Carnage had more than one chapter in tonight and some of them are as old-school as they come. They won't take kindly to a fully patched member being attacked on Carnage property," he explains as he fills each glass. I just stand there staring at him in shock.

"I was supposed to let him rape me against the front door with a room full of bikers behind us because he has a jacket with a badge stitched onto it? Are you fucking kidding me with this, Gage?"

He spins around and slams one of the glasses down on the counter, making the water spill over the rim.

"We live in a different world than the one you're used to, little girl. The rules are there for a reason. Every brother has the club at their back. Anyone else is expendable."

Fire floods my veins as my temper boils my blood.

"You're right, Gage. I live in a world where it's not okay to force yourself on a woman, or a man for that matter, just because *you* have decided you want them. I live in a world where no means fucking no. I live in a world where men are men because of their actions, not because of their words or their brute strength."

The door opens behind me, making me spin around as Orion and Halo walk through it with grim expressions on their faces. Orion walks straight up to me but I hold my hand out, making him freeze.

"Don't touch me. Am I allowed to even say that? Or do you have more rights to my body than I do?"

"That's not fair, Luna. I haven't done anything to you that you didn't want me to." I look at him and force down the tears that spring to my eyes.

"You left me there."

"I left you with Gage," he reasons, but I'm not having any of it.

"You. Left. Me. There." I swing my hand out toward Gage. "You left me in the care of a man who hates me."

"I don't hate you. I just don't think you're cut out for the MC lifestyle," Gage answers, shrugging his shoulders.

"You are absolutely right. This shit is not okay no matter which way you want to dress it up. The funny thing is, I could handle just about anything else, but not this, never this."

"You shouldn't have left my fucking side!" Orion roars in my face.

I look up at him, saddened that he just isn't getting it.

"I was eight steps away from you. Not eight feet, not eight miles, eight steps. Maybe you should have brought me a shorter leash."

"Or a fucking muzzle," Gage mutters around his glass.

"Fuck this shit, I'm done." I turn to storm off but Orion steps forward and grabs my arm.

"I decide when we're done, cherub." I look at him in disgust.

"If you don't let me go, I will gut you like a fish and wear your entrails as a trophy," I warn him calmly. I must sound like a psychopath because he lets go of my arm in shock, letting me storm away.

I head to the room farthest away from them at the end of the hallway and decide to stay in here for the rest of the night. I spot a white chair in the corner so I grab it and wedge it under the door handle before throwing myself down on the gigantic bed. As soon as I inhale, a scent I recognize from being pressed up against his back earlier invades my senses. I realize this isn't a spare room like I had originally thought, it`s Gage's. Fuck it. He can sleep out there with his buddies. If anyone comes near me right now, I'm liable to kill him. I slip into the little attached bathroom and splash cold water on my face before thinking "fuck it" and remove my makeup as well. I head back out to the bedroom, slipping off my boots and wiggling out of my jeans before pulling off my top and bra. I grab the first T-shirt from the dresser I can get my hands on and slip it over my head. I remove my jewelry and climb onto the bed, dragging the comforter with me. I bury my head under the pillow while I try to formulate a plan. I have a feeling tomorrow is going to be a clusterfuck.

* * * * *

I'M HOT. Really freaking hot. I try to kick the comforter off but find my leg pinned down under someone else's and a large hand spread across my stomach where my T-shirt has ridden up in my sleep. I feel him tense so I know he's awake.

"I thought I locked you out," I mumble.

Orion's deep voice rumbles over me. "We're bikers, cherub. It will take more than a door and a chair to keep us out."

Good to know. I open my eyes and find myself face-to-face with Orion. He's so close I can feel his breath on my skin.

"Halo or Gage?" I ask him. He cocks his head before looking over my shoulder.

"Halo," he answers.

"Want to tell me why you seem okay with me waking up with either of your friends wrapped around me?" See, there is no way the leg pinning me down or the hand on my stomach can belong to Orion if he's in front of me.

"Halo and Gage are my best friends. I trust them with my life and with yours."

"That's not an answer to the question, Orion. You might have alluded to sharing me with Halo before, but you never mentioned Gage. Any more you want to bring out of the woodwork or are you just expecting me to fuck everyone?"

He scowls at me but eventually sighs, shaking his head like he doesn't know where to begin.

Yeah, well, welcome to my world, Orion.

"It's only Halo and Gage. Nobody else, I promise. I just didn't know how to throw it all out there. You can trust them, Luna, I swear it." I look at him, trying to read between the lines of what he's saying as the fingers on my stomach start to stroke around my belly button.

"Trust them with what, Orion? My body? My heart? What do you all want from me?"

"We want everything," Halo whispers in my ear before sliding his hand down to my underwear. He trails his fingers around the edge of the material and, despite my confusion, I can feel myself growing wet.

"You want to share me with your friends?" I clarify yet again. I sound like a broken record, but at any second I expect him to tell me he's joking. I watch Orion lick his lips but he doesn't answer. He just pulls the comforter off my overheated body, fixing his eyes on Halo`s fingers.

"I don't understand. Why not just get a club whore to

share?" There is no way I'm going to come out of this without feeling used.

"Because we don't want a club whore, cherub," he tells me, sliding his hand up under my T-shirt to cup my breast as Halo's fingers dip just below the waistband of my underwear.

"We want an old lady," Halo continues before sliding his fingers through my small patch of blonde curls.

"I don't know if I'm staying yet," I say, panting.

"Then at least give us a chance to convince you of all the reasons why you should," he whispers in my ear before slipping a finger inside me. I gasp in surprise. Surprise that I didn't stop him, surprise that I don't want to.

I watch the fire blaze in Orion's eyes. He wants this badly. I don't know what I want and with his hand tweaking my nipples and Halo's fingers inside me, I can't think rationally enough to consider all the variables.

"What happened to, 'we're just going to pretend you're a virgin cuz I can't think about someone else's hands on you without wanting to kill them?'" I mock, trying to emulate Orion's voice. He pinches my nipple hard, making me squeal and back up into Halo more.

"That statement still stands but it's different with Halo and Gage." He looks down at Halo's hand working me beneath my panties.

"Seeing his hands on you does nothing but turn me on." He slides my T-shirt up a little more to reveal my breasts before leaning forward and taking a nipple into his mouth.

Halo picks the same moment to suck on a spot behind my ear before driving another finger inside of me.

"Fuck!" I slide one hand down and grip a handful of Orion's hair as he flicks over my nipple with his tongue. I lift my other arm to reach back and grip Halo's hair and hold him against me as he sucks on my neck.

"Say yes, Luna," Halo whispers against my skin.

"Where's Gage?" I choke out on a moan as my resistance slips away from me.

Orion lifts his head to answer me. "He went back to the club to see what happened after we left. Say yes, cherub. I know you want to."

Fuck it, I hate it when he's right. Oh god, am I going to do this? Halo crooks his fingers, rubbing against a place inside me that makes me see spots.

"Yes," I give in with a sob. Orion yanks me up out of Halo's arms and whips my T-shirt over my head before slamming his mouth down onto mine. I hear the rustling of clothes behind me but I pay it no attention as Orion tongue-fucks my mouth with as much vigor as when he fucks my pussy. I feel warm hands on my hips a second before Orion breaks the kiss and climbs off the bed, stripping out of his T-shirt and jeans. The hands behind me slide their way up my body to cup my breasts. I tip my head back against Halo's shoulder and thrust my ass against his now naked cock.

"Fuck," he grunts in my ear. I tilt my head up to see him watching me with such a look of intensity on his face that I almost come just from that look alone. He slants his head down before his lips graze mine in a soft, feather-light kiss. It's enough to light a fire inside him, as a second later I'm flat on my back with a very sexy Halo bearing down over me. This time his kiss is hot, scorching me from the inside out. His lips are soft but firm, forceful yet teasing, and they are driving me out of my mind.

"Are you going to share her or what?" I hear Orion ask as he climbs naked onto the bed beside us.

"Fuck you. You've already had her all to yourself. Have some fucking patience," Halo growls at him. Orion just laughs and sits behind me with his back flat against the headboard.

"You need to get a taste, Halo. I swear you'll lose your mind," Orion tells him, making me squirm. Oh, I like this idea.

"I'm already losing my fucking mind," Halo grumbles, sitting up so Orion can snag me under my arms and pull me up so my back is against his front.

Halo slides my underwear off before he opens my legs and lifts each one over each of Orion's thighs, leaving me wide open to him. When I try to cover myself up, Orion grabs both my wrists and pins them between our bodies.

"Tsk, tsk, cherub. Trying to hide what belongs to us."

"Fuck you, Orion. I don't belong to anyone."

"Is that right, sugar?" Halo smiles at me but it's nothing like the sexy smiles he usually bestows upon me. Right now, Halo looks every inch of the hardcore biker he is. I just unwittingly made myself a challenge, a challenge that Halo has no intention of backing down from. He lowers himself between my legs, blowing gently against my exposed pussy, making me squirm.

This is about to become a battle of wills to see who can hold out longer. Who is the strongest out of the two of us, who—"Fuck!"

Never mind, Halo wins. When he swirls his tongue over my clit for a second time, I'm not only ready to declare him the winner but I want to give him a gold fucking medal too.

With my arms pinned behind me, Orion takes advantage of my position by sliding his large, rough hands around to cup my breasts. He drags his thumbs over my erect nipples as Halo sucks hard on my clit, making my back arch at the duel sensations. I whimper at the explicit pleasure these two men are giving me, knowing they are playing my body like an instrument. At this point, I'm willing to sing any tune they ask of me.

"You like that, cherub?"

I moan in response to Orion's stupid question.

"Tell me," he demands.

"You want me to have a chat while Halo's tongue is inside me?"

Halo laughs against me, blowing hot air over me. Oh my.

"I want to know you're enjoying it. I don't want you to feel like we backed you into a corner."

"I swear to fucking god, Orion, if you don't shut up, I'm going to kill you." I pull myself forward and yank my arms free. Reaching down, I grip Halo's hair harder than necessary in my frustration, making him moan and tip his head back so Orion can see his face glistening with my juices.

"Look at his face, Orion. Now tell me, do you think I'm enjoying it?" I look down at Halo who is smirking at me and something snaps inside me.

"Fuck me, Halo, hard and fast. I want to feel you inside me." The smirk slips off his face, only to be replaced with a feral expression of need. He reaches over to the bedside table and snags a condom, ripping it open with his teeth before sliding it on his impressive but thankfully slightly smaller than Orion's length. Halo kisses me softly as he nudges his cock at my entrance. He slides his tongue into my mouth and surges inside me. I can taste myself on his lips, making me feel wanton and wild. He pulls almost all the way out before surging in again and again. His strokes are slow but forceful. Each thrust pushes me back into Orion who is pinching my nipples and licking up the side of my neck.

"Oh, god, faster, Halo." I try to tip my hips up to meet his thrusts but Orion lifts his thighs, preventing me from moving.

"You will take exactly what I give you until you admit you belong to us," Halo tells me, making me squirm and mewl like a newborn kitten. I'm so close to the edge I just need a little bit more.

"Please, please, please, Halo," I beg.

"Say it, Luna." He thrusts into me hard, bumping something inside me that makes my legs spasm.

"Say 'I belong to you.'" He holds still inside me, letting

me know he has all the power to let me come and the power to take it away. He rests his forehead against mine, his arms shaking with the restraint he's showing.

"Say it," he whispers, making me realize something. He doesn't just want this, he needs it. He needs me.

"I belong to you," I whisper. His eyes blaze for a second before his lips devour mine as he begins hammering into me. Orion slips his hand down between us and strums my clit, setting off an explosion within me. I clamp down hard on Halo and scream my release into his mouth, capturing his roar when he comes just after.

"Jesus." Halo collapses flat on his back. I'm not given any time to recover. I find myself pushed over on top of Halo, my sensitive breasts brushing against his heaving chest and my hair falling around us, curtaining us away from the rest of the room. He kisses me softly, completely at odds with the wild biker from a second ago. I don't have time to think about it as Orion slides inside me. I grunt at the invasion. Despite the fucking I just received from Halo, Orion's sheer size pushes my body's boundaries to the limit. I break the kiss, unable to concentrate on anything other than breathing. Orion thrusts become erratic, shoving me forward a little, which lines my breast up with Halo's mouth. Not one to miss an opportunity when it's presented to him, he snags a nipple between his teeth.

"Oh god." There's something about a pinch of pain that always seems to enhance my pleasure.

"Come now, cherub!" Orion orders as I feel him pulse

inside me. Halo takes that as his queue to bite down on my nipple. Hard. Motherfucker. My orgasm crashes over me, stealing the last of my energy and sanity along with it. I collapse on top of Halo and vow I shall remain here for the rest of my days.

"Tell my brothers I love them," I manage to croak out

Halo chuckles underneath me. "Not sure now is the best time to talk about your brothers, sugar."

"I'm dying. It might be the only chance I get."

Orion laughs as he pulls out of me, making me groan. "You're not dying, cherub. Not now that we're finally getting shit sorted out."

"Don't be so sure about that. I saw a white light there for a second and I'm pretty sure I just had an out-of-body experience." They both laugh at me again. Assholes.

"I need you to roll off me for a sec, sugar, so I can get rid of this condom," Halo says softly.

"M'kay," I mumble, burrowing further into his chest.

"Sweet after sex. I'll have to remember that." I can hear the smile in his voice. I haven't got the heart to tell him it's because I'm too shattered to flip him off.

"I got her." Strong arms lift me and cradle me so Halo can slip out from beneath me.

"Shower, cherub?"

"Is sleeping all day an option?" I ask, hoping he says yes.

"'Fraid not. We've got shit to do and we need to sit down and have a chat." And just like that my glow starts to dim.

"Yeah, shower sounds good." He carries me into the

bathroom and places me down on my feet, leaning forward to start the shower.

"I'll leave you to it. I'll go use the other bathroom after Halo is done to give you five minutes to breathe by yourself, okay?" I nod, not sure what else to say. He bends and kisses my forehead.

"We'll figure shit out, cherub. Don't worry so much." He turns and walks away, showing me a glimpse of that sexy ass of his. My libido wakes up and starts shaking her hips. I smack the bitch upside the head and climb into the shower, turning the water to cool. I freshen up and rinse off before climbing out and snagging the world's smallest towel. A quick search shows no more towels but I do find a spare toothbrush. I dry myself as best I can on the scrap of material and brush my teeth. My hair is dripping down my back by the time I'm finished and there is no way this towel is going to cut it. I sigh and head out the door, hoping one of the guys can help. I let out a startled scream when I find Gage looking at the bed. He turns when he hears me. His eyes move up my legs to the apex of my thighs, pausing for a second before continuing to my breasts and finally connecting with my eyes.

"Is it my turn now?" he sneers, making me itch to cover myself up but I refuse to let this asshole make me feel ashamed.

"You have nothing I want, Gage, besides a towel," I say with a nonchalant shrug of my shoulders.

"Hey, Luna, how..." Halo trails off when he sees me and Gage in a weird kind of standoff.

"Hey, Gage. How'd it go?" Orion walks in behind Halo with a towel in his hand. I walk over to him and take it before wrapping it around my body. Fuck my dripping hair.

Gage rubs a hand over his face and sits on the end of the bed. "It's sorted out for now. Luna was under our protection so it was Pipe's fault for starting shit. At least that was the general consensus. There are still some pissed off assholes that wanted retribution but King sorted it out. The other chapters are heading out today anyway. King said to tell you to get your asses up there to see them off."

Halo and Orion both nod, looking relieved. I hate to think what retribution would have been dished out otherwise.

I grab my clothes from where I left them last night and take them into the bathroom with me. I forego underwear. Nobody needs to be wearing day-old panties. That's just nasty. I pull on my jeans, bra, and tank but don't bother with any of my jewelry, sliding it into my pocket instead. I use the towel to squeeze the extra moisture out of my hair and give it a finger comb to separate the curls a little. This is about as good as it's going to get, I'm afraid.

I open the door and listen to them talking quietly to each other, oblivious to the fact I can hear them.

"All I'm saying, guys, is I'm not convinced she's the one," Gage mutters.

"Yeah, we know but we agreed it was majority rules. You

were the one who picked Jules and I hated that bitch from the start," Halo tells him. Who the fuck is Jules?

"Yeah, and look how that turned out. She was only in it for a good time. When the summer was over, she left to marry some yuppie asshole from the city."

"This Luna chick screams high maintenance. Do you really think she's going to be happy slumming it with a trio of fucking bikers? Wake up, Halo. We'd be better off training a club whore. At least she would know what she was doing and know when to keep her mouth shut."

"Jesus, Gage. You really want to swap Luna for a club whore? I think you've taken one too many blows to the head lately. I don't mind sharing with you guys but I don't want to share pussy with the rest of the damn club," Orion snaps at him. Ha, you go, Orion.

"It's never stopped you before," Gage quips. Ah, balls. Orion, you suck.

"There's a big difference between dipping my wick so I can get off for the night and making someone my old lady," he tells him, pacing back and forth in front of the bed before turning back to Gage.

"You just need to fuck her already. Trust me, you'll get where I'm coming from then."

Oh, I'm going to murder Orion in his sleep.

"It will take more than a golden snatch to convince me. She is too fucking soft and doesn't know her place. She isn't cut out for this world and I don't want to waste my time when we could be working on someone else." I count to ten in my head and when that doesn't work, I count to twenty, trying to talk myself down from shooting Gage in the face.

"Well, I like her and it's got nothing to do with her pussy." Okay, Halo, you are now officially my favorite.

"I mean, sure, it's snug as fuck even after she's been stretched out by this fucker." He laughs, hitting Orion in the chest.

Stretched out! Stretched out! I'm going to kill everyone. Murder. Kill. Die. A red haze descends over my eyes.

"But she is also funny, sweet, caring and so fucking beautiful I have to blink before I'm blinded by it. I swear to Christ, it's like looking at the sun." Okay, maybe I won't kill Halo. Today at least.

"Fine, I'll give her a shot. It's one month. If it doesn't work out or I still don't like her, then we move on. This chick better be able to suck like a fucking Hoover after the headache she's given me. I don't want to have to go and find Stacey afterward or it defeats the point in having a house mouse in the first place."

They both nod and agree, like shopping for a woman is an everyday occurrence for them.

So wait, if Gage decides to vote me off the island, they'll toss me aside and go find someone else, regardless of my feelings toward them? I don't fucking think so.

I push the door open hard, making it slam against the wall behind it. All three of them freeze before slowly turning to face me. I ignore them, walking over to the side of the bed where I left my boots last night. I slip them on as the silence stretches out between us all. I grab my jacket and shrug it on, pulling my hair free of the collar before walking past them.

I just make it to the door before my arm is snagged, tugging me back.

"Let go of my arm." My voice doesn't shake, it's threaded with steel and determination.

"Luna, wait a second—" I look at Halo. Whatever he sees makes him let go of my arm and sigh.

"Come on, cherub. You're overreacting," Orion tries to cajole. If I could start a fire with my eyes alone, Orion would be nothing more than a pile of ash right now.

"Just let her go. She doesn't want to be here anyway," Gage tells them with scorn in his voice.

"Your manipulations won't work on me, Gage. What, you think if you twist things enough I'll start questioning myself? Start agreeing you're right and I'm wrong so I will... what? Try to prove myself to you?" He doesn't say anything but I don't miss the tick of his jaw.

I step right up to him, between his spread thighs where he sits, and lean down so my face is inches from his.

"Better men have tried and failed. I have nothing to prove to you, any of you. Loyalty shouldn't just be given blindly, it should be earned. In your attempt to decide if I was worthy of yours, you failed to notice you are not worthy of mine." I stand up and head to the door again but they don't try to stop me. Probably realizing this time they had pushed me too far.

"Chose better next time, boys, but a word of advice. You

might want to take a long hard look in the mirror and decide how deserving of loyalty you are."

With that parting shot, I walk out the door and through the sitting room, snagging my bag from the table as I pass it. Out in the blazing summer sun, I close my eyes and tip my head back, soaking in the rays and letting go of the last of my anger. What's the point? They had their shot. They blew it. I'm not going to be that girl. The one who cries over what could have been. Nah, I have my ways of getting over shit like this. At least I can say I got some pretty spectacular sex out of it all. If nothing else, it will be material for my finger vault. But treating me as an option leaves me with no other choice than to walk away.

I figure I have about ten minutes before they come out to see if I've calmed down. They know I'm in heels in the middle of nowhere without my truck, so I'm betting they think they have just enough time to come up with a new plan of action while I cool off. Silly boys. I swing the keys around my finger that I picked up with my bag on the way out and head over to Gage's cherry red bike. I swing my foot against the kickstand while holding on to the handlebars and silently push the bike toward the end of the road. It wouldn't do to alert them to my plan, now, would it? The heavy bike crunches over the gravel as I finally make it to the road.

See, when Orion asked if my brothers rode, it never dawned on him to ask if I did. All these guys see is the girly clothes and the big blonde curls before making up their mind about me. If they only knew. I climb onto the bike and slip the helmet from the handlebars over my head. The bike is a little bigger than I'm used to but I can make it work. I start the engine and tear out of there, leaving behind a tiny piece of myself in the process and unknowingly taking a tiny piece of them with me.

CHAPTER EIGHT

Two months later

I shut the door to Megan's shop behind me and slip my bag off my shoulder so I can hunt for the keys to my truck, which always sink to the bottom. Out of the corner of my eye, I spot the bike parked across the street beside the coffee shop and sigh. Well, doesn't that just make an already shitty day worse. I hook my keys with my finger and quickly unlock Gramps's old truck before climbing in and sitting with the bag on my lap. I slip my hand back inside, palm my gun, and wait. I don't have to wait long before the passenger door opens and a big burly biker with black eyes stands there, glaring at me. Now I might have been lenient if it had been Rebel or Gecko but it's just my luck it's Gage and, unfortunately for him, I'm not feeling very charitable.

I pull the gun, flick the safety off, and point it at his head. I cock the trigger, the distinctive sound making him freeze. He swallows hard as he takes me in and I swear for a split second I see relief flash through his eyes before he masks it.

"What are you doing here, Gage?"

"Do you want to put that thing away first?" he asks, with a deep and rough voice.

"Not really, no. Now tell me what the fuck you're doing here."

"Where have you been, Luna? And what the fuck are you wearing?" A little of the fire I've come to associate with him begins to bleed through as his eyes rove over the exposed skin of my stomach that my little black crop top and skinny jeans leave bare. The long gray shirt I had hastily pulled on over the top is wide open and offering little protection from Pervy Mcpervisson.

"My eyes are up here and if you keep answering my questions with questions, I'm going to shoot you just for the fun of it," I snap, making his lip twitch before he can stop it.

He rubs his hand over his face before indicating the seat beside me. I look at him incredulously. On a scale of one to ten, how dumb does this guy think I am?

I don't answer him but I move my aim from his head to his dick. He sighs but steps back a little. I guess his dick is more important to him than his head. What a shocker.

"You just left, Luna, not telling a soul you were leaving."

"Not sure it would have been much of a getaway if I had told you three I was leaving. I'm sure you were so cut up about it you called my name while bouncing Stacey up and down on your dick." I roll my eyes at him.

Gage glares at me but carries on when I wave the gun at him.

"The agreement was that you stayed for thirty days and you broke it."

"I was supposed to be safe there, Gage, but you guys made it perfectly clear I was always going to be expendable." He shakes his head but doesn't deny it because we both know I'm right.

"You need to come back. You need to honor the agreement."

I throw my head back and laugh. "It's funny you should mention honor." His jaw flexes again, this time in anger. "Give me one good reason why I would ever willingly put myself in that kind of situation again?"

"King's sick, really sick and Orion is losing his mind. He needs you, Luna." Well, fuck. Orion is an asshat but King kind of grew on me like a fungus or something.

"What's wrong with him?" I lower the gun a little but make sure he keeps the distance between us.

"I just told you, his father is sick." He cocks his head at me in confusion when I swing the gun back up to his head. I forgot how much this guy gets on my last fucking nerve.

"King, you asshole. What's wrong with King?" I say through my clenched teeth. He looks over my shoulder for a split second and though it tells me everything I need to know, I'm too late to maneuver out of the way. My door is yanked open a second before something comes crashing down onto the back of my head. I crumple in my seat like I'm made of paper, only missing conking my head on the steering wheel because I'm shoved over toward the passenger seat and into Gage's waiting arms. I try to blink the fuzziness away as I feel blood trickle down the back of my neck, just so I can catch a glimpse of the man I'm going to kill.

Kibble looks down at me with no expression on his face whatsoever but it's enough to ingrain itself into my memory. I won't forget, even as the blackness pulls me under, I vow.

I drift in and out, catching snippets of conversation before drifting off again. I can tell I'm in the front of the truck still, even without opening my eyes. I can hear Gage and Kibble arguing but I can't make out their words, only their harsh tone. I wake again when I hear the screech of a metal gate. I wince as I crack my eyes open a little to see both bikers looking out the window, oblivious to me, so I take a second to hit the GPS on my watch and an SOS. Unfortunately, I know my brothers are on a mission in the middle of bumfuck nowhere at the moment. They won't get this until they're already halfway home so I'm going to have to wait this shit out for a little while. But they will come for me, and when they do, these bikers are going to be in for a rude awakening.

"I'm just telling you to prepare yourself. If you think because you're a patched member now that Orion, or Halo for that matter, won't kill you, you are severely mistaken," I hear Gage tell Kibble as the gate screeches closed behind us.

"And yet you don't seem too bothered," he correctly points out.

"Yeah, well, she was pointing a gun at me and I'm not entirely convinced she wasn't going to pull the trigger."

Kibble laughs as the truck comes to a stop. "All this fuss for a piece of gash. I just don't get it." I feign unconsciousness again when the truck doors open.

"Grab the bikes out the back of the truck and park this piece of shit over there by the other one she left here," Gage says as he carefully drags me out of the backseat and swings me up into his arms. His hands feel rough against my bare skin as he holds me tightly to his chest. The flurry of movement has me fighting back vomit but I keep my body loose and limp so as not to give myself away. Every step he takes sends a shard of pain through my head.

"What the fuck?" I recognize that voice. It's Rebel.

"None of your business, man," Gage tells him gruffly as we make our way farther inside the clubhouse.

"This is my fucking club too, Gage, so explain to me why she's lying unconscious in your arms and bleeding everywhere?" I have never heard that tone from Rebel before. He sounds lethal.

"She pulled a gun on me, Rebel, what the fuck was I supposed to do?" Gage tells him.

Rebel snorts. "And what did you do, Gage, huh? Let me guess, you were waiting for her, right? So she was protecting herself. Seems like something she has had to do a lot around us." He sighs and even I can hear the disgust in his tone over the throbbing in my head.

"Why is she here?" he asks something I would really like to know myself.

"She has to serve out her thirty days."

"We both know that was a trumped-up, fake as fuck sentence handed out to save face. It was thanks to her stirring shit up that we figured out Weasel had been double-crossing us."

"I'm just following orders, Rebel. If King wants her here, that's the end of it. You know the score."

"I want no part in this, Gage. I might be complicit in a lot of fucked-up shit but I won't be a part of this." He storms off. On one hand it's nice to have someone point out how utterly fucked-up this shit is, but on the other hand, he still left me here.

Gage continues walking when his name is bellowed from across the room.

"What the fuck is she doing here?" Whoever it is, sounds furious but I doubt very much it has anything to do with the fact I'm hurt and more to do with the fact I'm back here to begin with.

"King's orders, Joker. I thought you knew."

"If I had fucking known, I wouldn't have asked. Why is she unconscious?" He doesn't sound upset, just curious. Asshole.

"King said by any means necessary. Kibble decided this

was necessary." You didn't exactly stop him there, buddy, I think to myself, trying to keep my breathing even.

"And you couldn't have just fucked her into submission?"

Gage laughs loudly, making me bite my lip in agony. "You have met, Luna, right? I'm pretty sure she hates my fucking guts. She would have sliced my cock off if I had tried anything. Not to mention, she had a gun pointed at my head."

"Of course, she did. Stupid woman doesn't know her place anymore, not that she did before," Joker mutters. I would love to smack him upside the head, preferably with a tire iron.

"Orion and Halo are still out on a run and won't be back until late tonight. Rebel and I have to leave before that to get to the meeting with the new potential suppliers in time. We can't afford to miss it, what with Gemini cutting us out like that."

Joker growls. "Orion and Halo are looking for answers as to why our biggest supplier would suddenly up and leave but Gemini is like a fucking ghost. He only ever sent his lackeys to do his bidding and even those are proving to be elusive."

Joker takes a deep breath before blowing it out. "Strip her and stick her in the cells."

"What? Joker, come on," Gage protests.

"I'm the fucking president now, Gage, and you'd do well to remember that. Now strip her and stick her in the cells. If I have to repeat myself again, I'll do it my fucking self and, word of warning, Gage, I'm pissed off enough not to care what King's plans are for her." Joker's the president? What the hell?

"This is fucked-up, Joker. Orion and Halo are going to lose their minds."

"So be it," Joker answers before disappearing.

Fuck, this is so not good. I could try to fight now but I know I won't get far, especially if it turns out I have a concussion. I could let Gage know I'm awake and try to reason with him but I know he won't go against Joker's orders. Plus, he might end up restraining me. If he thinks I'm still out of it, I stand a much better chance of protecting myself if I need to, as well as trying to find a way out of here.

The first thing I notice when we reach our destination is the smell. It takes every ounce of willpower I have not to throw up everywhere. This place stinks of blood, decay, and feces. The next thing I notice is the cold. It seeps through my thin shirt and jeans, straight into my bones. Fuck, I hope Orion and Halo don't take too long to get back. They might not be my favorite people but I still have enough faith in them to know they wouldn't want me dead.

I keep my eyes closed, fighting back the sting of tears over my humiliation as Gage carefully undresses me. His movements are thankfully clinical, robotic, almost as if he has shut off every emotion and for that I'm grateful. There's no way I could just lie here and take someone's unwanted advances.

Finally, I hear him move away and the sound of the cell opening and closing behind him. I swear for a second I thought I heard a whispered "sorry" but realize it must have been my imagination. I doubt Gage is ever sorry about anything.

I wait five minutes but when I don't hear anything else, I open my eyes and look around. The room is dark and damp, some kind of sub-basement if I had to guess from the lack of windows. There are three cells including mine but I'm the only person down here. The floor is cold hard concrete and there's a bucket in the corner. That's it, the entire contents of my cell. There isn't a bed or even a blanket for that matter. Something tells me it's all a psychological move from the Kings of Carnage viewpoint but I never envisioned I would end up here.

I touch the back of my head gently and wince when my fingers come away damp with blood. It's not bleeding much anymore but the fact it's still bleeding at all is worrisome. The rest of me seems fine, which, given the circumstances, is a blessing. I'm so fucking mad at myself. I knew going to see Megan was risky but I'd been going stir-crazy out on the ranch and figured the MC would have lost interest in me by now. I never thought it would pan out like this. I manage to get myself up into a sitting position but I finally lose my battle at fighting back the vomit. I manage to lean forward and avoid getting any on myself. Fuck, this is not good. My head has a brass band playing inside it and my vision keeps fading in and out. I need to come up with a plan, something to get out of this fucking mess, but I can't focus enough to concentrate. I crawl into the corner, needing the walls at my back and the protection they offer, and curl into a ball. I wrap my arms around myself and give in to the descending darkness.

I wake up with a still banging head but the sickness seems to have eased off a little. Every bone in my body aches from sleeping on the cold unforgiving floor. A glance at my watch, which Gage didn't bother to take off, reveals it's two o'clock in the morning. I hit SOS again, knowing it's unnecessary but it feels like I'm doing something at least. I walk over to the corner farthest from the one I slept in and relieve myself in the bucket. As much as I feel like a fucking animal, this bucket is the only weapon I have at the moment. If someone tries getting handsy, they are going to seriously end up regretting it.

I walk the length and width of the cell, over and over, backward and forward, trying to keep myself warm even as my body wracks with shivers. Where the fuck is everyone? Did they seriously just bring me here to die? Because that's what's going to happen if it gets much colder down here.

Eventually, it becomes too much and my shaky legs threaten to give out. Not wanting to risk falling and banging my head again, I walk back to my corner and fold myself up as small as possible and wait. Wait to be saved, wait to die. At this point, I'm not sure which is going to be the lesser of two evils

CHAPTER NINE

The sound of gunshots wakes me. I back up as far into the corner as I can but it isn't long before I can feel unwelcome hands on my body. I lash out with what little strength I have left but there just isn't enough force behind it to do any damage.

"Shh... I've got you, Luna." Gage. Shit, now what? I struggle as he wraps his arms around me and swings me up into his arms. I hold on as my body shakes so hard I'm sure he's going to drop me. He runs to the bedrooms, every movement jarring me and making my head throb. He finally takes me into an unfamiliar room but I know straight away from the smell it belongs to him. He places me gently on his large bed and drags the thick comforter over me. I burrow down into it and squeeze my eyes tightly closed as I try to get my convulsing body under control.

I hear Gage moving around before the bed dips and he slides under the covers with me. As soon as I feel his naked flesh against mine, I freak out and try to throw myself off the side of the bed. He must have anticipated my move as he wraps his arms tightly around me and pulls my chest to his. His heat hits me instantly, making my body and mind war with each other as one fights to get closer to him and the other battles to get away.

"I know you don't want me anywhere near you." His deep voice fills the room. "You have every right to hate me, and you should, but we need to get you warm as quickly as possible. I swear to god, I won't hurt you and I won't let anything else happen to you while you're here. My word might not mean anything to you right now but I *will* prove it to you." I still my movements, angry at him, angry at me, angry at the whole fucking world.

"Wh...hh...y did y...you bring me... herrre," I stutter out, struggling just to form the words. I can feel sleep threatening to drag me back under as his heat starts to soak into my skin but I fight it, not trusting him at all.

He sighs, pulling me closer and pressing my face up against his neck. I feel the vibrations when he starts to speak and find it strangely comforting.

"I told you King was sick but it's bad, Luna. He has an inoperable tumor on his brain. He doesn't have long left. Joker has stepped up as president, which makes Orion the new vice president. However, with everything going on, he's been losing his shit and refuses to deal with it. I think King thinks you'll give him something else to focus on.

"So I got thrown under the bus by King because Orion having his favorite chew toy back means less focus on him," I manage to whisper without stuttering, even though my words still sound a little slurred.

"I don't know, Luna, maybe. I think he saw how happy Orion was when you were here and he wanted to give that back to him before he was gone."

"And having me kidnapped, knocked unconscious, stripped naked, and locked in a freezing cold cell is the key to Orion winning me back?" I ask, dumbfounded.

He tips my head back so I can see into his eerie black eyes.

"King just wanted you back here. He knew you would argue but he's a stubborn asshole and insisted. He had a rough night, though, and spent it at home or he would have been here to see you. Fuck, Luna, I didn't expect everything to turn to shit like that. Halo and Orion should have been back an hour after I left you there but they got stuck on a run. The meeting Rebel and I had ran a lot fucking longer than we thought it would but I honestly didn't know you were still down there until I got back and King started barking like crazy near the door.

"Doesn't really matter now, does it? I could have died."

"Joker never meant for this. He probably thought it would stop you from running again, that's all. It was only meant to be for an hour." I don't answer him because I have no idea what Joker is really like but leaving me so vulnerable has not endeared the man to me in the slightest.

"He lives offsite or he would have known everything had been fucked up and let you out himself. As soon as I realized why King was barking, I shot the fuck out of the lock, not bothering to waste time looking for the keys, and brought you up here."

His face is so close to mine I can feel his warm breath blowing against my lips.

"You can't just go around kidnapping people, Gage."

"Of course I can. I'm a biker. It's part of the job description."

I fight the urge to smile at his ill-timed joke. I can accept they didn't mean for me to come to harm—this time at least—but it's always something with this place and it doesn't change the fact that I have no intention of staying.

"Besides." He slides his hand under my chin, tipping my head back gently. He's lucky my head has stopped throbbing or I would have kneed him in the dick. "It wasn't kidnapping," he tells me, staring into my eyes with his onyx ones.

"Well, what the heck would you call it then?"

"Bringing my woman home."

"I was never your wo—" Before I can protest further, his lips are on mine. His kiss is soft and sensual and completely at odds with the Gage I'm familiar with.

I don't move for a minute, my body locking down as shock races through me. Every sensible neuron in my brain screams *run away* but I never was good at playing it safe.

When he licks the seam of my lips, demanding entrance, I pull away. There is zero chance of me kissing him open mouthed before I've had chance to brush my teeth. He doesn't push for more, even though the evidence of how much he's enjoyed the kiss so far, is pressed up against me. Finally, he pulls back and kisses me softly on the forehead.

"Get some sleep, Luna. I'll watch over you." I don't know this version of Gage. All I know is the fucked-up one, but as sleep threatens to drag me under, something instinctual inside me tells me that for now, at least, I'm safe.

Maybe the bump on my head did more damage than I realized. This man never wanted me despite Orion and Halo trying to convince him otherwise. Would I have entertained the idea of the three of them? Maybe. There's something about Gage's darkness that calls to me but he made up his mind about me long before I left. Now he thinks of me as his woman? Maybe he hit his head too.

I guess I should be grateful he isn't holding a grudge about me borrowing his bike. I'm sure he was surprised when I had a courier deliver it back to the compound the day after I left but I didn't want to give them any more incentive to find me. And yet, here we are.

I must have drifted off again because the sound of arguing stirs me, ripping me from one of my favorite dreams. That and the tingling sensation in my feet and legs, like tiny ants crawling over my body. What the fuck happened to me? I crack my eyes open and see a very pissed off looking Orion glaring down at me. Ah, I must still be dreaming. Well, this is different than the usual X-rated shit that has been haunting me for the last two months. My stomach swirls, making me feel sick, so I snap my eyes closed again.

"What kind of fucked-up dream is this? We're supposed to fuck against the wall," I whine as the sickly feeling gets worse.

"What the fuck?" Orion's voice grumbles. My mouth starts to water and not in a good way.

"I'm going to be sick," I manage to get out as I try to untangle myself from the blanket.

"I've got you," I hear Halo say from somewhere in the room before picking me up and carrying me to the bathroom. I just manage to grab hold of the sink before I start throwing up. Thankfully, I don't have much to expel and after a few heaves, I'm done. I wash my face and accept the toothbrush Halo hands to me. I brush my teeth and check him out in the mirror. He looks tired and his hair, which is usually tied back in a sexy man bun, is down, framing his handsome face. I finish brushing my teeth and realize for the first time that I'm naked.

"Finally, we must be getting to the good bit of this dream," I mutter as I walk toward Halo and slide my hand down the waistband of his jeans. He stops me by gently grabbing my wrist.

"Luna?" I look up at him, wondering why he's stopping me.

"This is the part where you bend me over the sink, right?"

I ask, confused. He groans like he's in pain. I swear this dream is shit compared to some I've had. Fuck it, maybe I should just wake up instead.

I sigh and head back to the bedroom, feeling Halo following right behind me. I push the door open wider and freeze. This isn't Orion's room where my dreams always take place. I see him though, standing over by the window. He turns when I enter and drags his eyes over my naked body. I turn and see Gage on the bed wearing a pair of jeans and nothing else. He looks at me with apprehension in his eyes and it reminds me of how he looked at me after—

"Sonofabitch. I'm not dreaming, am I?" I ask him.

He stands and makes his way over to me with a T-shirt in his hand. He slips it over my head and snags my hand, pulling me into his arms like this is the last chance he'll get.

"Well, isn't this cozy?" Orion sneers, making me look up from Gage's chest in confusion. I don't think I've ever heard him use that tone before, even when he was angry.

"Finally figured out bikers do it better, huh? You weren't interested in old lady status because you were more interested in becoming a club whore? Guess it all makes sense now."

"Orion, that's enough," Halo snaps at him but Orion is on a tangent.

"Why's that, Halo? She isn't anything to me. I can say whatever the fuck I want."

Gage swings around to face him, his hands fisted at his sides.

"You have no idea what's going on, so shut your fucking mouth before we lose her for good this time."

"Well, you sure changed your tune. Must be the golden snatch. Didn't I tell you she was a good fuck?"

Gage's fist comes out of nowhere, catching Orion on the side of his jaw. Orion's head swings to the side before he turns back with a thunderous expression on his face. Halo quickly pulls me behind him and stands guard but does nothing to stop the fight that breaks out in front of us as Orion throws a punch of his own.

"You just wanted her for yourself, you fucking selfish bastard," Orion spits out as he punches Gage again and again.

Oh, fuck this bullshit. It's entirely possible I might be losing my sanity but as I slide my hand up the back of Halos T-shirt and snag his gun, all I can think about is helping the demon who dragged me back here in the first place. Go figure. Halo spins around but I have the gun up and pointed at him before he can speak.

"Move, now." Halo steps back until he's next to Orion, who has frozen with his fist pulled back. He's in such a rage-fueled blackout, it's almost like the lights are on but no one's home. I spare Gage a quick glance and wince. He's going to be sore as a motherfucker tomorrow. I could tell straight away he was holding back. Whether that was some kind of loyalty at play for his new VP or because he's paying his penance after his role in what happened to me, I don't know. But I refuse to watch it anymore. I doubt Orion will stop before killing him.

"If you so much as breathe on Gage again, I will shoot you." Orion doesn't move but he seems to focus on my words more before looking at my face.

"Gage, come here." Gage looks at me like I'm nuts. Yeah, tell me something I don't know. He humors me and climbs to his feet before dragging himself over to me. I push him down onto the edge of the bed gently, not taking my eyes off them. Orion snorts, making me glare at him, my anger urging me to shoot first and yell later but I tamper it down.

"What the fuck is wrong with you?" I really need to know what his goddamn malfunction is.

He looks at Halo incredulously. "Is this bitch serious?" he asks him

"This bitch is going to shoot you between the fucking eyes if you don't start explaining."

"Well, let's see," he sneers. "Our girl disappears without a trace for two months and the next time we see her she is banging one of our club brothers like she doesn't have a care in the world. Does that explain it enough for you?" His chest is heaving up and down as he tries to rein his own temper in.

"Gage?" I call his name softly. He has one shot to prove his loyalty to me. If he lies now, there will be no going back. I hear the bed creak as he stands a second before I feel his hands on my hips. I let out a relieved breath.

"Where did I spend most of the night?" I ask him quietly, but I never take my eyes off the guys in front of me. Which is lucky, really, or I would have missed Halo's arm move slightly. I point the gun at his chest.

"Don't even think about it." He raises his hands in surrender. Yeah, shit face, I saw you reaching for the gun tucked behind Orion's back.

"Gage?" I prompt.

"Luna spent the night in one of the holding cells." Both Halo's and Orion's eyes shoot to Gage over my shoulder.

"Explain," Halo barks.

"King ordered me to collect her by any means necessary. Kibble coldcocked her and we brought her in. The trouble was, you two were still on a run and Rebel and I had a meeting set up we couldn't miss, so Joker decided the cells would be the best place to stop her running before you got back." Orion's eyes flick back to mine. The look in them isn't one I'm familiar with but I can't say I'm a fan.

"So, what, you decided to fuck him as a thank you? I didn't know you were so messed up." I swing the gun from Halo back to Orion and move to press the trigger when I feel Gage's hand around my wrist. He doesn't squeeze like I know he could, he just leans down and whispers in my ear.

"I can't let you shoot my VP, Luna." I curse under my breath, knowing I can't shoot him but really, really, wanting to.

"Fine," I mutter. A warm fuzzy feeling washes over me when he takes me at my word and slides his hands back down to my hips, leaving me pointing a fully loaded gun at his club brothers. I guess that answers the loyalty question.

"I haven't fucked anyone since you two. I bet you can't say the same, though, can you?" Neither of them speaks but they don't need to. I'm not stupid. I'm not even angry about it really. I left with no intention of coming back, so I have no rights to them but it doesn't mean I have to like it.

"Yeah, that's what I thought. The only reason I was naked in Gage's bed was because he was trying to warm me up." Shit. As soon as the words leave my mouth, I realize exactly how they sounded. Gage just chuckles in my ear, not helping at all.

"Not like that, for fuck's sake. Get your minds out of the gutter. You try spending the night naked in the freezing cold with a concussion. Gage probably saved my life, although he was the one who put me there, so that kind of negates it a little," I admit. Halo looks like he's fighting back a smile while Orion just looks as confused as fuck.

"I do have a question for you though, jerkface. Why the fuck are you so bent out of shape at the thought of me sleeping with Gage when you wanted to share me among all three of you before? In fact, I distinctly remember you telling him to just fuck me already." He opens his mouth to speak but snaps it closed again.

Yeah, probably a wise move there, buddy. I lower the gun when my arm starts to shake, realizing I have pushed myself a little too far. The tension in the room has dropped to a low simmer so I don't think I need to kill anyone just yet.

"Here." I flick the safety back on and hold the gun out in the flat of my palm for Halo to take. He steps forward slowly like I might change my mind before taking it and sliding it back into his jeans. I turn toward Gage and feel a wave of nausea creep up again. I sidestep him and make it to the bathroom just in time. I have virtually nothing to throw up, making my stomach cramp violently.

"Fuck." I lean over the counter to catch my breath as my stomach starts to settle once again.

"You doing okay?" I jump when I feel Gage's hands gliding up my back.

"Urgh, sure. I'm just peachy." I lift up and brush my teeth again, looking behind me at Gage's swollen face. What am I going to do about these guys? I finish off and rummage through the cupboards until I find some cotton balls and some antiseptic.

"Sit." I nod to the closed toilet seat, grateful he doesn't argue with me. He spreads his legs so I can step between them and gently dab at his cuts. He doesn't flinch once, even though I know it must hurt like a son of a bitch. I leave his eyebrow till last, thinking that it might need some stitches, but when I clean it up I realize it's not so bad. I dab it gently, cleaning away the blood before blowing on it softly like I remember my mother doing to me when I was small. When Gage's hands slide their way under my T-shirt up to my bare hips and squeeze, I realize it's definitely not having a soothing effect on him. No, soothing is not the word I would use at all. He pulls me down onto one of his thighs, holding me still when I try to protest.

"I need to check your head. If you keep throwing up, we're going to have to call the doc."

"I'll be fine. I just need some painkillers and some sleep," I grumble.

"And something to eat and drink. I suspect you're a little dehydrated."

"Probably," I concede. I wince when he touches my bump but I let him look.

"It looks like it's stopped bleeding but it's hard to tell with all the blood in your hair. Think you can manage a shower?"

I think I would sell my soul for a shower right about now. I just nod, feeling drained. I stand up, letting him out from under me and watch as he turns on the shower for me.

"Are you sure you can manage?" he asks, worry threaded through his voice.

"Yeah, I'll be fine. I'm just going to wash my hair and then I'll be out." He nods, trusting me to know my limits.

"I'm going to go and grab you some food. Are you gonna be all right with those two assholes out there?"

I shrug. "Who knows? Maybe you should leave me your gun, just in case." He laughs but shakes his head no.

"Not a chance. I have a feeling I would end up having to dig two graves and I just don't feel up to it today."

"That's probably for the best."

He smiles at me, something I had yet to see on him. It's odd. His smile itself is sexy as fuck but teamed with his eyes, it kind of makes me think of one of the villains in a slasher movie.

A pulse of awareness washes over me, making my clit throb. What is it about a bad boy that makes a sensible woman stop and throw their panties at them? Is it the primal instinct he will bend and break any rule to protect what he sees as his or is it simply the duality of knowing the killer everyone else encounters is soft as shit in the hands of his girl?

I know some might want to domesticate the untamable, to be the one to change them, but, well, I never was a normal girl. There is nothing wrong with soft and sweet but sometimes a woman just wants her hair pulled and her ass smacked.

I smile at him and slip his T-shirt off over my head and climb into the shower, ignoring his growl. The water feels good on my skin. I turn it up a touch and watch the steam swirl around me, soothing away the last of the cold. I stand there and just let the water beat down upon me, figuring out pretty quickly that I'm just too tired to wash my hair or do anything other than crawl back into bed.

I'm about to call it quits and turn the shower off when the shower door opens. Expecting Gage, I jump when I realize it's Halo. A very, very naked Halo.

"If you think you can come in here and fuck me into some kind of sex coma so I'm easier to deal with, I would rethink your plan. I'll make sure you can never father children," I grumble, taking in his sculpted body and the intricate web of tattoos that run up and down both sides of his ribs and over his chest.

"I come in peace. I can see you're dead on your feet. Let me help you." He takes a step closer to me but I'm focused on his little friend who has decided to say "hey" too.

"Sugar, you really need to stop looking at me like that."

Huh? I look up and realize I zoned out staring at his baby maker.

"Shit, sorry. It's been a long day, no pun intended, and well, if you wave it around, I'm going to stare." I turn my back to him and pass him the shampoo.

"Think you could wash my hair for me?" I ask him, hating how small my voice sounds but, fuck, I'm going to fall asleep where I am in a minute.

"Sure, thing, sugar," he says softly. He makes quick work of it before grabbing the shower gel. He soaps up his hands and washes my arms, legs, and stomach. His hands slip down and wash over my ass before climbing up to my chest. He washes each breast, spending a little longer than necessary before sliding his hands down between my legs. He doesn't push his luck, he just washes me and nothing more before rinsing me off. I'm fighting now just to keep my eyes open. He reaches around me to turn the shower off before helping me climb out. He grabs a couple of towels from the rail, twisting one around my hair before wrapping the other around me. He reaches over to grab another one for himself. I feel hands on my hips and turn to find Orion looking down at me.

"I've got her, Halo." Before I can protest, he has me up in his arms and back out into the bedroom just as Gage walks through the door carrying what smells like soup. My stomach rumbles in response, reminding me it needs feeding. Shit, I can't even remember when I last ate. Orion sits on the bed with me on his lap and pushes himself back so he is leaning against the headboard. I flush, remembering the last time I was in this position with him, a lot less clothes, and Halo between my thighs. Fuck. Gage sits down on the bed in front of me with the tray of food in his lap.

"Think you can handle a little bit?" Say what now? Right, soup. Focus, Luna.

"Yeah, I'm starving. Soup sounds really good."

"When was the last time you ate?" Halo asks as he strolls in with a towel around his waist, rubbing his hair with another as tiny little water droplets slide down his abs. I whimper a little. I just can't do this shit right now.

"Okay, that's enough. You—" I point at Halo. "Put some clothes on. I don't have the brain capacity to deal with all this shit right now and all this man meat on display is making me even foggier. I forget that I'm pissed off with you all and I deserve to be pissed for a little longer yet."

"You—" I turn to face Gage who is full out smiling at me again. "Knock that shit off. Stop the smiling thing right this damn second. It makes my hoo-ha start doing the Macarena and I swear to god I'm in no fit state for anything other than food and sex—shit, I mean sleep—right now."

"Orion, don't think for one second I can't feel your monster cock trying to break free and invade me. If you don't get him under control, I'm going to snap it off before he tries to storm the keep. My body is on lockdown until further notice." He shifts behind me a little, leaning down so he can whisper in my ear.

"What did I say to you about your attitude? If you wanted my dick to go down, you really should have kept your sassy mouth shut." I close my eyes and ignore him as best I can before opening them and focusing on Gage.

"Soup, please," I tell him. They must hear the strain in my voice because they all wisely stop teasing me. Big, bad Gage feeds me spoon after spoon of tomato soup until the bowl is empty and my stomach is full. He hands me a bottle of water, which I down in one.

"Okay, cherub, time for some sleep. I need to call church and fill everyone in on what's going on. Are you going to be okay up here by yourself?"

I ignore the sting I feel from the familiar use of my nickname. I missed it more than I realized.

"Of course. I'll be asleep before my head even hits the pillow." Gage moves the tray off the bed and fetches me a clean T-shirt to wear. He slips it over my head before pulling the towel away.

"You need anything else?" he asks, tucking a curl behind my ear. I stare into his eyes and as the light catches them, I notice for the first time his eyes aren't actually black.

"You have brown eyes." Well done, Luna. Good job of pointing out something I'm sure he is well aware of.

"I do," he confirms with a smile.

I hear Halo laugh and look up to find him clothed, thankfully, and looking between Gage and me.

"What?" I ask when he doesn't say anything else.

"I was just wondering what nickname you gave Gage before you found out his road name." I look away chewing my lip.

"What nickname?" Gage asks, looking at him.

"Apparently, Luna here has a thing for naming us bikers in her head so she doesn't have to call us biker one and biker two or whatnot. I'm Pretty Boy." He winks at me before nodding his head toward Orion.

"Dickhead over there is Adonis." I feel Orion squeeze my hips at that. Maybe I wasn't the only one who missed their nickname.

"So, it stands to reason she has one for you, too," Halo continues telling Gage. Gage looks back to me and I feel the heat creep up my face. He leans forward until his face is right in front of mine.

"Is that true?"

"Ermm... oh, look, a squirrel." I point behind Halo but, of course, none of them listen to me.

"Do you have one for me, Luna?" Crap. I can't tell him I call him Demon, especially when I'm still not entirely convinced he isn't one. He'll think it's a bad thing and, okay, maybe in the beginning, I was worried he might steal my soul or something, but now I kind of want to see just how bad my demon can be. Gage's breathing picks up as Halo lets out a strangled laugh.

"What?" I question. Why is everyone acting so weird? Orion just snorts into my shoulder.

"Your demon?" Gage asks, his voice sounding deep and seductive, leaving a trail of goosebumps across my skin— wait, shit. I look over my shoulder at Orion, who is fighting a smile.

"I said that out loud again, didn't I?" I whisper.

"Your demon?" Gage repeats. I turn to face him, ready to apologize, when his mouth is suddenly on mine. Gone are the soft kisses from before. This kiss is the kind of kiss they write stories about. The kind of stories that get really, really dirty. Just as I melt into him, he pulls away.

"When you're feeling better, I'll show you how bad I can be. Now rest, before I forget about trying to do the right thing."

I nod, climb off Orion's lap, lie back down on the bed, and shut my eyes. I feel Orion stand and pull the blanket over me but true to my word, I'm asleep before they even leave the room.

CHAPTER TEN

I wake up feeling a really eerie sense of déjà vu. A hard body is pressed against my back and a large hand is splayed across my stomach. I open my eyes slowly and blink as Orion comes into focus. His eyes rove over my face, waiting to see how I'm going to react.

"Halo or Gage?" He knows I'm referring to the body pressed up against me. We've played this game before.

"Gage. Halo is working on something but will be back in a bit." I nod, happy to find my headache has finally gone. "How are you feeling?"

I think about it for a second before answering. "Okay. I'm a little stiff but my headache is gone and I don't feel sick anymore."

"Good. I need you to get better." Aw, that's kind of sweet. "Why's that?"

"So I can put you over my knee and spank the shit out of you."

"Excuse me?"

"You left, Luna. You fucking ran away like a coward. You promised me a month and bailed when things got tough."

I reach out a hand to wrap it around his fucking throat when Gage's hand reaches round to snag my wrist. He links his fingers through mine and pulls our joined hands back to my stomach.

"Can't let you kill the VP, remember?" his sleepy voice tells me. He's lucky he has sharp reflexes because I'm making no promises.

"I'm really starting to think you have a death wish, Orion," Gage tells him something I wholeheartedly agree on.

"Well, what the fuck do you want me to say? She's here again, messing with my fucking head when we both know she has no intention of staying."

Gage lets go of my hand and nudges me. "You know what? Luna, do your worst. Maybe you can beat some fucking sense into him."

He doesn't need to tell me twice. I jerk up before either of them can stop me and straddle Orion's waist. Using his surprise to my advantage, I grip both of his wrists and pin them above his head. I put my face right into his and snarl.

"If you need to put all the blame on me to make yourself feel like a big strong man, then go for it. All you're doing is proving I did the right thing by walking away. What really makes me fucking laugh is that you are so butthurt about it.

Did you really think I would stay with what you were offering?"

He frowns and I can see he's starting to get angry. "What's the matter, cherub? Did you look around and decide a biker wouldn't be able to buy you all the pretty little labels you seem to love so much?"

"Gage, who is next in line for VP?"

"It'll be up to the club to vote but it would more than likely be Diesel. Why?"

"I wanted to know who was going to step up when I murdered the current one." I glare down at Orion and feel him start to harden against me.

"For your information, asshole, I can buy my own stuff, thank you very much. I never asked you for anything, so the crap you're spewing is bullshit and we both know it." He flips me so I end up flat on my back with him pressed down on top of me.

"I warned you about your attitude, cherub."

"Fuck you!" I squirm underneath him, very conscious of the fact that I'm not wearing any underwear and his rock-hard length is pressed up against me.

"Well, if you insist." He dips his head and bites down on one of my nipples through my T-shirt, making my back arch. He rubs his boxer-covered cock against me and I can feel myself getting wet.

"Sex won't fix anything between us, Orion." I pant as he trails his lips up my neck.

"Orion!" I shout when his hand starts descending south.

He stops and looks at me before sighing. He presses his forehead against mine in a surprisingly sweet gesture.

"We've already given you a million reasons to leave," he whispers. I look into his eyes and see the Orion I know, a version of himself I suspect he keeps only for me.

"I just need one good reason to stay," I remind him.

"Stay because I need you. Stay for Halo. Stay for Gage." He means it. I can see every single emotion he usually keeps locked up clear on his face.

Ah, fuck. I must have a screw loose but the truth is, I've felt hollow since I left. Maybe I overreacted or maybe I didn't react enough, who knows? I'm not sure it even really matters anymore. I could leave if I had really wanted to get away once I was free from the cell. I could have. I would have been back at the ranch before they even realized I was gone. But lying here with my heart beating out of my chest, I realize for the first time since I left, I feel something other than regret.

This will be the only second chance I get. Should I stay and run through the gauntlet of shit that comes with being a part of an MC or should I go back to the life I had loved right up until I realized what I had been missing? One road, two choices. One would be safe. There would be no angry words, fighting, or possible heartache. The other would be fraught with trials and tribulations and littered with carnage—literally. The choice should be obvious, so why, when I picture the paths in my mind, do I see one in black and white and one bathed in color?

I close my eyes and remember my gramps's words from years ago.

It's better to regret the things you lived for than to die regretting that you never really lived at all.

I open my eyes and stare into Orion's crystal blue ones. "There needs to be some ground rules."

He rears back in shock, giving Gage an opening to slide his hand around my jaw and turn my face toward him.

"You'll stay?" he asks, waiting for confirmation.

"If you guys can agree on some ground rules and I need to tell you—" He cuts me off with a kiss.

They need to stop doing that. It makes it really hard to finish a fucking sentence around here. Orion shoves my T-shirt up, exposing me from the waist down. I squirm when he slides down, anticipating his next move. I feel a soft kiss on the inside of my thigh before his tongue splits the seam of my sex and dives into me. He groans in pleasure at the taste of me on his tongue, sending vibrations through my body. I gasp into Gage's mouth, letting him swallow it down before he pulls away so he can whip my T-shirt over my head. Orion slides a finger inside me, making my back arch.

"Fuck." Gage dips his head and sucks one of my nipples into his hot greedy mouth. I grip his hair and pull him hard against me, loving the scratch of his stubble against my skin. Another finger pushes in beside the first, scissoring inside me, opening me up for what's about to come.

"Oh god, oh god," I chant, thrashing my head from side to

side when Orion sucks hard on my clit at the same time Gage sucks on my nipple.

"Feel good?" Gage asks, letting my nipple slip from his mouth. I groan in answer.

"What's he doing to you, Luna?" I ignore him, concentrating on the pressure building inside of me.

"Tell me!" Gage barks, making me jump

"He's flicking my clit with his tongue," I answer in short pants.

"What else?" Fuck, why do they always want me to talk?

"He has his fingers inside me." I push down on them as Orion starts sliding them in and out.

"How many?" Huh? A bite to my breast has me focusing back on Gage.

"Two, he has two fingers inside me, oh god."

"Think you can handle three?" I nod rapidly. Yes, please. Only Orion doesn't add a third finger, Gage does. He leans down and slides one of his thick fingers in right beside Orion's. He pushes it inside, rubbing the front wall, making everything so intense for a second. I think I'm going to come but he slides his finger out, moving his lips back to mine. He dips his tongue inside my mouth, stroking it against mine before pulling away and replacing it with his finger. I taste myself and groan when I realize this is the finger he just fucked me with. I suck it hard before Gage is licking at my lips and slipping his tongue over my finger too. It's hot, too fucking hot.

"Gage!" I gasp. Orion stops licking and pulls away. Damn

it, I need to come. I rub my legs together but a slap to my thigh stops me.

"Behave, cherub," Orion tells me. Gage pulls away and I finally take them both in as they stand there stripping out of their boxers. I slide a hand down between my legs but find my ankle snagged by Gage as I'm spun on the bed so I'm lying across it.

"You need some relief, Luna?" I nod in answer as he grabs a condom from the drawer of the bedside table and crawls back onto the bed and between my thighs. Forgetting about Orion for a second, I watch as Gage covers his impressive rod with its latex sleeve but a yank on my hair reminds me real quick Orion's there.

"Gage is going to fuck your tight pussy but me, well, I'm going to fill that sassy mouth of yours."

Gage pushes me farther across the bed until my head is hanging over the edge and perfectly placed for Orion's dick. He glides it over my lips, staining them with pre-cum as I open my mouth a little and lick the tip. Maybe licking is the way to go. I would need a hinged jaw to handle that thing.

Gage chooses that moment to thrust inside me, gliding all the way in and not stopping until there is nowhere else for him to go. My mouth opens on a silent scream, which Orion, the bastard, takes advantage of, pushing his cock into my mouth.

I open as wide as I can to accommodate him. He gives me no time to adjust as he pulls back and pushes in again a little harder. It doesn't take long for me to figure out these guys have finished taking it easy on me.

"Fuck, cherub, just watching my cock sliding between your lips has me ready to shoot my load down your throat."

I'm guessing he isn't expecting a response from me, which is just as well, as Gage pulls almost out before slamming back into me. Lucky for me, they seem to have their rhythm down, so when one pushes in the other pulls back. Thank Christ because, at this point, I'm just hanging on for dear life. I feel Gage lean down over me, never slowing his thrusts, and suck a nipple into his mouth.

"Fuck her hard, Gage, just the way she likes it." Gage fucks me like he has something to prove, fuck, maybe he does, but the pace he sets is too much for me. I lift my hips as he thrusts and clamp down around him as I come, dragging him over the edge with me. I scream around Orion, setting off a chain reaction as he erupts in my mouth and follows us over the edge seconds later.

I lie there for a second gasping for breath until I feel Gage pull away. He goes to get rid of the condom, leaving me alone with Orion for the first time since I came back.

Everything feels different between us now. Everything is as electrically charged as it always was but there is an awkwardness too. I hurt him, he hurt me, and now there's a wariness that wasn't there before. It's hardly surprising, given everything that happened, but I find I really don't like it.

"Cherub?" His eyes roam over my face as he climbs onto the bed beside me. He pulls me close until our noses are almost touching, staring into my eyes as if he can figure out what's wrong without having to ask me.

"It's nothing. Just, everything is intense when it involves you guys." His fingers that were drawing lazy circles on my hip pause briefly before drifting around to the base of my spine, leaving a trail of goosebumps behind.

"I'm no good at figuring out the female mind. Give me your body and I can make you feel like a goddess but anything that goes on in here," he taps the side of my head gently with his finger, "is Sanskrit to me. You're going to have to spell it out because I won't get it otherwise," he tells me, looking a little lost.

"Failing that, you can always smack him upside the head. It's not like you need him for his stimulating conversational skills. You've got me and Halo for that," Gage suggests, walking out of the bathroom before climbing on the bed behind me. He pushes up against me and nips my ear between his teeth, making me squirm.

"This fucker had you to himself while Halo and I had to wait to find out if you were open to the idea of the four of us. I'm just petty enough to tie this fucker up and make him watch while Halo and I fuck you until you can't breathe." I resist the urge to remind him he didn't want me as I feel Orion's cock start to harden against my stomach at this idea. Interesting.

"Hmm... That does seem a little unfair. The trouble is, I am rather fond of his monster cock." My breath hitches as Gage grinds into the back of me.

"Well, he would be tied up, so you could just treat him as your own personal buffet and serve yourself," Gage whispers and his hard length presses against my ass. I don't take my eyes away from Orion, whose own eyes are ablaze with lust.

"Well, when you put it like that..." I don't get to say anything else as Orion leans forward and closes the tiny gap between us, sliding his lips over mine. His tongue doesn't ask for permission, it demands it as it slips inside my mouth. I feel Gage's hand skim around to cup my breast but before I can lose myself in the moment again, a cough catches my attention. I pull my lips from Orion's and find Halo standing at the foot of the bed, looking a little turned on and a whole lot of pissed off.

I don't think he's pissed at us, though, which can only mean one thing. Club business. I sigh and dislodge myself from the guys and climb off the bed.

"What's wrong?" Orion asks on alert, obviously catching the same look I did.

I leave them to it for a minute as I snag the pile of clothes I spot folded on the dresser. I head to the bathroom and clean up before slipping on my freshly laundered underwear. Next, I slide my legs into my black jeans and top and slip the shirt over my shoulders, buttoning it up so the guys don't lose their minds. Everything smells fresh, so I'm guessing Gage must have had this stuff cleaned and ironed for me. I'm certainly not complaining. I brush my teeth and tame my hair a little before heading back into the bedroom.

"Morning, Halo," I call out softly as I slip my feet into my pumps.

Halo doesn't answer, so I look up and see him doing some weird silent communication thing with the guys. Right, and so it begins. I walk over to him, lift up on my tiptoes and kiss the scruff on his cheek. I notice a smear of red near his ear and wipe it off.

"Hey, sugar, how are you feeling?" he asks, looking down at me. He tenses when he sees the blood on my fingers but I just wipe them on his T-shirt.

"You missed a bit." I can tell he's been in the shower, his hair is still wet, so lord knows how much blood was on him to begin with. "I'm feeling better, thanks, but I'm starving. You going to feed me, Pretty Boy?" His smile is angelic but only a fool would take him at face value. Even the devil wore a halo once.

"Absolutely, sugar." He takes my hand and tugs me toward the door. I turn back around to face the other two when I realize they aren't following. "Are you guys coming too?"

"We'll be there in two secs. We've got something to take care of first," Gage answers. I shrug, no worries. I follow Halo down to the kitchen and park my butt on a barstool at the kitchen counter as he makes me some scrambled eggs.

The curious part of me wants to ask about the blood. Not because I'm overly bothered by it but because I'm nosy as fuck. I rein it in though, knowing he won't tell me anyway. Instead, I watch him move around the kitchen with a confident ease that tells me he genuinely likes to cook. He's slipping some eggs onto a plate when I sense someone approaching behind me.

"Shouldn't you be the one in the kitchen, darlin'?" I look up and find an older biker looking down at me. His black hair is threaded with gray and his face is lined and weathered. I don't answer him, just turn back to Halo who slides some silverware and a cup of coffee toward me before placing down a plate full of fluffy eggs and toast. I smile big and genuinely.

"My hero," I tell him, making him wink at me before he heads back to make himself a plate.

"So, what's so special about you that you've got Halo here making you eggs?" The biker I'm trying to ignore sits on the stool beside me. He leans one hand on the bar as he turns toward me.

"Must be my stellar personality," I say with a small smile. Kill them with kindness, Luna.

He places his large beefy hand on my thigh and squeezes. Okay, kill him with a fork, Luna.

"I don't doubt that for a second, sweetheart, but I'm willing to bet that's not what's got him making you eggs." He starts to slide his hand a little higher, so I grab my fork and bring it down onto the back of the hand he has resting on the bar. His bellow has Halo snapping around to face us, eggs abandoned. He checks me out eating my scrambled eggs with my fingers and frowns until he spots my fork sticking out of the back of the biker's hand.

"You touched my woman?" Halo's voice sounds deadly.

"Your woman?" The biker looks a little pale now but he doesn't back down. "I don't see a patch on her, Halo. Besides, I thought you, Gage, and Orion were sticking to whores." I lean over and yank the fork from his hand.

"Call me a whore again and I will jam this fork in your eye next time." Halo snags the fork from my hand and drops it on the counter, stealing my fun. He walks around to us and stands in front of me, blocking me from the asshole. Whether that's for his protection or mine, I don't know. I go back to eating my eggs and let Halo handle it.

"As you said yourself, I'm making her eggs. How many whores you see me make eggs for, Slick?" Slick? Yeah, that name totally fits.

"Come on, Halo." The guy doesn't know when to back down. Halo finally has enough and reaches out to grab the guy by his throat.

"Don't push me, Slick. You're lucky she's not armed." Now, that's a true story.

"You're picking her over a club brother?" he chokes out. Fuck me, this guy is stupid. Halo leans in close to him and whispers.

"I'm picking my old lady. She sucks dick better than you do. Now fuck off and keep your hands to yourself. I'm not fucking around here either, Slick. If I find out that you've even breathed in her direction, I will choke the rest of the air from your lungs. You get me—*brother*?" The guy doesn't speak, thankfully, just nods and when Halo lets go of him, he walks away.

Halo spins to face me but before he can speak, I throw myself at him. He catches me and picks me up with his hands under my ass. I seal my mouth over his and slip my tongue inside when he parts his lips. I only have control briefly before he takes over, nibbling, sucking, biting, and making me practically beg him to take me on the kitchen counter.

"So, my temper turns you on, huh?" he questions, his voice thick with desire. I groan and bite up the column of his neck to his ear, pulling his lobe between my teeth.

"I'm so fucking wet right now, you'd be able to slide right in."

"Fuck, is that an offer?" he asks, his breath coming out in pants. Damn, I like the effect I'm having on him.

I breathe against his lips. "Oh yeah." He doesn't need another invitation. He strolls back out the way we came in and heads up to the rooms, never once breaking the kiss. Now, that takes some skill. I pull away when he opens the door and stand up, recognizing the room instantly as Orion's. I don't have time to think of anything else as Halo is taking his cut off and hanging it on the back of the chair, and then the T-shirt is off and the thinking thing becomes even more of an issue.

"If you keep looking at me like you want to eat me, I'm going to shoot my load before I even get inside you."

Eat, you say? I look at him with a coy smile before shimmying out of my jeans and underwear.

"But, Halo, I do want to eat you."

"Later, sugar, right now I need to be inside you, filling you up." He stalks toward me with his jeans open and his hand on his cock as he slips a condom from his pocket and slides it on. He hoists me up into his arms so I wrap my legs around his waist and wait for him to toss me on the bed, but Halo has other ideas. He spins us around and pushes me up against the door as he takes my mouth again in another blistering kiss before pulling away. He supports my weight with one arm before reaching down and tugging on my small patch of curls and rolling my clit between his thumb and his finger.

"Be very sure, sugar, because once you take my cock inside you again, there's no going back." He dips his finger inside me, before swirling the wetness around my clit, making me pant with need.

"I let you get away from us once before but mark my words, Luna, if you chose to come on my cock now, you'll be choosing to come on it for an eternity because I will never let you disappear on us again."

He grabs his cock and runs it backward and forward through my slick folds, coating himself with my wetness and bumping deliberately against my clit as he waits for an answer. I forgot he doesn't know I agreed to stay. I reach around and grab his hair, pulling his mouth to mine as I return the kiss he gave me with just as much vigor. I rip my lips away from his and tell him what he needs to hear.

"Fuck me, Halo, make me yours."

He surges inside me at my words, not giving me a chance to change my mind and back out.

"Thank fucking Christ. Hold on tight, sugar, this is going to be hard and fast."

He presses me against the door as he thrusts up into me hard, before retreating then slamming into me again and again. I lock my ankles behind his back as my head bangs the door but I can barely feel it. I slip my hand down between us and feel his cock sliding in and out of me, before strumming my clit harder and faster than Halo had previously. I don't know if it's the angle or if it's just Halo but I can feel my orgasm rapidly approaching and call out Halo's name, warning him.

"Come, sugar, come, now," he roars as he pushes inside me one last time and buries his head in the crook of my shoulder. Watching him lose control like that shoves me over the edge. My whole body tenses up as I shudder and shake, gripping onto him for dear life.

"You're really staying?" his muffled voice asks as he places a soft kiss on my collarbone.

"I'm really staying," I confirm.

"What changed?"

"I did, I guess," I tell him as he lowers me to my feet. I leave him to think on that while I freshen up and slip the rest of my clothes back on. When I come back out, he's fully dressed and waiting for me. He looks subdued somehow, not really the look you want to see after fucking.

"What's wrong?"

He waits until I'm close enough to wrap his arm around my shoulder and tugs me out of the room.

"I don't want you to hate me but I meant what I said before about not letting you go. You only know one side of me. When the coin flips and you decide I'm not the man you thought I was, it won't matter one bit to me. I'll cuff you to the bed if I have to, trust me, it won't be a hardship." I tug on his hand so he stops and faces me.

"I'm stronger than I look, Halo. You guys have a habit of writing me off as weak but that just isn't true. I have my lines I won't cross but they're less than you might think." He looks at me, considering my words but I can tell he isn't convinced.

"And what are these lines, Luna? Being part of an MC means we don't exactly frolic in the park."

I laugh at him. "I'm sorry, did you just say frolic? I didn't know anyone under the age of eighty even used that expression anymore."

He slaps my ass, making me squeal. Fucker, that hurt.

"To answer your question though, about my lines—no children get hurt, ever. They didn't choose this life. I'm a firm believer that the sins of the father stop with him." He nods at that in agreement.

"That, I can agree to. We keep kids out of all MC business and we don't drag other people's children into it either. I can't promise you other clubs follow those rules, Luna, but that's not how Kings of Carnage work." I get that. You can't control other people, unfortunately.

"What else?" he questions.

"Don't lie to me. If you can't tell me something, then just say so. I might not like it but I'll understand." He looks at me but doesn't answer, which doesn't bode well for me.

"That's it?"

"No, lastly, I have a major issue with how women are treated around here." When he opens his mouth to answer, I silence him with my hand.

"The MC is a man's world. I get it but that doesn't make me at best a second-class citizen and at worst just a pocket for you to slot your cock into." He barks out a laugh at that but I'm deadly serious. "I'll follow the rules, wear the vest, or whatever marks me as all of yours, but don't ask me to stand around and watch someone get abused if they decide they want out."

"Rape is and always will be a hard no for me and, honestly, it should be for you too. If I one day end up carrying your daughter, I want her to be able to grow up knowing all her pseudo uncles will *have* her back, not that they will be waiting for her to turn eighteen so they can have her *on* her back."

"Club kids are protected, sugar, but I get what you're saying. Things need a bit of a shakeup. Most of the guys are younger and will be fine with it. It's the old-timers that have issues with women more than anything. It's a generation thing."

"It's a dickhead thing," I counter.

"I have friends and family I care about that I want to be able to invite over. I need to have their safety guaranteed. They won't have a vest as a deterrent, so I need your word that when protection is offered, it will be adhered to. Standing up afterward and saying 'I didn't know' won't cut it."

I sigh but I don't relent.

"There are some good men here that could do with a good woman beside them but all they will ever be able to score with these outdated views is club pussy. No sane woman is going to put herself on the line for a club that treats her as an afterthought." He studies me. I know he can tell I'm serious. The question is, what will happen now?

"I'll bring it all up to Orion and Gage. If they agree, we'll take it to church for a vote. But, Luna, the vote is final. If it doesn't go your way, you'll have to deal with it."

"No, I won't," I tell him straight up.

He growls like he's expecting me to give him an ultimatum.

"I won't leave you guys, especially if you go to bat for me, but I won't be a part of the club either. I'll be your old lady, wear your patch, and come to the functions expected of me but that's it."

"I won't bring a single friend here. I will go elsewhere to meet them and I will never raise a kid here. You want to come share my house or something, the four of us together, I'm down with that but if nothing changes, this place will never be my home." I walk back to the kitchen and leave him to think about it.

"Hey, sweetheart, I heard you were back. Are you staying this time?" Gecko is standing at the counter eating a bowl of cereal when I walk in and I smile a genuine smile at the guy who has always been nothing but nice to me.

"That's the plan."

"Well, where are those men of yours? Tired them out already, huh?" I laugh at his easygoing nature.

"What can I say? It's a hard job, Gecko, but someone has to do it."

"What's a hard job?" Halo steps up behind me and wraps an arm around my waist.

"Keeping up with you three," Gecko answers him. "Congrats, Halo, I always knew Luna here was a keeper."

I look up at Halo and smile. "I like him. He's my favorite biker, well, out of the ones I'm not bumping uglies with, of course."

"Of course," Halo replies wryly.

"Hey, if you're looking for a fourth…" Gecko trails off, taking a sip of his juice and smirking at the look Halo is throwing him.

"Thanks for the offer, Gecko, but I only have three holes, you know?" Gecko chokes on his juice and a little dribbles down his chin.

"You know, sweetheart, you're my favorite non-biker, well, out of the ones I'm not bumping uglies with," Gecko tells me with a cheeky smile.

"Hey, what's going on?" Orion walks up beside me, pulling me away from Halo and grabbing a fistful of my hair and a handful of my ass before planting a hot wet kiss on me. I sink into him until he pulls back.

"I don't know how you expect me to answer you with your lips all over me. Is that the biker version of a peck on the cheek?" He winks at me, walking around the counter to the coffee pot.

Gage walks over to me, scanning me from head to toe before picking me up and sitting down with me in his lap in the seat I vacated before my quickie with Halo. I look at Gecko, who looks like he's fighting back a laugh, and shrug. It's easier to just go with it.

CHAPTER ELEVEN

After washing my hands, I wipe them on my dress and look in the mirror, taking in the sparkle in my eyes and the flush of my cheeks. I hadn't realized I had been going through the motions until I came back here. The last two weeks, though, have been amazing. I turn my head a touch and see the little line of bite marks running from the swell of my breast up my neck to my ear. Gage had found a way to drive me crazy, him biting my neck led to me losing my mind. Plus, the smug bastard loved seeing his mark on my skin. Mind you, they were each as bad as the other. Orion had left a rash of red on my cheek and chin from his beard and I had a set of Halo-shaped fingerprints on my hips from the night he spent fucking me from behind.

They played well together and they played *me* well together but when someone else's eyes lingered on me just a little longer than any of them deemed necessary, they lost their shit quickly. The feminist in me wanted to slap them upside the head. I was more than capable of taking care of myself but the other part of me, otherwise known as my vagina, well, she loved being fucked into submission.

I straighten my long red and white striped dress, one of the ones Orion bought for me during my first visit that he had kept for some reason. I pull my hair over my shoulder, covering the worst of the marks, before opening the door to Orion's room. The three of us had been staying at the house I had run from, which I preferred. It meant I didn't have to feel self-conscious about screaming and begging when the guys decided to work me over.

Still, using Orion's bathroom here at the clubhouse was a godsend. No woman would willingly want to use the communal toilets here. I swear you could catch an STD just walking past it.

I close the door behind me and turn, colliding with whoever had been coming around the corner. I look up ready to apologize and find myself face-to-face with Kibble.

I had seen him around over the last two weeks but never near enough for me to say or do anything. Kibble, I had come to realize, was a bit of a lurker. He tended not to stray too far from Joker and considering there was something about the president I didn't like, I stayed clear. But here we were.

"Look, before you start, remember where you are. I was

just doing my job. It was nothing personal." He shrugs unapologetically.

"Tell me, Kibble, do you have a mother? A sister?" A dark look flashes in his eyes. It's there for a second before it's gone but the pain I saw was so stark for a second, I felt it too.

"A sister, huh? How would you feel if someone hit your sister so hard she blacked out, only to wake up and find herself naked, vulnerable, and surrounded by bikers?" He doesn't like that, I can tell. It's easy to compartmentalize until you think about that shit happening to the people you care about.

"Let me tell you something you should already know, Kibble. It's always personal when a man puts his hands on a woman's body." I look him up and down, distaste coating my features, letting him see exactly what I think of him.

I place one hand on his chest and beckon him to bend slightly so I can whisper in his ear. He hesitates for a second before bending down.

As soon as he is slightly off-balance, I lift my knee and connect it with his balls as hard as I can. Lucky for him, the dress restricts my full movement. It's enough, though. He drops to the floor and grabs himself while swearing enough to turn the air blue around us.

"It's nothing personal, Kibble. Just a taste of what I'll do to you if you ever put your hands on me again." I turn the corner and see Joker walking toward me. I ignore him. There's something about him that just sets me on edge. Kibble groans behind me, making Joker's head snap up. Joker grabs my arm hard before I can walk past just as a stumbling Kibble turns the corner and sees us.

"What the fuck happened?" Joker barks.

"He fell," I tell him defiantly.

"Do not try my patience, Luna," he spits out, turning to Kibble.

"What did she do?" Joker asks him.

Kibble's eyes flash to mine before flashing back to Joker's.

"Nothing. It's like she said, I fell. I came to tell her Orion is waiting for her and tripped." He looks at Joker's hand on my arm before lifting his head to mine.

"You'd better go. Orion was pissed about something." It's a lie. We both know it but I pull away from Joker and head back downstairs, wanting to be anywhere the douchebag isn't.

The bar area is filling up and I notice a few more club girls here than usual so I figure it's going to be one of those kinds of Friday nights. I'm not fazed by it. The few girls I've spoken to seem cool with the exception Stacey, who thinks her shit doesn't smell. I look around for one of my guys and spot Gage sitting on one of the three faded leather sofas that line the back wall. He's talking to Inigo and Half-pint but from his expression, it's nothing too serious. I make my way over, smiling at Gecko when he winks at me from behind the bar, and ducking around hulking men who seem to forget that some of us are vertically challenged. Finally squeezing through the crowd, Gage spots me and smiles, making the two guys with him look around perplexed.

People are still adjusting to seeing this side of him but I fucking love it.

"Hey, sexy demon," I call when I'm close enough. He reaches up and pulls me down onto his lap.

"Cherub." Everyone seems to be calling me that these days. He pulls my hair aside and admires his handiwork for a second before placing a soft kiss on my neck that has me shivering.

"Hey guys," I greet Inigo and Half-pint who watch us with smiles on their faces.

"Hey, darlin'. How are you doing?" Inigo asks.

"I'm good." I smile. "Is this a regular Friday night fuckathon or is there a celebration going on?"

Half-pint laughs at me, shaking his head. "Not all of us are interested in the free snatch."

"Yeah, that shit gets old when you get to my age," Inigo answers.

I spot Halo making his way over to us and smile before replying to Inigo.

"Please, you are not old and you're hot as fuck. You're just at the age where you need exclusive pussy, not one that contains more sperm samples than a fertility clinic," I mutter as Stacey steps up to Halo and runs a hand down his chest. He grabs her wrist and pushes her away, shaking his head. She pouts, actually fucking pouts like a child, before turning on her heel and stomping off.

Gage bites my neck hard where he had previously been kissing.

"Hey, fucker!" I yell, pinching his rock-hard thigh through his jeans.

"Stop telling people they're hot," he rumbles. I roll my eyes at the jealous bastard but I don't miss the smile Inigo tries to hide behind his beer bottle.

"Thanks for that, Cherub, nice to know I'm still a hit with the ladies." He winks at me as Halo sits down beside us.

"Inigo, stop flirting with my woman," Halo tells him before turning my head and devouring me with a blistering kiss that has me squirming against Gage.

"Shit, I think I just came in pants," Half-pint grumbles before standing up and heading over to Tasha, one of the club girls.

Halo pulls away from me with a smile. "Want to get out of here for a bit?" he asks.

I nod. "I'd go anywhere with you," I tell him.

The look on his face is one I'll remember forever.

"You got stuff you can get changed into here or do we need to make a detour?"

"I'm good. I have a bunch of stuff up in Orion's room still. Are we taking the bike?" I ask, excitement zapping through me.

"Yep, so dress accordingly." I don't need any further encouragement. I hop off Gage's leg. Twisting, I plant a quick kiss on his lips before heading back the way I came. I've enjoyed my time here. Most of the MC has been welcoming and I've gotten to see a softer side, the side that makes it easy to see they really are just one big family.

Even so, getting away for a little while with Halo sounds perfect.

I make my way up the stairs, passing Joker's office, but slow my steps when I hear angry raised voices.

"I don't appreciate my orders being fucking questioned," Joker spits out.

"And I don't appreciate you getting our men to pull stunts like that. We all have blood on our hands but we've never crossed that line before. I'm not okay with this, Joke, not one little fucking bit. We rough up douchebags who don't pay up when they know the score before borrowing cash from us, I get it. But Fredricks is a single dad paying medical bills for his dying daughter. She slipped into a coma. I would say it's understandable he forgot about us. He had the money when we asked for it and you knew it, so why the fuck did you double his interest? It was unnecessary unless you were setting him up to fall. Why would you do that Joke?"

I hear Orion blasting Joker. What a fucking tool. Who does that? I hear shuffling and the sound of a fist hitting the desk.

"I'm not running a fucking charity. If you make an exception for one, you have to make it for all of them and we are not a bunch of pussies. Halo needs to man the fuck up. If he can't handle the role of enforcer, someone else will be more than willing to step up and do it for him."

I close my eyes in distress, remembering the blood on Halo's ear. Halo must have been the one who beat Fredricks and the guilt was eating him alive.

"If you were so fucking convinced of your actions, you wouldn't have kept that shit from him to begin with. Instead, you rubbed it in his face after. You got an issue with Halo I need to know about? Because I suspect this has less to do with Fredricks and more to do with Halo himself."

"I don't answer to you, Orion, now get the fuck out of my office." It's quiet for a moment and although I want to stay and hear whatever Orion has to say to him, I don't want to get busted for eavesdropping.

I make quick work of changing into gray ripped jeans, a simple white T-shirt, and my black leather jacket. I slip my ballet pumps back on, they would have to do, and pull my hair up into a messy ponytail. I hurry back downstairs, passing Joker's office without stopping. It's packed downstairs, girls grinding on guys as the evening progresses and the alcohol lowers everyone's inhibitions and panties. I head back to where I left my guys but turn my head when I feel eyes on me. I see Joker sitting at the bar next to Chewy. Chewy is talking away to him, oblivious to the fact that Joker isn't listening to a word he's saying. No, his focus is all on me. He doesn't even hide it. He drags his eyes up my body, hovering over my chest for a minute or two before meeting my eyes. It takes everything in me to stop my body from shivering but I'll be damned if I'll let him know the effect he has on me.

There are a few guys in the MC I haven't really warmed up to. Maybe that will change, maybe it won't. Some people just don't gel but Joker is the only one I can say hands down makes my skin crawl.

I don't give him any kind of reaction. I just turn and continue without looking back until I reach the table. Orion has joined the guys so I slip my hand into his back pocket and lean into his side. He looks down at me with a smile before dipping his head and pressing a surprisingly soft kiss against my lips.

"You okay?" I ask him. He doesn't answer for a minute as his eyes scan the crowd. When they focus on the bar I know exactly who he's looking at. I can feel the animosity coming off him in waves.

"Yeah, Cherub, I'm fine." I pinch his ass with my hand in his back pocket, making him jerk.

"Yes, you are." I wink at him. He turns fully into me and before I can process his next move, he picks me up so my legs are dangling off the floor and kisses me hard and deep. By the time he puts me back down, my legs are wobbly and I'm a panting mess.

"You want to dance?" he asks, nuzzling my neck.

Doesn't he realize when he kisses me like that I can barely stand, let alone dance? He lifts his head, showing a large smile that spreads across his face, dazzling me with its intensity, wiping away the frown from moments before and making me realize I had yet again said that shit out loud.

"Halo is taking me for a ride." I stop for a second when everyone at the table just stares at me. I play the words back over and figure out why they all look so amused.

"On his bike, you perverts. Although, that being said..." I trail off and wink at Halo, leaving him to fill in the blanks.

"Do you want to come?" I look up at Orion and see him focusing on Halo, a slight frown on his face, before looking back down at me.

"No, you two go and have fun. I think Halo needs to blow off some steam. Go shower him with some of your sparkle." He winks at me.

"You got it, Adonis." I turn back to Halo, who is talking to Gage, and whistle. When he looks up, I beckon him over with my finger.

"Come on, Pretty Boy, show me what you got." Laughing and jeers erupt around us but he only has eyes for me. He pulls me close, throwing an arm over my shoulder and angling us toward the door. I ignore Joker as we pass him and thankfully he returns the favor. I feel the nip in the air as we walk over to Halo's bike. I snuggle into him a little more since he always seems to run a few degrees hotter than the rest of us. He hands me his helmet, which I put on begrudgingly. I know from a previous fight with Gage I wouldn't win the argument. Thankfully, my own helmet should be arriving tomorrow so I won't have to feel guilty for taking away theirs. If anything were to happen to them—I shut off that train of thought. Nothing was going to happen. I know it, but the more attached I become to these guys, the more I worry. I am falling hard and fast for them all, spiraling headfirst into something wild and reckless, already knowing that losing one of them would kill me. It's too soon, Luna. My brain knows this but my heart doesn't care about logic. It wants what it wants.

"You good?" Halo asks as I grip his shoulder and climb on behind him, wrapping my arms tightly around his waist.

I nod against his back and give him a squeeze. We wait for the prospect to open the gate before tearing out of there. I don't think the thrill I get from being on a bike will ever diminish. The world whips by at dizzying speeds where nothing else seems to matter. I close my eyes and empty my mind of everything other than this moment.

All too soon, I feel us slowing down. I open my eyes and see us pulling into the diner Orion had taken me to once before. Halo parks and climbs off before lifting me off as if I weigh nothing. He gently unfastens the strap and pulls the helmet from my head, hanging it on the bike as I pull my ponytail loose and shake out my hair.

"I'm starving. I figured we could grab something to go. There is somewhere I want to take you," he tells me, grabbing my hand and tugging me inside.

"Sounds good to me."

All eyes turn to us when we enter but when they see Halo's cut, they quickly turn back to their meals.

"Trust me?" He looks down at me.

"Of course," I answer without having to think about it.

"Good. This place does the best burgers, hands down. Is there anything you don't like?" he questions, pulling his wallet from his back pocket as a teenaged boy hurries over to take our order.

"Nah, I'll eat pretty much anything." He glances down my body slowly and back up again, making me squirm as a bolt of need flashes through me.

"I'll remember that," he mumbles for only me to hear before turning to the boy whose hands shake slightly as Halo places our order. When the boy disappears into the back, I watch as Halo turns and scans the room. Seeming happy with what he finds he hands me his wallet.

"Be right back," he tells me before heading to the restroom.

The wandering eyes feel a little braver now that my biker has disappeared. I feel people looking at me, some out of the corner of their eye trying to be discreet, some just blatantly staring, but I'm not bothered. It's nothing more than what I got in school whenever I was with my brothers. Even back then they had towered over everyone else and with their looks and air of menace, other guys had wanted to be them and the girls wanted to do them.

The sound of a bike draws my attention to the huge window. Wondering which club brother would be joining us and praying it's not Joker, I'm surprised when the bike slows but continues past. It isn't until the rider turns that I realize the emblem on the back of his cut is different. I can't make out the symbol from here but it's definitely not a deck of cards and the colors are black and white, not the blazing red and yellow of Carnage.

"Hey, everything okay?" I turn when I feel Halo wrap his

arm around my waist and take in his frown, remembering Joker and Orion's argument earlier.

"I'm all right but what about you, Pretty Boy? You doing okay?" He flashes me his dimples, making my vagina wake up and start preening. She's so fucking needy.

"Got my bike, great food, and my girl. It doesn't get much better than this, sweetheart," he replies, dipping his head and kissing me. He grabs a handful of my hair and slides his tongue along mine, making me moan, then he smiles against my lips before pulling away.

I feel him take his wallet from my hand and open my eyes to find the bag of food on the counter. Halo pays as I turn and head toward the door. I hold it open as Halo grabs the food and heads over to me. I look at the people openly staring and can't help but laugh. Halo—any of the guys from the MC for that matter—has this effect on people.

"As you were," I call out to them before closing the door behind us.

"So, where are we going?" I ask.

"You'll see."

CHAPTER TWELVE

"It's so peaceful here." I lean against Halo, shoving the last of the burger into my mouth as I look out over the eerie calm of the lake. We are completely hidden from the road, sitting within the copse of trees that concealed this beautiful scene the many times I'd passed by here.

"I come here to think or just for the quiet. I love my brothers but as you know, they're a rowdy bunch of assholes," he explains, making me laugh.

"No! Really? Can't say I noticed." I snort.

"We're not that bad." He nudges me.

"Nope, you guys are a family. Families are crazy. Trust me, I know." I look up at him when I feel him staring down at me.

"What?"

"You are so fucking beautiful." I suck in a sharp breath at his words and feel my face flush. "Any regrets?"

"Regrets? You mean about staying?" I clarify.

"That and having to put up with me and Gage for Orion." I frown at that. That's not how it is at all.

"Is that what you think? That I want Orion so badly I let you fuck me to keep the peace? What the fuck, Halo? Are you serious?" He sighs and leans back, taking his weight on his elbows as he gazes up at the darkening sky.

"Yes, no, maybe. I don't know. What do you want me to say, Luna? I get this is a fucking weird situation for all of us and part of me can't help but wonder if Gage and I are second best."

I lean over and punch him in the arm before standing up and kicking him in the leg, which in these shoes means I hurt myself more than him. I'm blaming him for that too.

"You are such a douche," I yell at him.

"Tsk. Always so violent, Luna."

"Give me one good reason why I shouldn't rip off your cock and smack you repeatedly over the head with it."

"Erm… maybe because you like bouncing up and down on it so much." He grabs my knee and pulls hard until I topple over and end up straddling his lap.

I look down at his chest, pissed off, and if I'm honest with myself, hurt too.

I don't want to look at him but he can't even give me that. He slides his fingers under my chin and tilts my head up until my eyes meet his.

"I didn't mean to upset you, sweetheart. I just…" He sighs before carrying on.

"I don't want to be someone's second choice, Luna, their consolation prize. I don't mind sharing you with my best friends but I want it to be an equal thing. I don't want the girl I'm crazy about wishing she were with one of the others when she's with me."

"Have I treated you that way? Have I made you feel like you don't matter as much?" I swallow hard, feeling tears well up with the thought I might have unintentionally hurt him.

"No, Luna, not even once. It's just that… we should have been straight with you in the beginning instead of letting Orion lock you in first. It was a dick thing to do but we didn't know how else to go about it. We never really thought it through. Now I just can't help but feel like you stayed for Orion and I'm always going to be playing catch up to my best friend."

I look at him, really look at him, and decide to just tell him the truth. What's left to lose?

"Halo, I'm in love with you. You stupid pig-headed pain in my goddamn—" His lips are on mine, rough and unyielding, swallowing the rest of my words as his hands yank my jacket down my arms. I sigh in sweet agony when he pulls away but it's only long enough to rip my T-shirt over my head. Then his lips are back on mine as his hands deftly unclip my bra one-handed. My breasts bounce as he pulls my arms free and tosses the bra aside. The cool air makes my nipples pucker, acting like a target he can't resist.

He dips his head and sucks one nipple into his mouth while palming the other, dragging his rough, scarred hands over my sensitive skin. Each coarse callus has me whimpering with barely contained need, proving these hands that bring pain can also bring mind-numbing pleasure.

"Halo," I moan as my head falls back.

"You love me? You're sure?"

I lift my head and glare down at him. "No, actually, I take it back. Oopsie." He bites down on my nipple in response, making me cuss him out.

"You love me?" He lifts his head to meet my eyes and whatever smartass remark I was going to say dies on my lips.

"It was you who stood between Weasel and me, you who fucked him up for hurting me. You were the one who defended me against Slick in the kitchen, knowing I wouldn't have started something without provocation and it was you, Pretty Boy, who washed blood from my hair when I couldn't lift my arms to do it myself. Those moments are just the first three things that pop into my head and not one of them had anything to do with Orion. If he left me, I would be devastated but, Halo, I wouldn't walk away from you and Gage because of it. I don't love you because of Orion, I love you, Pretty Boy, because you are Halo."

His lips take mine again, ravaging me with an almost desperate need. Standing up with me still in his arms, he walks us the few steps to his bike before setting me on my feet and bending me over the seat. He reaches around me and pops the button on my jeans, yanking them down with my underwear to my ankles before slipping my feet through the legs, my shoes sliding off with them.

I hear the clinking of his belt and the rip of a foil packet as he drops his jeans and presses against my back.

"I can't do slow and soft right now, Luna, let me know if it's too much. Hold on tight."

I don't answer, I just tip my hips up, ready for him. He slides a finger in first, grunting when he feels how slick I already am.

"Goddamn it, baby, always so wet and ready for me."

He doesn't waste any more time, swapping his finger for his cock. He nudges the head against me, coating himself with my wetness before gliding all the way home. We both groan this time as he bottoms out inside me. He drags his cock back out as my walls squeeze him tight, desperately trying to keep him inside.

"Fuck, Luna, if you keep doing that, I'm going to come in two seconds," he grits out before slamming back inside me.

The bike wobbles a little but it doesn't topple over, which is just as well because Halo doesn't let up after that, hammering into me, each push and pull harder and faster than the one before. I can feel the heat building, a swirling mass of want and need desperately trying to claw its way out before I explode around him with a scream that rips from my throat.

I feel Halo pulse as he bites down on my shoulder, masking his groan as he rides out his own orgasm. His movements slow, his energy spent, he presses a kiss between my shoulder blades and gently pulls out.

"How does it keep getting better and better with you?" he grunts. I don't answer him. I couldn't even if I wanted to.

I hear him fumbling around but I don't move or even open my eyes as I try to catch my breath. I flinch when I feel something cold against my folds but Halo holds me in place. It takes my brain a second to realize he's cleaning me up. No, it's more than that, he's cleaning me up with baby wipes.

The giggle of laughter that erupts from me startles us both. He spins me around when he's finished, looking at me with a mix of amusement and bewilderment.

"What?" he asks but I just keep laughing. Every time I try to speak, another bout of laughter escapes me.

"Just what every guy wants to hear after he fucks his woman," he says drolly as I finally manage to calm down.

"Oh, behave. You know your dick makes me do-lally. I just wasn't expecting my fearsome biker to whip out a pack of baby wipes from the saddlebag of his Harley." That sets me off again.

"Laugh it up, Luna." He picks me up and sits me in his lap, chuckling along with me.

"Look, bikes are messy. I'm on the road a fair bit, which means eating on the go. Some of the places I stop should be fucking quarantined. I think I'll stick with carrying the wipes and risk having my man card revoked than risk catching—who the fuck knows what—out there."

"Eww, good point. Hey, you can use me as an excuse now.

If anyone asks, you can just say they're pussy wipes for when you make your old lady come so hard, she sees stars."

"Stars huh?" he asks, amused.

"A whole galaxy worth." I nod.

"Sweet after sex. I remember now." I elbow him as the cold finally makes itself known now that I'm not running on lust.

"Come on, let's get you dressed before you get sick." He helps me up and then, I kid you not, he helps me get dressed. There's something sweet and endearing about it and if I didn't already love this man, I think this moment would have done it.

"I love you," I murmur as he holds my jacket out for me to slide my arms into.

He turns me in his arms and pulls my hair free from my collar. Looking into my eyes, he swallows hard. "I've never told anyone I've loved them before. I'm not sure…"

I reach up and squeeze his arm with my hand. "Hey, you don't have to say it back. It's soon, I know it is. I'm not saying it so you'll say it back. There's zero pressure, I swear." I try to reassure him, not liking the lost look on his face one little bit.

"It's not that… it's, fuck!" He runs a hand through his hair before pulling me even closer. It isn't until he starts speaking that I realize he's trying to draw comfort from me.

"I was found by a dumpster when I was a couple of days old, detoxing from god knows what. I had no name, parents, or birth certificate. I was just nothing. The papers dubbed me 'Angel' on account that it was a miracle I was even alive, and it kind of stuck. Anyway, long story short, nobody wanted a baby that had a whole heap of medical problems. I spent a lot of time in and out of the hospital as a kid and the rest of it bouncing around the foster system. Nothing shady happened to me, there was no abuse of any kind, but there wasn't any connection to those people either. I was just a way for them to make cash. I've never had someone tell me they love me before and... I just don't want to fuck it up and have you take it back."

I feel my heart breaking for him but I refuse to cry. That's not what he needs right now. I hate that, after all this time, he sees himself through tainted lenses. Dirty, unwanted, undeserving of love. I need to show him he's worthy of so much more.

"First of all, you are not nothing. To me, Halo, you are everything." I cup his face with my hands as his eyes blaze into mine. Even if he can't find the words to say it, it's there in his eyes for all to see.

"Second of all, I'm honored that I'm the first person to get to say those words to you. They are yours now. I'll never take them back because, even if the world falls down around us and this relationship crashes and burns in the wreckage, right here, in this moment, I love you with every breath in my lungs and every beat of my heart." He kisses me, stealing any other words I might have wanted to say. It's soft and full of intent and, dare I say it, love.

He pulls away, resting his head against mine and breathes me in for a second.

"We should head back," he finally says, breaking the moment. I squeeze his hand and look out over the lake and nod.

"Take me home, Pretty Boy."

* * * * *

The party is in full swing by the time we get back. Walking into the clubhouse is a shock to the system after the placid calm of the lake. Being here surrounded by black leather-encased bodies and mostly naked women laughing, joking, and fucking to the sound of Lynyrd Skynyrd playing in the background threatens to burst the bubble Halo and I had been in. But when he links his fingers through mine so he can pull me through the crowd toward the bedrooms, I realize he isn't ready for our night to be over either.

Before we even make it halfway, I'm convinced I've already seen more vaginas in the three-and-a-half minutes it took us to break through the crowd than I have in my entire life.

After a text telling us that both Orion and Gage are at King's place across the back of the lot, we crawl into Orion's big old bed and pass out wrapped up in each other.

I wake once when a hard body climbs in behind me in the early hours of the morning but settle when I realize it's Gage.

"Where's Orion?" I ask sleepily as he wraps his arm around my waist.

"He's staying with King tonight. He had chemo today so he spent most of the night throwing up. Orion didn't want to leave him."

"I'll go see him tomorrow," I say softly.

It's a dire situation but he has people here who care about him and I want to get to know the man a little better before it's too late.

"Okay, Cherub, just remember he can be a grouchy fucker when he's feeling crappy," he warns me.

"Men always are when they're sick. It's okay," I whisper as sleep pulls me back under.

Now I'm waiting for the coffee to finish brewing, standing with a smile on my face at all the groaning I can hear coming from the other room. Not the sex kind of groaning but the dear-god-in-heaven-why-did-I-drink-so-much kind of groaning. I decide to take pity on everyone and throw a load of bacon on to cook, letting the smell permeate the air.

Gecko is the first to stroll in, looking sleepy and a lighter shade of green than his hair.

"Rough night?" I ask, assembling a stack of bacon sandwiches on a large platter.

"Urgh. My mouth tastes like ass." I snort at that lovely description.

"Well, you are what you eat," I joke.

"You wound me, darlin'." I shake my head at him as I pour us both a mug of coffee.

"One day, Cherub, you'll listen to me and wake one of us the fuck up before wandering around the clubhouse alone," Gage grumbles as he walks in behind me and picks me up before plonking me down on his lap.

"Sure, I wasn't busy at all," I grumble. "Besides I knew it was only our chapter in last night. I wouldn't have come down otherwise."

He doesn't say anything but he grabs my coffee off the counter and takes a sip.

I glare at him. "I will cut you," I growl out.

Who does that? What kind of psycho steals someone's first coffee of the day? Someone with a death wish, that's who. He just smirks at me and continues to drink it. I spy a fork on the counter and lean forward but another hand scoops it up and tosses it into the sink.

I look up and find Halo looking down at me, laughing.

"Traitor," I snap.

Seeing Orion behind him, I climb off Gage's lap and walk over to Orion, wrapping my arms around his waist.

"How's your dad?" I ask, looking up into his tired eyes.

"Better this morning. He's sleeping now, thank god."

"I'll go and sit with him for a bit today." He looks down at me gratefully before dipping his head and kissing me.

"Thanks, Cherub."

"It's no problem," I tell him honestly, turning when a prospect pokes his head in. He spots Orion.

"Trouble at the gate."

Pulling away from me, Orion heads outside quickly, followed by Halo and Gage.

"Watch her," Orion barks over his shoulder at Gecko. He needn't worry. I have no intention of going out there. I walk over to the coffee machine and pour myself a fresh cup, ignoring the rising voices coming from outside, confident the guys can handle it. I catch snippets but ignore it, choosing instead to enjoy my cup of magic goodness when I catch the last part of a conversation.

"....burn this place to the ground."

"Shit, fuck, shit." I place the cup on the counter and sprint outside, ignoring Gecko shouting from behind me. I see two men standing just inside the gates pointing guns at Halo, Gage, and Orion who are returning the favor.

"You don't get to come into my club barking your orders and making threats. Give me one good reason why I shouldn't shoot you where you stand? How the fuck did you get in here anyway?"

"Fuck, fuck, fuck," I chant as I sprint down the steps and speed around Gage who spots me too late to grab me.

"Luna!" he roars. I ignore him and the few other men littered around the yard with guns pointed at the two troublemakers. I fling my arms around the slightly taller of the two men who has lowered his gun to catch me.

"I missed you," I whisper in his ear before I'm snagged up in a bear hug from the man beside him.

"What the fuck?" I hear Halo ask. I wait until I'm lowered back to the ground before grabbing a hand of each of the men. I turn to face my guys and freeze at the looks of anger and betrayal on their faces. Whoops.

"Shit, sorry, guys. Gage, Halo, Orion, meet my brothers Zig and Oz." Nobody moves for a second but eventually, everyone lowers their guns, sensing the threat is over.

"Brothers?" Orion asks, eyeing Ziggy and Cosmic up and down. I know what he sees. Where I'm tiny and blonde, they are massive in height and breadth with dark, almost black, hair. They take after our dad whereas I'm all our mother.

"Afraid so. I'm so sorry. I forgot to check in and let them know I was okay."

"How did they even know where to find you?" Gage asks, looking backward and forward between me and them

"My watch." I hold it up dumbly like they don't know what a watch is.

"It has GPS and an SOS function. I hit it when I was in the cell." Instead of looking angry, Gage looks impressed.

"Cell?" Zig grits out. Oops.

"Erm… maybe we should take this inside," I say, looking around at all the guys watching us. Unlike my guys, they haven't lowered their guns.

"Cell, Luna? Really? You let them lock you in a cell?" I snap my head around to face Oz and flip him off before stomping ahead of them.

"I was tag teamed," I shout over my shoulder and pause for a second as everyone turns to look at me. A flush creeps up over my cheeks.

"Not like that. He got me from behind. You know what? I

hate you all. I should have just let you shoot each other. Then I could have enjoyed my coffee in peace."

I stomp up to my guys and find myself tossed over Gage's shoulder. I don't protest, knowing he won't listen, but I spend my time on his shoulder making a solid plan about smothering him in his sleep later. We head into the bar area and I find myself unceremoniously plonked on a chair between Halo and Orion. I sit quietly and fume while everyone else sizes each other up.

Well, if nobody is going to talk, I'm going to go grab my coffee. I try to stand and find Halo's arm around my shoulder and Orion's hand possessively on my thigh.

"I was just going to get my coffee," I grumble. Orion gives my leg a squeeze so I shut up and let the big babies—sorry, I mean big strong men—deal with everything. After five minutes of posturing, I'm ready to throw myself out the nearest available window.

"For the love of—if we could move this along, that would be fucking awesome. Some of us aren't nearly caffeinated enough to deal with this shit in the morning."

"Still as bitchy as ever, I see, Luna," Oz teases. I pick up the empty beer glass someone was nice enough to leave behind for me and launch it at his head. The asshole ducks at the last second, letting the glass shatter on the wall behind him.

"I will drop all your guns off at the police station without wiping your prints if you keep pissing me off," I threaten him.

"Ouch, that's harsh, Luna, even for you." He places his hands over his heart, acting wounded.

"Guns?" Gage questions.

"Huh? Oh, Oz has quite the collection."

"Prints?" Orion hones in on that tidbit of information.

I shrug. "Not every job is strictly legal."

"Job? I thought you said these guys were soldiers," Halo points out.

"They are, just of the soldiers for hire variety."

"So, mercenaries." Gage correctly puts the pieces together. "Guess that explains why the MC doesn't freak you out as much as it would others. You're used to the rules being bent. How the hell does none of this come back to you?"

Oz opens his mouth to answer but I give him a small shake of my head.

"Just lucky, I guess. Besides, it's the same kind of risk I take being here in a relationship with you three. Other MCs will see me as a weak spot."

"Well they would be in for a rude awakening," Ziggy mutters under his breath

"So, do you want to explain what's going on or what?" Oz asks, clearly bored with this conversation. "Are they the reason you spent those two months moping around?" I'm going to seriously kill him.

"I do not mope," I bite out.

Orion squeezes my thigh, making me look up to see him smiling. Yeah, laugh it up.

"You've seen that I'm fine. You can go home now. I'll call you when I need you," I tell my brothers.

"Good enough for me." Oz stands and Zig follows suit.

"That's it? You're really not bothered about leaving your sister in the care of a bunch of bikers?" Gage asks, angry on my behalf.

"Ha. I'm more worried about you guys. Luna can take care of herself." Zig winks at me and turns to leave.

"You do know she could have died, right?" Gage asks sarcastically. I wonder absently as I check my nails if he wants to get shot.

"But she didn't die, did she? Now she knows to adjust her expectations to pussy fucks who hit girls from behind." Zig squares off to Gage.

"Enough, Zig. Thanks for checking on me. Can you take my truck back with you? You can sling your bikes in the back. I've got Gramps's truck here. I don't need both."

"Done. Anything else you need?"

"What do you think?" I answer cryptically, knowing he will know exactly what I mean. I don't like being unarmed but I know Zig will take care of it.

"Right, let's go. I can feel my balls starting to shrivel knowing my sister's getting fucked more than me. I need to go and get laid before heading back," Oz adds.

"You're a pig, Oz."

"Jealous? Oh, what's the matter, wrong time of the month?" Halo stops me from launching myself across the table at him. Oz's laughter echoes around the room, making me want to throw another glass at him. I scan the table but quickly find myself in Halo's lap with one of his arms around mine and the other on my stomach, stopping me from throwing anything else.

"You're a menace," he whispers in my ear but I can hear the laughter in his voice. He bites my ear, making my body shiver before focusing back on my brothers. They finally start talking to each other, yet I can't make out any of their words. I feel like the bottom just dropped out of my world.

Everything was fine until Halo rested his hand against my stomach. Then Oz's words suddenly took on a whole new meaning.

I haven't had my period. I hadn't given it much thought as I'm not the most regular person but by my calculations, it's been—fuck, it's been nearly three months.

"Luna?" I look up and see Ziggy's eyes roving over my face.

"What's wrong?" he asks, drawing the attention of the guys around the table. Orion turns my head toward him and frowns at whatever he sees.

"Cherub?" I open my mouth to answer but nothing comes out, so I close it again.

"Fuck, Luna, you're as white as a sheet." He lifts me from Halo's lap into his so I'm straddling his thigh. Both his hands cup my face as he stares into my eyes for answers I'm not sure I'm ready to say out loud yet.

"Nothing. Sorry, I just felt dizzy for a minute. I think I need to eat something." The words are barely out of my mouth before Gage clicks his fingers at one of the prospects against the far wall.

"Prospect, bring Luna one of those bacon sandwiches and some juice." The prospect leaves and I offer Gage a wobbly smile in thanks. Orion tucks my head against his shoulder and rubs a hand up and down my back, not caring in the least about the bikers surrounding us. The move brings a tear to my eye and has me snuggling into the side of his neck, breathing him in. Maybe, just maybe, everything will be okay.

CHAPTER THIRTEEN

T hings were definitely not okay.
Well, fuck! Megan signs from the floor beside me. We're both sitting with our knees up and our backs to the wall of the small bathroom at the back of her shop, staring down at the six pregnancy tests that confirm I am indeed pregnant.

What happened to no glove, no love? She smirks at me, making me shove her.

"For your information, they always suit up but these guys seem to defy the freaking odds. Orion's lightsaber probably destroyed it with his super sperm." I shove her again when she laughs at me.

What are you going to do? Well, that's the million-dollar question, now, isn't it?

"I don't know, Megan. It's not that I'm opposed to having

kids, I just didn't want them yet. I mean, how will this even work? Me and the guys are still trying to figure things out between us and how I'm going to fit within the MC. Things have been up in the air with King being sick. I don't know what to make of the new president but he has sway with the others, obviously. Even if my guys are willing to make changes, they can't go against the president, so what kind of life does it leave for me and nugget here?"

Don't borrow trouble, Luna. That's a lot of what if's, but the truth is, you aren't going to know how this is going to go until it plays out. You know I'm not the biggest MC fan but not all of them are bad. Answer me this, do you trust them? After everything that's happened, I know most people would think I was nuts and who knows, maybe I am, but there is something instinctual that says yes, I can trust my guys.

A hammering at the door has me looking up even though I know it's locked.

"Everything okay in there?" a new prospect named Parker calls through the door.

"Everything's fine. We'll be out in a sec," I yell back. He walks away muttering about bitches going to the toilet together. I lay my head on Megan's shoulder and take a deep breath, thankful she could help me out today. We sit quietly for a minute before she climbs to her feet offering me her hand. I scoop up the tests and grab her hand, letting her help me up. I dump the tests into the small zipped pocket inside my bag on the counter before washing my hands and nodding my head that I'm ready.

We head back into the store where Parker is waiting for us. Another prospect is sitting outside. The MC is having a barbeque later, a sort of thank-you-for-being-a-great-leader kind of thing for King. It feels more like a congratulations-on-not-dying-yet kind of thing to me but what do I know? My brothers are coming, so I know tonight at least I won't feel like an interloper.

This is the first time I've been out without one of my guys since I came back. I suspect the only reason Orion even agreed to let me come here today was because I asked him mid blowjob.

Megan and I walk out together, coming out behind the glass counter. Parker spins to say something, when there is the unmistakable *pop, pop* of a gun firing outside.

"Down, now!" he roars at me. I yank Megan to the floor, quickly signing to her what's going on before I rummage through my bag for my gun. I really do have the best brothers in the world. Before they took my truck, Zig left me a gun under the seat of Gramps's truck since Gage still hadn't given mine back after the fiasco from before.

I pull out the gun and switch the safety off as the bell above the door chimes.

A gun fires again, closer this time, so I peek around the edge of the counter and see someone drop to the floor by the door. I take a deep breath in relief that Parker managed to get the drop on him, when a second gunshot rings out. A body crashes into the counter and slumps to the floor. Fuck. Tears spring to my eyes thinking about Parker but I swallow it down and focus. I have two lives to save, no, three now, with nugget. It's all the incentive I need to shut off my emotions. I watch from my spot as someone else steps through the door. I glance up and am surprised to see Weasel looking around.

"Come out, come out wherever you are," the psychotic dickhead calls. I feel an arm against mine as Megan leans up against me to see what's going on and, as much as I want to snap at her to move back, I can't imagine how terrifying it must be to have one of your senses stripped from you and not know what's going on around you.

Weasel starts laughing maniacally like the creeper he is.

"Oh, that's right, you can't hear me, can you, bitch?" he mocks, pulling one of the shelving units over so it crashes to the floor.

I look at Megan and realize he's here for her, not me. What the fuck is going on? Megan is white as a sheet and shaking like she's seen a ghost. I grip her face with my free hand, needing her to keep it together. I mouth that I need her to distract him. Her eyes widen but she takes a deep breath and nods. She crawls away from me as Weasel systematically destroys the store around us. She makes it to the farthest part of the counter before standing up on shaky legs and pushing a jar of pens off the counter to get his attention. I watch from my spot as he spins around and his ugly face breaks into a smile.

"Well, well, well. Look who it is. Little bird, I've missed you." She knows him but I can tell from every twitch of her body this is not a happy reunion.

"I hear you've made friends with that bitch that got me booted from Carnage. Tsk, tsk, Birdy. Have you no loyalty at all?"

"Fuck you!" I hear Megan whisper and for a second I'm so shocked, I can't move. I've never heard her speak before. I wasn't even sure she could.

"Well, if you insist, Birdy. Come over here and get on your knees. Show me how much you've missed me and I might refrain from cutting out your tongue."

She turns toward the opening, moving her fingers behind her back. It takes me a second to realize she's signing.

I'll distract him so you can sneak out the back.

If she thinks I'm leaving her here, she is fucking delusional. She lifts the counter flap and heads toward him. When she's close enough, he grabs her by the hair and forces her to her knees.

He puts his gun on the shelf behind him so he can open his fly without letting her go and I take advantage of the only shot I might get. I stand up and shoot him right between the eyes without any hesitation. He crashes back into the shelving behind him and slides to the floor. I'm up and around the counter two seconds later with a shaking Megan in my arms. I check her over and after determining she's okay, I crawl over to Parker.

He's lost a lot of blood but I can feel a faint pulse. I run back to Megan and drag her over to Parker with me. I press her hands against the wound on his neck but it's doing little to stop the blood from flowing. She nods that she understands what I need from her, leaving me free to run and snatch my purse from behind the counter. I grab it and head back to Megan, skidding in Parker's blood and nearly falling. I pull out my phone and hit speed dial with shaky hands as the adrenaline floods my system.

"Oz's crematorium, you break 'em we bake 'em." Fucking Oz and his stupid sense of humor are strangely fitting for once.

"Oz," I whisper.

"Luna?" Oz reacts to the tone of my voice and the joker is replaced with the lethal killer he's trained to be.

"Where are you?" I hear shuffling in the background. I reel off the address before taking a deep breath.

"I'm pretty sure I've just started a war and I need someone on my side to have my back. I have to call the guys but I *need* you," I say, not having any idea how this is all going to play out.

"On my way." He hangs up, leaving me to dial Halo who, out of the three, might be the easiest to talk to.

"Hey, sugar, we've just got back from collecting King who is his usual charming self again."

I can hear King in the background shout, "Fuck you!"

"Halo." My voice shakes even though I feel a little calmer hearing his voice.

"What happened?" he shouts.

"Weasel shot Parker and I think the prospect outside too but I don't want to go out and check in case anyone else is out there. Parker is in a bad way, Halo, he's been shot in the neck.

He needs an ambulance but I don't know what you want me to say to the police," I ramble.

I can hear running and bikes starting up and I know they are on their way, thank fuck.

"We'll be there in five, sugar, don't worry about the police. Rebel is calling an ambulance now but we'll probably beat them there. Doc is with us, so don't panic. Where is Weasel now? Are you safe?"

"Yeah, me and Megan are fine. I… Weasel's dead. I shot him." I hear his sharp intake of breath.

"I've gotta hang up but I'm on my way, sugar, I promise." He hangs up and I crawl back over to Megan who has managed to stem the worst of the bleeding by shoving her fingers inside Parker's neck. I look at his face, surprised to find his eyes open and watching me.

"Hey." I grab his hand and squeeze. "You're going to be fine. The guys are on their way. Just hold on for me okay?" He squeezes my hand so I take that as a yes.

We stay exactly as we are, time crawling by agonizingly slow until the door crashes open behind us. I turn my head and see Carnage bikers flooding in but my eyes are focused entirely on Gage as he barrels toward us with a face like thunder. He scans me from top to bottom, checking that I'm okay before his shoulders finally relax a little. He comes directly over to me and picks me up, squeezing me tightly. He hands me over to Halo who wraps his arms around me, kissing me softly and wiping the tears of relief from my eyes.

"Orion is with King and Joker. He wanted to be here so

badly but he had to stay and protect them in case this was a trap." I nod, I get it.

"It's fine, Halo. It was the smart thing and the right thing to do."

"I need you to move now!" someone barks from behind me. I turn and see an older MC member shouting at Megan's back but of course, she doesn't hear him. I watch as he shoves her and she lands sprawled to the side of Parker with her fingers still inside his neck. Something inside me snaps. I shrug out of Halo's hold and walk over to the crouching Doc, who is berating Megan for getting in his way, and kick him in the face. He falls as I pull my leg back to kick him again but find myself restrained by a pair of strong arms.

"Enough!" Halo roars at me. "He's trying to save him and she's in the way. We don't have time for sensitivities right now."

"She's keeping him alive, you fucking motherfuckers. Her fingers are in his neck and they're the only reason he's still breathing." He must look to see what I'm talking about because he lets me go.

"Shit!" He crouches down next to her and tells her to move so he can take over.

"She can't hear you, she's deaf," I explain, crouching down on the other side of her. I rub her arm gently to get her attention and sign that she needs to let go. She shakes her head at me.

"Megan, let go. Halo has him. I swear it," I sign.

I watch the tears drip down her face before she turns to

Halo and nods. He slides his fingers down beside hers. She watches his mouth and on the count of three, they switch. She pulls away and turns into my arms, sobbing. I stand with her and pull her away before Gage wraps his arms around us both. I hear a commotion at the door and look up to find Oz and Zig shoving their way inside.

"This is club business, Luna," Gage scolds me.

"They weren't looking for me. They were looking for Megan," I tell him, making him look down at her suspiciously, which is another reason I called my brothers.

"Luna." Oz snatches me away from Gage, much to Gage's disgust, and wraps his arms tightly around me. I let go and move toward Zig when I notice Gage still has hold of Megan, only this time, he has his massive hand wrapped around her wrist.

"Let go of her, Gage." I step forward and take her free hand.

"Club business, Luna. I have a dead prospect outside and one down in here and you want to let go of the only connection we have to the traitor over there?" He nods in Weasel's direction.

"This is one of those times, Luna, where you are just going to have to shut up and deal with it. This is an MC, not a fucking knitting club." He seethes.

I feel my brothers stand beside me, flanking me and having my back like they have done a thousand times over the years, and stare down one of the men I'm falling for.

"She sacrificed herself to get me out," I point out softly,

making him look down at her and swallow. She's shaking so hard I can feel her body vibrating through our connected hands.

"I only managed to get a shot at Weasel thanks to her. The only reason Parker is still alive is because of her. Now let her go so she can get checked out. You want to talk to her, I get that, but let her get cleaned up and looked over first," I say softly, not wanting to make a scene in front of his club brothers, knowing instinctively that will be the wrong move to make. I walk up to him and slide my hand over the one of his holding her wrist.

"I'm not going anywhere. She can stay with me." He looks at me like he wants to give in but when the paramedics turn up I know the police will be hot on their tails, signaling our time is up.

He looks over at the biker I vaguely remember being called Agro and nods for him to take Megan. He comes up and takes her, grabbing both of her arms behind her. She looks at me scared and confused for a second so I sign that I will sort it out. She nods, trusting me. God, I hope that trust isn't misplaced.

"Take her to the cells," Gage tells Agro, never taking his eyes from mine, waiting for me to protest. I say nothing. Nothing I say will make any difference right now. I let every ounce of my disapproval show though. Agro walks her outside. I turn to follow but Gage grabs my arm.

"Don't interfere. Gecko will take you back to the

clubhouse. Stay there and keep out of the way. Orion will want to see you but he won't be able to stay for long."

I don't answer him, say goodbye to him or Halo, or even acknowledge Gecko when he walks over to me offering me his hand. I turn to face my brothers who both have neutral expressions on their faces. Guess the bikers must be fools because if they really knew what was going on beneath my brothers' placid expressions, they would have all pulled their weapons by now.

"*Chosaint,*" I tell them in our native tongue, knowing they will understand me. They both nod in unison before I slip my hand into Gecko's and let him lead me outside to my truck. I climb into the passenger seat and toss my keys onto the driver's seat as he puts his bike in the back. I lean my head against the cool glass beside me and close my eyes. I take a deep breath and prepare myself for everything that's about to go down. Why does everything always go to shit so fast?

"Everything's gonna be okay, Luna. You have to trust your guys to sort it out," Gecko tells me as he starts the engine. He pulls out just as I hear sirens approaching in the distance.

"Okay, for who, though, Gecko? My friend is being locked down in the same place that nearly killed me after she just saved both mine and Parker's life. The MC sure has a fucked-up way of showing their gratitude. I'm sure next time she'll just sneak out the back and leave me to fend for myself."

"They're trying to tie up loose ends. It's been quiet for the

Carnage for a while but then you show up and, no offense, Luna, things start fucking up."

"I love it when someone says no offense before offending you. It's such BS and you know it. Weasel was a traitor. I think we've safely established that so my turning up only helped there. King being sick has fuck-all to do with me. My friend and I were minding our own business when we were attacked by a former MC member. But please, feel free to blame me if it makes you feel better, Gecko."

He wisely stops talking and we drive the rest of the way back to the compound in silence. The gate is more heavily guarded than usual but I guess that's to be expected. Gecko parks the truck. As soon as he turns off the engine, I hop out and make my way inside. The bar area is busy but I can't see King or Orion. I head upstairs to Orion's room but can't find him there either. Fuck it. I don't have time to chase after him. Considering how worried about me he's supposed to be, he's making it impossible to find him. I grab two hoodies from his wardrobe and slide them both on over my T-shirt. I head down to the cells without anyone seeing me. I walk in just as Agro is locking the cell closest to us and slips the key into his jacket pocket. He turns to me and frowns.

"You shouldn't be here, Luna. Get your ass upstairs now." He steps toward me so I dip my head, making myself look nervous and unsure.

"I just wanted to make sure she was okay," I tell him, making my voice quiver. He shakes his head at me like I'm nuts but nods for me to go and follows me back upstairs.

"I'm going to go and lie down. It's all been a bit too much today, you know?" His face softens a little now that I'm acting like a good little girl. He nods and holds the door open for me to head back to the rooms. I give him a little wave and head off, ducking around the corner to wait for him to disappear. When I'm sure he's gone, I head back down to the cells.

My heart breaks a little when I hear Megan crying in the corner of her cell, still covered in Parker's blood. Technically, I'm not breaking the rules being down here because I'm not letting her out but I'll be damned if I let her suffer down here without me. She must see the movement as she looks up sharply, showing me her tear-stained face before her lip wobbles when she notices it's just me. I crouch down beside her, slip my fingers through the bars, and grip her hand tightly in mine. I wait for her crying to subside before pulling away and signing for her to tell me everything. She sighs and leans back, nodding. I pull one of the hoodies off and slip it through the bars to her. I watch her slide it over her head, knowing better than anyone how much she's going to need it. She smiles at me gratefully but I don't miss the sadness in her eyes or how she folds in on herself as she begins her story.

The official story is that my mother was a club whore who belonged to the Chaos Demons. The president got her pregnant but he already had an old lady so she was made to stay but was never given the protection that came with old lady status. She was to live out her days as a club whore whether she wanted to or not.

They were never going to let her leave. It was only as I got older that I realized there were some major holes in the story.

I was always treated like a pariah, the unwanted club princess, but it still should have given me the protection that comes along with being a club kid. The problem was that when fucked-up shit started happening, nobody believed me. They thought I was an attention-seeking whore like my mother. I was trapped within an MC that was supposed to have my back but, instead, they hung me out to dry based on a bunch of secrets and lies I wasn't privy to.

My father hated me. Confiding in him earned me a slap around the face. I remember him screaming at me that I was just like her. After that, I just kept quiet.

I stop her for a second. "Kept quiet about what, Megan? What happened?"

Crogan happened. Crogan was the son of my father's old lady. He had his sights set on me and he didn't give a single shit I was underage and not interested. Every time he was nearby, he would find any excuse he could to touch me or grind up against me. He always found ways to get me alone so he could kiss me and grope me. The older I got, the worse it became until I turned sixteen. That's when he decided I was old enough to become his. He went to my father and his VP, Rock, to tell them he was making me his old lady. Rock—who was actually my father's step-brother—was against it from the start but my father said he would think about it. When Rock pointed out how the other members would react when they realized their own teen daughters would be painted as targets from members when they hit the same age, he denied him.

Crogan was furious. He convinced himself if he got me pregnant they would have no choice but to allow it. I grip her leg, offering her some comfort, not liking where this story is going.

I woke up to find him on top of me. He was so heavy. I could hardly breathe. I remember it had been freezing that night so I had gone to bed in sweatpants and a sweatshirt and wrapped myself up like a human burrito. I had no idea that in the long run, they would save me, buying me extra time.

He forced his tongue into my mouth as he tried to dig me out from under the blanket so I bit him. He slapped me in the face but he never stopped trying to get to me. He finally managed to pull the quilt out from between us and went to work on getting his hands down my pants. He stopped kissing me to bite down on my neck, hard enough to draw blood, so I screamed as loud as I could. I screamed so loud it hurt my ears but I didn't stop until he started punching me over and over and over. She looks at me with tears in her eyes.

My scream was the last thing I ever heard. When I woke up in the hospital a month later, it was to find that I would never hear again and that my mother, father, and Crogan were dead. I stare at her in complete shock.

"H...How... what the fuck?"

My father was the one to find Crogan just as he was about to fuck me. He dragged him off, pissed that he disobeyed a direct order, and beat the shit out of him. Crogan was given a warning to stay away from me or they would take his cut. A warning—that's it. For beating his daughter to near death and almost raping her. My mother lost her mind. When Crogan decided if he couldn't

205

have me that night, he would have her, she stabbed him to death. She took his gun and shot my father before turning the gun on herself.

Rock became President. He knew what had happened and let me leave the MC, knowing I would never be safe there. He paid my hospital bills and gave me both my and my mother's possessions before they were destroyed. I've seen them ride by a few times over the years. Their black and white colors make them hard to miss but it's been six years since I've heard from them, until today. I know there was a protection order placed on me. As long as I didn't betray the club in any way, I would be safe. I guess having Kings of Carnage at my place of business was considered an act of treachery.

She looks up at me and suddenly she looks so much younger than her twenty-two years.

"Shit, this is all my fault. I should never have brought the Kings to your place." I'm truly kicking myself now.

How could you possibly have known, Luna? Besides, you're the only friend I've got. I was willing to take the risk to keep you.

"I swear to you—" I'm cut off by the clanking of the door and Orion's furious voice.

"Then where the fuck is she, Gecko? You brought her back here. She was your responsibility until you handed her over to me. I swear to god, if anything has happened to her, I'll gut you myself. Why do you think this bitch will know where she is?"

"Because they're friends, Orion, or at least Luna thinks

so." Yes, because I'm such a simpering idiot that my instincts can't be trusted.

"That's because Luna is—" I cut him off before he needs a shovel to dig himself out of the grave I will put him in.

"Luna is what, honey lumpkins?" I mock, my tone saccharine sweet.

"What the fuck are you doing down here?" he fumes as he stomps down the last of the creaky steps.

"If Megan is expected to stay down here for saving my and Parker's life, then I deserve to be down here for placing hers in danger."

"You don't know what the fuck you're talking about. Do you know what cut Weasel was wearing?

"I'm going to go out on a limb and say a Chaos Demons cut."

"Right, and if he was there for her, then she's tied to them somehow. I don't want you anywhere near her."

"Well, that's just not going to work for me, Adonis," I tell him as he finally stalks his way over to me. "If you touch me, Orion, I will shoot you in your sleep."

He doesn't listen. Instead, he bends down and picks me up and tosses me over his shoulder, barking out an order for Gecko to watch Megan. I have to have faith that Gecko won't hurt her, but Gramps didn't raise no fool. The hoodie Megan is wearing is also the hoodie with the gun in its pocket.

CHAPTER FOURTEEN

Orion drags me up to Joker's office where the man himself is sitting behind his desk. Gage and Halo are standing, looking angry with me, and King is on the sofa looking tired and pissed off. Rebel, Half-pint, and Chewy are all gathered around too and none of them look happy to see me. So be it.

I'm tossed unceremoniously onto the chair in front of the desk and Orion takes his place next to Halo. I sit up straight, refusing to let them intimidate me, and watch King. Despite his tired appearance, I know he is anything but frail and weak.

"Hi, King. You look like shit."

He shakes his head at me. "You're becoming a liability, Luna."

"Then perhaps you shouldn't have had me kidnapped."

"Watch your mouth, lady. Don't think because you're fucking the VP you have any sway over this club," Joker barks at me from behind his desk. This guy is something else.

"The thought never crossed my mind, Joker. All I care about is protecting someone who has earned it. I am nothing if not loyal."

"Yes, but the question is, Luna, who are you loyal to?"

"Pres?" Halo speaks but shuts up when Joker glares at him.

"I'm loyal to the people who have earned it. Isn't that how loyalty is supposed to work?"

"And have we earned your loyalty, Luna?" Joker sneers at my name. I stare at him a beat before I realize he's serious. I burst out laughing, not caring how disrespectful it is. Even when Joker bangs his fist on the desk, I can't stop. The tears are streaming down my face as I try to get the hiccups under control enough for me to speak.

"I saved your dog. That got me a thirty-day stay. I got thrown in at the deep end when I found myself filling in a club sandwich but I just rolled with it. I was almost raped a few feet from where you all stood and yet I was labeled the troublemaker because, what? I stopped him? I left and solved your problem but you guys dragged me back here. Oh, and let's not forget I was knocked unconscious and locked in one of the cells overnight naked. I was lucky to make it through but I still gave you all the benefit of the doubt and agreed to give it a go with the three guys next to you. And here we are, yet again. Isn't it funny how after being attacked, shooting a guy to death, and almost watching my friend get sexually assaulted, I get the interrogation chair instead of the protection this club keeps saying it's all about?"

"Trust and loyalty runs both ways, Luna. You haven't earned it either," King says softly from the sofa.

"And how was I supposed to earn it, King? Tell me what I should have done differently. Should I have let canine King get killed? No, wait, then you wouldn't have met me at all and you would have been none the wiser about Weasel being a traitor. So that leaves, what? Me getting raped. Was that how I was supposed to earn my loyalty, on my back?"

Joker stands and pulls his gun and points it at my head.

"Joker!" Orion barks. I watch as Halo, Gage, and Orion pull their guns and point them at their president. Relief so immense I have to fight from bursting into tears rushes through me.

"Oh, come on, Orion, haven't you learned anything about women leading you around by your cock from your mother?"

"Don't!" King barks at him.

Orion doesn't break Joker's stare but laughs at him nastily. "Maybe my mother was the smart one after all, 'cause let's face it, Luna's right about all of us. We threw things at her left, right, and center and expected her to do as she was told. We gave her a pat on the head and expected her to comply but failed her every step of the way. Now she's sitting here with a gun pointed at her," he states. "No fucking way."

"I'm with Orion, Pres, that's my old lady," Gage replies.

Joker sneers at him. "You weren't bothered when you

were stripping her naked and locking her in the cell. But then, maybe you enjoyed her when she was a little more compliant." Everyone freezes at his words. Even Chewy looks at him with an odd expression on his face.

"Did you just imply I fucked Luna when she was unconscious?" Gage asks, shocked.

Joker shrugs like it means nothing to debase one of his men's characters. "You three keep calling her your old lady but I don't see a cut or a tattoo. Maybe you should rectify that before I decide to take her from you as is my right as President." Who the fuck is this man?

"Like hell, you will!" Halo steps forward and lays a hand upon my shoulder.

"It's in the bylaws, Halo, as you well know. I'm the fucking president. I can do whatever the fuck I like."

"It's also in the bylaws that we claim old ladies in our group of multiples. Two at a minimum, but I don't remember you claiming Melinda. King did but you and John were happy to fuck your way around the club without committing yourselves. So maybe you should practice what you preach, old man. You don't get to pick and choose which rules suit you. You're pissed that John split and Melinda left with him but you had no right to her. King got to mourn the loss of his old lady but she was just another whore to you. And yet you act like she did you a huge disservice when it was the other way around. It's been over twenty years, old man, let it go," Halo snaps at him.

"I will do whatever I damn well please," Joker yells, spit

flying from his mouth. "Get the fuck out of my office and take your whore with you. I have someone to see." The look on his face makes my blood run cold.

"You might as well shoot me now," I tell Joker, looking him dead in the eye. "Because the only way I'm going to let you harm Megan is over my dead body. So fucking shoot me!" I stand up even as Halo grips my shoulder hard enough to leave bruises.

"You don't get to call the shots around here, missy, I do. You'd do well to remember that. I need answers only she can give and I plan on getting them."

"Let me guess, by any means necessary, right?" I feel Gage step up behind me and wrap his arm around my waist.

"Well, good luck with that." I laugh in his face before continuing. "Megan's deaf, Joker, and can't speak." No way will he ever learn any differently from me.

"What were you gonna do when she didn't answer you, beat her to death?" I demand. King looks over my shoulder to Halo who must nod in confirmation.

"And let me guess, you just happen to know sign language?" Joker asks, his voice full of sarcasm and spite. I sign to him that he is a giant asshole and I hope he gets eaten by a crocodile. He raises an eyebrow at me in question.

"It just happens that my gramps was deaf so I do indeed know sign language, thanks for asking." Rebel coughs into his hand to hide his laugh but I just smile sweetly at Joker.

"Fine, you can come but you three have shit to take care off."

"Not a chance. I'm coming too and before you say anything else, as VP, I need to be there," Orion says.

Joker relents. "Fine, fuck it."

Everyone finally lowers their guns. Gage and Halo kiss a cheek each, forgetting they were mad at me. They let me go with Orion, who links his fingers through mine. We make our way down to the cells again. Gecko is standing sentry against the wall outside the cell. Megan is sitting with her knees pulled up to her chest and her head tucked down, her long black hair hiding most of her face.

Gecko opens the door when we approach. As soon as it's open, I let go of Orion's hand and scoot around Joker to get to her. I drop down on my knees in front of her and tap her shoulder, leaning back out of swinging distance. Now her reactions makes more sense.

"Hey!" Orion shouts but I hold my hand up to him.

"She has a startle response and didn't know who it was." Her eyes connect with mine and she takes a deep breath, checking me over.

You okay? she signs. I nod. She dips her head and looks at my belly. *You sure?*

I nod in response, not having had time to process nugget yet with all the shit going on. "How you doing? Think you're up to answering a couple of questions?" I sign and say out loud for everyone else's benefit.

Okay, she agrees.

I step aside so she can see Joker and Orion properly, and

can read their lips if she wants, when I hear Joker suck in a sharp breath.

"Melly?" he whispers, staring at Megan like he's seen a ghost. She isn't looking at him, though, she's looking at Orion. I take in her face and turn to look up at him and find him frozen on the spot.

"Erm... I feel like I've missed something here." I make sure Megan can see my hands so she knows what I'm saying.

"That fucking cunt didn't take long, did she? Jesus, she fucks off and leaves the kids she has so she can make another one with the asshole she left us for. Bet the apple doesn't fall far from the tree." Joker's voice is scathing.

I have no idea what he's talking about but I sign what he says so Megan can shine some light on the situation. I watch her turn to face him as I finish signing. I'm surprised when her fear and uncertainty melt away, only to be replaced with white-hot fury. She climbs to her feet with a look of murder on her face which, given the long black hair and the fact she is covered from head to toe in blood, makes her look like the killer from one of those creepy Japanese horror flicks.

I wait for her to sign something but instead, she shocks the shit out of me by launching herself at Joker. She punches and kicks and bites, making a wild keening noise before he backhands her and she tumbles to the floor.

"Fucking psychotic bitch." He seethes, wiping blood from his split lip with the back of his hand.

I wrap my arms around her as she sobs inconsolably. I

look up at Orion, who is looking at Joker like he doesn't recognize him at all.

"That is the last time you touch her, Joker," Orion tells him in no uncertain terms, his anger barely held in check.

"She attacked me!" Joker yells.

"She's my fucking sister!" Orion roars back.

Holy fuck. I pull away from Megan's embrace and look at her, really look at her, and see what was right in front of me all along.

Melly is Melinda, Orion's mother who left.

"Fuck me," I whisper, shocked, as I swipe her tears with the pad of my thumb. She tenses when Orion crouches down beside us.

"That won't happen again, Megan, I swear," Orion tells her, making sure she can see his lips.

"I'm Logan. I'm your brother." Two seconds later, Megan is in his arms with her head buried in his shoulder. He looks at me in a state of panic for a moment, before wrapping his arms carefully around her.

"How fucking touching. Tell me, how is mother dearest?" Joker asks spitefully. I stand up but Orion reaches out and snags my arm.

"She can't fucking hear you, Joker. Which part of that don't you understand?" This fucking guy makes me so mad.

"You will show me some respect!" he shouts at me but I just shake my head in disgust.

"You are not my president."

He smiles before nodding at Orion. "Maybe not, but I'm

his. I can strip that pretty little cut of his and then what will you do?"

"Is that right?" Orion tucks Megan under one arm and grabs my hand with the other, walking us toward the cell door, but Joker steps in front of us and blocks the way.

"What, you think because our prisoner is your sister, she can just stroll out of here? I don't fucking think so." He reaches forward and grabs Megan's arm hard, making her yelp.

"Let go, old man, before I put you on your ass," Orion growls at him.

Joker eyes Orion, weighing the pros and cons of persisting but must realize he's no match against him and lets go. Orion walks us out of the cell with Gecko looking between us and Joker before following us out. It looks like lines are being drawn. Now it's time to see which side people will choose.

We make our way up to Orion's room. He hands Megan off to me and asks Gecko to round up the other few he knows will be loyal to him. I pull Megan into the bathroom and sit her on the toilet seat. I grab a washcloth, gently scrubbing away the blood from her skin. What she really needs is a shower but this room is going to be full of angry men in a minute, so that's not an option. Orion pokes his head around the door and scans us both to make sure we're okay. I can't help it, I'm so fucking proud of him right now I walk up to him and plant a big smacker on his lips.

"You're the bomb, Orion." He kisses me a little harder before grabbing my ass and pulling me closer.

A cough makes us pull apart as Megan makes a gagging motion, making me laugh. Orion smiles at her. He walks over and bends down in front of her.

"I didn't know about you, Megan, I swear." She nods and offers him a small smile. I'm guessing she didn't know about him either.

I can hear rowdy voices coming from the bedroom. I guess everyone is here already. He stands and gestures for us both to follow. We head into the now packed bedroom, Megan hovering a little behind my back trying to blend into the background. I maneuver us into the corner so she has nothing but her back against the wall, to make her feel a little safer.

"What's going on, Orion? Joker's calling for church and we're all up here." Diesel stands with his arms folded over his chest.

"Megan, come here," Orion asks and I sign for her. She looks at me with wide eyes but she swallows down her nerves and walks toward him. When she's close enough, he hooks his arm around her shoulder, making a few of the men look at me funny.

"Diesel, this is Megan, our sister." The room is so quiet for a second you could hear a pin drop.

"What?" Diesel asks in shock.

Orion slips a finger under her jaw, lifting her head so she can look at him before he speaks.

"Megan, this is your other brother, Leo, or Diesel." She turns her head to look at him, waiting for acceptance or rejection. It's clear on her face. She's an open book and everyone in this room can read her.

"Does this mean I'm not the baby anymore? Well, thank fuck for that," Diesel states as he tugs her gently from Orion's arms and hugs her. She grips him tightly and I can see her shaking from here as she cries silent tears. Diesel mouths over her shoulder to Orion, "What the fuck?"

"Well, I don't even know where to begin. I think Joker's starting to lose it. I don't know whether it's the fact that King is sick or if he has always been this much of a dick and I just never noticed but something's got to give."

"Orion, watch what you're saying, man," Gage warns as he walks into the room with Halo behind him. They spot me in the corner and make their way over to flank me, much like my brothers did earlier.

"No, Gage, enough is enough. It's time for him to step down. I need to know who's going to support me and who's going to be against me."

There is a banging on the door before "church" is hollered out.

"I have a feeling this meeting is to ask for my cut. He alluded to as much in the cellar after he smacked Megan in the face. He's already pulled a gun on Luna tonight and don't even get me started on all the other crazy shit. I love my club and I love my brothers but it's time for a change before Joker turns us into something we're not," Orion tells the room.

"What you're talking about is treason," Rebel warns him.

"What he's talking about is survival. I was given orders to teach a man a lesson." Halo looks down at me as he says that and squeezes my hand a little tighter.

"Nothing new there. I didn't think anything of it. People know the score. If you borrow money from us, you better be prepared to pay it back, in cash or blood." He's talking to the room at large but he never looks away from me, waiting for my reaction. I'm guessing he's expecting me to look at him with loathing and pull away. I'm not naïve. I didn't exactly think he knitted sweaters for the club.

When I don't react, he continues.

"I found out, after the fact, the guy's six-year-old daughter is in the hospital battling leukemia. He borrowed to pay for her treatment. He hadn't left her side until one of us snagged him from the cafeteria. He actually had the money to pay back until Joker doubled his interest. Now he's in a bed beside his daughter, thanks to me. I'm a lot of things, I've done a lot of things, but I've never been more disgusted with myself than I was when I found out. Joker found the whole thing fucking hilarious."

I let go of his hand and watch as a look of shame passes over his face before I wrap my arms tightly around his waist. He lets out a shuddering breath when he realizes I'm not pulling away but holding on tighter.

"You know I'll always have your back," Halo tells Orion.

"Me too," Gage agrees, watching me and Halo, making me breathe out a sigh of relief.

"You sure about this, brother?" Diesel asks him, torn between his loyalty to his club and his brother.

"He put his hands on our sister. To him, she's expendable, to me, she's family." I watch Megan's eyes flood with tears as she watches Orion's lips move.

Diesel nods. "Family."

Orion looks around the room at his club brothers, each of them looking to him like the leader he was born to be.

"Things have been off lately, even before King got sick. The Kings of Carnage has always been a club I have been honored and proud to be part of. As you all know, my grandfather was a founding member but we have been getting complacent. Luna and Megan have been abused—there is no other way to put it—while in our hands. Tell me how that makes us any better than the Chaos Demons?" He lifts his hand when the room starts getting loud.

"Tell me how many of you have been ordered to do something lately that didn't sit right with you but you did it anyway because it was the president's order, like Halo?" I can see a few people nodding and agreeing but my eyes are on Gage who looks at me with remorse. I guess he's thinking about the night I spent in the cells. I grab his hand and pull him closer to me.

"We need to go down to church now but I'm warning you all what might be coming. I won't go down without a fight. I love this club and I used to love everything it stood for but lately, I think a lot of us have been going through the motions. Luna is my old lady and Megan is my sister and I will not sacrifice either of them for this place." He turns to me and steps forward, cupping my face before placing a soft kiss on my lips.

"I'm going to have Gecko lead you out the back and down to the woods. The spot you broke King free from now has a gate and a keypad. The code is the date we met. If this goes bad, you take my sister and you run." I try to protest but he kisses me again and signals for Gecko. Halo kisses me, holding me tight for a moment before Gage moves in and does the same. They both leave without saying a word and yet it feels strangely like goodbye.

Not today, that is not going to happen.

All the men file out and we follow behind, using them to shield us from sight. Gecko leads us away from the group and down to the spot Orion instructed. He ruffles my hair and tells me to be good, making me smile like I'm sure he intended, before running back to the club. As soon as he's out of sight, I type in the numbers on the keypad and pull Megan through. I drag her to the end of the small path I ran down that fateful day and hand her over to the two men waiting for us. She looks at me with wide eyes. I sign for her as quickly as I can but I don't have a lot of time to go over this right now.

"Trust me. That's all I'm asking for. There are things you don't know about me but everything you do know is true, including our friendship. I'm asking you to please just trust me so I can get your brothers out alive." She nods instantly, without even having to think about it. I give her a quick hug before leaving her with Zig, who signs that he wants her to follow him. She nods and with one last look at me, disappears into the trees with one of my brothers.

"Okay, Oz, what we got?"

"I managed to get a call in to the presidents of the mother chapter. Not real friendly but they were not happy to hear about the shit going down from an outsider. They're coming down themselves but I wouldn't expect a warm welcome."

I look around to make sure nobody else is around and lead us both back through the gate.

"What did you find out?"

"They go by the names of Priest and Bates. Bates because the guy is a psycho, apparently." I throw him an are-you-serious look, making him shrug.

"I know but here is where it gets interesting. They both took over the president's position by removing the former president from his throne." I stop and stare at him.

"How did they remove him?"

"They slit his throat after they found him raping a young girl who came to party and quickly realized she was in over her head." Well, fuck.

"They're hard asses from what I could find out but women and children are a big no-no for them. Also, each patched member of their club has either a partner or a trio they are part of—much like Orion, Halo, and Gage—only it's mandatory for their royalty. You can't move up into a royalty position without at least one partner.

"Royalty?"

"You have the president or presidents, in this case, then the royals. The royals are the VP, treasurer, road captain, enforcer, etc., then your regular patched members, followed by your prospects. It's a hierarchy thing."

"Right, okay. It's not like that here, not that I've noticed," I point out.

"No, and that's because of Melinda. Twenty years ago, King was the road captain, Joker was the sergeant-at-arms, and a guy called John was the enforcer. They had an old lady named Melinda. Rumor has it John and King had a major falling out and John left the club and formed one of his own."

"Let me guess, the Chaos Demons."

"Ding, ding, ding. We have a winner. When Melinda left to follow John, things started to deteriorate further, culminating in the death of the Carnage president in a shootout. King, who became the new president, was left raising two boys, and Joker, who became VP, went off the rails for a while. They didn't care if their men had partners or not, or about the hierarchy. The only people they trusted was each other, at least until Orion and Diesel came of age."

"How are they so sure that Orion and Diesel are actually King's sons?" It had been bugging me since I found out about these multi-relationships.

"Melinda and King met first. King brought her around the club when he quickly realized he wanted more than just a fling. He made her his old lady before telling her about Joker and John. She was not a happy bunny but, by then, she had discovered she was pregnant. I don't know the ins and outs of what went down between them all but King was the only one who officially named Melinda as his old lady. According to the rumor mill, Diesel was conceived when Joker and John were on a run a couple of years later."

"Wow, those are some odds. Regardless of that, how did things get so out of hand here without the mother chapter noticing?

"Well, the mother chapter had its own issues. They had two presidents at that point like they do now, twin brothers, but one was shot and killed in a turf war. That left one president. Nobody made an issue out of it because fuck, he lost his twin. How can you replace that? It would be like me losing Ziggy. The thing is, the guy was a loose cannon to begin with, his brother was the one to rein him in. It's one of the benefits of having a second or a third to rely on. Without him, he was unpredictable and pretty much a recluse, never leaving the compound." I look at Oz, impressed.

"You found all this out within a couple of hours?" He laughs.

"I've been checking shit out for the past few days. It's not every day your baby sister decides to become an old lady to a notorious motorcycle club."

I flip him off. "Bite me. Okay, is everyone in place?" He just looks at me disgruntled for insulting him. Jesus, he's so sensitive.

"Fuck, I was only asking. I've left the back gate unlocked, so refrain from blowing shit up." His shoulders deflate with disappointment, making me laugh.

"Ready?" I ask.

"I was born ready." My brother the comedian, everyone. Fucking hell. I walk back into the compound and Oz follows me inside before he disappears into the shadows. I make my way through the quiet clubhouse and into the main room. Walking behind the bar, I pour myself a Coke and wait for everything to play out.

It's maybe half-an-hour later that Joker comes storming out of the room they're holding church in with a face like thunder. Everyone spills out behind him and heads toward the bar. I start popping open beer bottles and sliding them down the bar before lining up shot glasses and grabbing the whiskey.

Halo is the first to spot me. Walking around the bar, he throws his arm around my shoulder and pulls me in for a kiss.

"How did I know you wouldn't listen? It's gonna be a toss-up between Orion and Gage as to who is gonna spank your ass later and, you know what, sugar? I'm gonna stand back and watch as your ass starts to glow red."

I roll my eyes but tuck myself against him so he can hear me better.

"How'd it go?"

"Joker is still the president for now. We just don't have enough on him to convince the old-timers to strip him of his title. That being said, when Joker tried to vote Orion out, he was shot down and lost the support of a few guys that would have otherwise been faithful to him. More than that, he pissed off King."

"So what happens now?"

"That will be up to Orion but I doubt there will be any way they can co-exist together now. Where's Megan?"

"Safe."

"Well, we need to figure something out because we're gonna have the Chaos Demons breathing down our necks soon enough. The last thing we need now is to be fighting among ourselves."

"I really need to talk to you guys about something, well, two somethings, actually."

"It's gonna have to wait, sweetheart. Heads up, Orion has spotted you and he does not look happy." He barely gets the words out before I'm pulled away.

"What the fuck are you doing here, Cherub, and where the fuck is my sister?"

"I'm fine and Megan is safe. Chill the fuck out," I growl lowly so only he can hear me.

"You!" The noise dies down as Jokers bellows. There are over a hundred people in this room but I know he's shouting at me.

"Yes, Joker?" I see King whip around at the sound of my voice.

"Fetch me a beer." I could tell him to fuck off but I'm curious enough to see where this is going. He must be touched in the head if he thinks I haven't noticed the gleam in his eye. I know I'm not the only one either when I see a few hands move to rest on their guns.

I snag an open beer off the counter and carry it over to where Joker has perched himself on one of the chairs. He has Chewy on one side of him and King at the next table over but I ignore them and head toward Joker, holding out the beer he asked for. He takes it with his left hand before grabbing my wrist with his right and pulling me onto his lap, twisting me so I'm facing everyone else in the room. Gage steps forward with a face of thunder, not stopping even when Chewy points his gun at him. He freezes, though, when Chewy turns the gun on me. I see Diesel and Rebel holding back a struggling Halo behind the bar.

"Back the fuck up," Chewy growls at him but Gage doesn't move until Chewy pushes the gun against my temple.

Orion lunges forward but Gage snags him and holds him back. "You piece of shit. This is why you aren't fit to be President," Orion snarls at Joker.

"And you?" Orion addresses his father, who looks away disinterested. "I'm ashamed to call you my father. The man who raised me would never let this shit happen."

King just sips his beer, ignoring him.

"You see the kind of man you agreed to keep on as your leader. This is the kind of man he is," Orion addresses the room while Halo keeps his eyes fixed on mine.

"Tut, tut, Orion. Maybe you should rein that temper in a little. I'm not doing anything wrong. Check the bylaws. No tat, no vest, makes her free pussy. Don't blame me because you dropped the ball and didn't claim her. Now it's my turn." He slides his hand up to cup my breast before squeezing it hard. I bite my lip, refusing to give him a reaction. I keep my eyes locked with Gage and smile.

"I claim her, right here and now in front of you all. Luna is now my old lady and as her first task, I think she should strip. I'm feeling generous. Who here would like to have a go with her? Anyone who has my back can have any of her holes."

I snort out a laugh making the men gathered around look at me strangely. I laugh until tears leak from my eyes and only stop when Joker wraps his hand around my throat.

"I doubt you'll be laughing when you're bleeding all over my dick," he grates out in my ear, loud enough for everyone else to hear.

He lets go of my neck so he can grab my hair at the nape of my neck and yanks it hard.

"Laugh all you want, Luna, I have nothing left to lose," he whispers.

"You fucking idiot. You have everything left to lose. Every man in here worshipped the ground you walked on. They would have walked over fire for you, taken a bullet for you but you are not the same man they pledged their loyalty to. You are not my president and you will never be my old man, so I suggest you get your hands off me before I kill you myself."

"Oh yeah, you and whose army?" He laughs and I notice Chewy is the only one that laughs with him.

"Mine," I answer. He freezes as a click sounds behind him and he finds himself with a gun pointed at the back of his head. He lets go of my hair to grab the gun sitting just inside his holster but I'm faster. I pull my elbow back and connect with his nose before grabbing his gun and pressing it against Chewy's forehead.

"What you gonna do now, Luna?" Joker laughs.

"You think these guys are going to just let you walk out of here? These are my men. They do as I say. The only way you and your little friend behind me will leave here will be in a body bag."

The main doors open and men in camo gear and grade A military assault weapons start pouring in but I don't move my attention away from the two threats closest to me.

"What the fuck?" I hear someone yell and the sound of multiple weapons being drawn.

"I wouldn't bother with the guns, biker boys. You're not a threat unless you're siding with Pres here," I tell them.

"Luna? What the fuck is going on?" Orion yells, walking closer to me and ignoring the guns completely.

"Meet my army."

"Shoot her now, Chewy," King roars. Chewy's finger twitches on the trigger. So be it. I shoot first and leave him with a hole matching the one I gave Weasel earlier. I stand from Joker's lap and in his shock he lets me. I roll my neck and walk the few steps to Orion and Gage. I kiss each of their cheeks while everyone in the overly quiet room stares at me in shock.

"Ermm... surprise?"

My brother starts laughing from his position behind Joker but the MC still looks confused as fuck. I look around at them and sigh.

"You've met Oz before. You know what he and Ziggy do," I tell a stunned Gage and Orion. I wave my arm around the room at the soldiers.

"This is the rest of my team."

"Your team?" Orion asks.

"Yeah. I took over the family business when Gramps died."

"Are you trying to tell me you own and run a team of mercenaries?" Gage asks me.

"Well, yeah. But I also make pretty gift baskets and sell them online. Life's about balance, right?"

"But... she's so... and a..." I turn at the sound of the confused voice and find Agro staring at me in shock.

"I get this a lot. It's the boobs, right?" I look over my shoulder at Oz who has his gun still trained on Joker, but he shrugs.

"Luna, you can't just walk into an MC and fucking kill someone without starting a fucking war," Halo yells, stomping over to me. His anger is at odds with the way he checks me over for injuries.

"Sure I can."

"Luna, this shit is serious," Halo says, like I'm playing freaking amateur hour.

"Just pointing out the obvious here but in case anyone

missed it, Joker started this shit. Before you start with the whole 'he's the president thing,' let me ask you this. Would you willingly bring your women around this man? Would you give him access to your sisters? What about your daughters?" Nobody says anything but I can see them beginning to look uncomfortable as my words strike a chord.

"You guys are supposed to be family, brothers that have each other's back. But why? What the fuck are you even protecting? Your right to drink and fuck? Well, congratulations. What an amazing legacy to leave for the next generation. Oh, that's right, there won't be a next generation because no woman in her right mind would constantly put herself at risk for a club that treats her like she's expendable. Not everyone is fortunate to have an army like me." I grin, my boys in green smiling back.

"I'm never going to fit the mold you guys want to squeeze me into. I'm done trying." I look at Halo, Gage, and Orion.

"I love you guys. I'm not leaving you but I'm not staying here in a place that will never be home and neither is Megan. I'm not asking you to leave, I would never do that, but you deserve better than what a tarnished president can give you." I step forward and cup Orion's jaw, imploring him to understand.

"You three will always be welcome in my home and in my bed." I grab one of Gage's and one of Halo's hands and give them a squeeze, hating that it's come to this, even though I knew it was inevitable.

I pull away and offer them a sad smile.

"You can't just leave, you stupid whore. You shot one of my men. Blood for blood," Joker yells.

"Oh, shut the fuck up, you idiot. You ordered him to kill me. I wasn't into that. The person at fault here is you. Shocking, right?"

"I say we take a second vote. I'm with Luna on this. I love this club but I never signed up for this shit," Rebel calls from the crowd, stepping forward.

"All those in favor of Orion taking over as President, say 'aye,'" he calls out, staring at Joker.

"Fuck you!" Joker yells as "ayes" ring out around the room.

"Fuck you all!" he screams as Oz pushes the barrel of the gun harder against his temple.

"Those in favor of Joker staying as the president." Silence envelopes the room, leaving no doubt as to which way the vote has swung.

"Congratulations, Orion, it looks like you're the new King of Carnage," Rebel tells him, shaking his hand as he recovers from his shock. The room erupts into cheers, making me smile.

"I thought I raised you better than that, boy." King's voice quiets the room in an instant.

"You agree with what he did? With what he was planning on doing to Luna?" Orion asks as Diesel steps up beside him.

"It's not about what I do or don't agree with. If you don't like the bylaws, bring it to church. You don't air shit in front of strangers." He waves his arm around the room. "This shows an utter lack of respect for the MC you swore to protect."

I snort, drawing his attention.

I walk back over to Oz and Joker but I don't look away from King, meeting his eyes and refusing to show him any mercy.

"What happened to you? You were supposedly this great man and yet you let Joker turn this club into something of a joke. And you." I turn back to Joker. "Some chick does you dirty so you just decide to punish all women for it? I don't get it."

"She didn't do him dirty, though. He was the one who fucked her over. He fucked you all over." I turn at the sound of Ziggy's voice and watch as he walks through the crowd with Megan. He's watching her hands and translating as she talks. Everyone turns to see what the hell is going on now.

"King, Joker, and John fell out over drugs. John wanted to sell them, King wanted to stick to running guns. Joker sided with King so John left and took a small bunch of nobodies and made them a formidable MC but he was pissed at King and wanted revenge." She offers Diesel and Orion a sad smile before continuing.

"He took our mother from the grocery store one day and sent word that the Kings of Carnage were not man enough for my mother and she had chosen John instead." I look on with trepidation as Orion and Diesel watch her, knowing it's their mother she's talking about as unease spreads through the room.

"She waited for you to come and save her. She knew if nothing else, you would know she would never leave her boys. But you never came for her." Megan looks straight at King while she signs.

"What the fuck is she talking about, Dad?" Diesel asks.

"Lies. Melly made her choice. She had to live with it," King rebuffs.

"He kept her locked up until I was born. Then he used me to keep her in line, passing her around all of his men and keeping her on the side while he went home to his old lady." Orion turns to face King.

"What is she talking about? You said she was John's old lady, that's why she left and why our club had nothing to do with each other." King glances over at Joker, a flicker of doubt crossing his brow.

"It's bullshit lies. Joker saw them playing happy family together. She sure as shit wasn't a prisoner when he saw them or he would never have left her and he sure as hell would have told me. I can't believe you would turn on your family like this."

"I'm protecting my family, something you failed to do. Joker fed you a line and you bought into his bullshit because your ego had been bruised. You let your pride get in the way of me having a mother," Diesel yells at him.

"You don't know what you're talking about, you sanctimonious little prick. Joker, tell them."

Joker shrugs like he doesn't have a care in the world. "She

made her bed. She doesn't get to cry when she's expected to fuck in it."

"She was fucking kidnapped, raped repeatedly, and tortured because of you and when she finally managed to sneak a phone call to ask for help, you laughed at her and told her to fuck off." Megan signs in an agitated flurry.

Orion walks over to Joker and punches him in the face. He pulls back and punches him again and again before Diesel grabs his arm and pulls him away. Then Diesel kicks the chair, knocking Joker to the floor before turning to King. "You're dead to me." Diesel moves to stand next to his sister.

King, frozen in shock, looks down at Joker on the floor.

"John's old lady had two sons from a previous relationship, Crogan and Stokey. Crogan made my life hell. He sexually abused me for years before I turned sixteen and decided he wanted more. I was lucky the only thing I lost that night was my hearing."

"Fuck!" Orion yells. And he isn't the only one pissed. None of the men in the room look any happier to hear this than I was down in the cells earlier.

"We have to get Mom out of there, Orion, but somewhere far, far away from this piece of shit." Diesel spits at his father.

"Oh, god!" The words are out before I can stop them. Fuck, they don't know she's gone.

"What?" Diesel looks between me and Megan in confusion but Orion has figured it out, I can already tell.

"Tell me," he grits out.

"Crogan was pissed he never got to fuck me. As I was in

the hospital, he decided to fuck my mother for the night and have her pretend to be me instead." Yuk. She failed to mention that last time.

"My—our mother stabbed him through the heart before taking his gun and shooting John. She then turned the gun on herself." Megan is breathing heavily by the end of it but everyone else is quiet. Diesel picks up a chair and throws it across the room before picking up another and throwing that. Gage wraps his arms around him while Ziggy blocks Megan.

Orion stares at me with an odd mix of anger and sorrow coating his features before drawing his gun and pointing it at Joker.

I walk over and wrap my arms around him, holding on to him as hard as I can.

"I'm sorry," I tell him and I truly am. Sorry for the boy who lost his mom and to the man who just realized his heroes are anything but.

"The VP let me go but I had to stay loyal to the club." Megan continues to sign as Ziggy translates. "I never heard from them until this afternoon and it was only because they had seen Kings of Carnage coming into my shop."

"Which brings us to Weasel," I sign and speak. She looks at me confused.

"Who?"

"The guy from the shop that I shot."

"You mean Stokey?"

"What? How the fuck does the stepson of the president of

the Chaos Demons become a patched member of a rival club without detection?" Halo asks.

"They don't, do they?" I spin to face Joker who is watching us from his spot on the floor.

"You knew who Weasel was but you had no choice but to throw him out when everyone else realized he was selling guns to the Chaos Demons. Except it wasn't just him, was it? It was you. Weasel was just your go-between." I look at him with revulsion.

"You have no fucking loyalty or respect for anything, do you? You had to know Weasel was filling them in on all the club business. You just didn't care."

"I made this club a fortune, you fucking cunt. Who I do or don't deal with is irrelevant." He looks at Megan briefly before looking away.

"Tell them," Megan signs.

He ignores her.

She walks toward him, empowered by her words. "Fine, then I will tell them myself." He makes a grab for her leg but Orion crunches down on his wrist with an audible snap.

"I saw you. I should have been in bed but I had a nightmare and I saw you. I was too young to understand at the time. You were just another man and lord knows I had seen more than any eight-year-old should have by then. You were with my mother but she was blindfolded and gagged while John sat in the corner getting himself off. She was crying but then she always was. You were mean to her and I was scared of you so I ran and hid. I saw you a few times over the years but I never knew who you were and I always saw you in places I wasn't supposed to be. Imagine my surprise when I found out years later who you really were."

"You were punishing her," Diesel says, cutting through the confusion that swirls around us.

"You were punishing Melinda because you believed she chose John instead of you. John gave you access to her in exchange for the guns." Halo seethes.

I look at King who isn't looking so good as he stares down at Joker like he has had his heart cut from his chest.

"No, that's not it at all, is it? I don't think you ever sided with King, to begin with. I think you sided with John. He gave you a cut of his profits from the drugs he distributed and you gave him guns that he couldn't get from your supplier himself." I stare at him, knowing he doesn't have a flicker of remorse within him.

"You gave her up. Offered her to John as a way to make King pay for not bending to your will."

"It was only a matter of time before she left anyway. She didn't want me or John. All she cared about was fucking King."

"But she didn't leave you, you left her. Again and again and again. You made her pay for sins she never committed. I wish she had never met you. I hope when you die, I'm the one who gets to do it," Ziggy speaks for Megan.

"You know nothing! She never loved me or John. It was always about King. Why do you think King is the only one with kids, huh? Because she wasn't interested in having

John's or mine." He roars but I can see he knows deep down it's not true. He just couldn't see through his hatred before.

"Well, John changed that, didn't he? He hated that Melly gave King sons but never gave him one. So he took the choice away from her. He must have been pissed when he realized his kid was nothing more than a piece of gash like her mother," Joker yells, trying to place all the blame on John.

"But that's just it. John wasn't really my father. You are. That's why he hated me because, even after everything, he still couldn't get that elusive son he craved."

He stares at her in horror. "No, that can't be true, no."

"But I'm afraid it is, Daddy."

"No!" he roars before pulling a gun from his boot. He never gets a shot off before King drills him with a dozen bullets.

When silence reigns again it's because the dishonored president is dead and everything is about to change.

CHAPTER FIFTEEN

The mood is somber when the guys arrived back at the clubhouse after disposing of Chewy and the almost torn apart body of the former president of the club.

"Hey. You doing okay?" I slip my hand into Orion's as he looks down at the burning embers of Joker's cut in the bonfire in front of him.

He looks up at me and pulls me to him, my back to his front, and wraps his arms around my shoulders.

"I'm doing okay. How's Megan?" I look over to the left and see her sitting on the ground stroking King's fur while watching Oz sign something to her.

"She's doing better than you, I think, but she already knew what kind of man her father was. For you and Diesel, finding out about Joker like this, it's different. Where is Diesel, by the way?" I know he was here earlier.

"I saw him head inside with Stacey." I scrunch my face up but I don't say anything. People deal with death in different ways. Some get blind drunk like most of the club around us and some fuck it out of their system. Who am I to judge?

"Do you want to get out of here?" I ask him.

He nods against me before pulling me toward his bike. I spot Halo and Gage making their way over to us so I tug on Orion's hand to get him to stop.

"Where are you two escaping to?" Halo asks, trailing his eyes over my legs. The high-waisted shorts and black tank leave plenty of skin on display.

"Away from here. Want to join us? I have a bone to pick with our woman," Orion tells him.

"Hey! What did I do?"

"You put yourself in danger!" Gage yells at me.

"Repeatedly," Halo adds

"And you never listen to a goddamn word we say," Orion finishes. My shoulders slump.

"Yeah, okay, I did do all those things but, in my defense, I had a good reason for all of it. Which reminds me, I really need to talk to you guys about something."

Orion leans down and whispers in my ear, "Later. You will take your punishment like a good girl first."

"Wait, are we getting to the fucking part of the grief thing?"

"As per usual, I have no idea what you're talking about, Cherub, but if it ends with fucking, I'm game."

I laugh softly.

"So, you're a mercenary?" Gage asks, walking beside us. He's been exceptionally quiet since this all went down.

I look at him, trying to gauge his reaction but he isn't giving me much to go on.

"Not me personally, no. I just have a team of them at my disposal. I pick up the cases, deciding who needs us and who doesn't. I organize everything and collect the cash. I mean, don't get me wrong, I'm a crack shot but I like my life the way it is," I tell him honestly. It's not like I haven't tried to bring it up with them before, it's just that something always came up.

"How did they even get here so fast?"

"Most of the team were on a rescue job with my brothers so they're on a little downtime at the moment. Almost all of them live up at the ranch so as soon as Ziggy called them, they mobilized."

"Yeah, but how did Ziggy know to call them?"

"I knew back at Megan's shop that things were going to go tits up. I wanted someone in place to protect Megan. I'm glad I did."

"Chosaint," Gage mutters, surprising me. "I looked it up after I heard you say it to your brother. You ordered them to protect Megan and they called in their squad."

I nod, not sure if he's angry or what. When he doesn't speak anymore, he leaves us all in uncomfortable silence.

"Gage, why don't you take Luna back to your place? Halo and I will catch up. I just need to see Diesel about something first," Orion suggests, looking at me.

Gage nods and heads for the bikes. I look at Halo and Orion, unsure what to do.

"Talk to him, sugar. Find out what's going on in his head. We'll be right behind you," Halo says with a quick kiss. I forget how in tune with each other these guys are sometimes.

"Okay," I agree, giving Orion a quick kiss too before heading over to Gage.

He doesn't say anything as I climb on behind him, reminding me of that night not too long ago. Let's just hope this has a better outcome.

By the time we pull up, the gray skies have opened and the rain lashes down around us. We're both soaked through to the skin before we make it inside.

"Shower?" I ask him, breaking the silence as I shiver lightly in the doorway.

"You go ahead, Luna, I'm going to make some coffee," He dismisses me and walks into the kitchen.

Fuck this shit. I follow him into the kitchen.

"Have I done something to piss you off?"

"No. Go take a shower, Luna, before you get sick."

"No, Gage. You obviously have a bone to pick with me about something so just spit it out already."

"Luna—"

I cut him off. "Gage."

"Fine, you want to do this now? Let's do it. Why are you here, Luna?"

"Excuse me?"

"Why are you here slumming it with a bunch of bikers when you have what you have at your disposal?"

"At my disposal? What are you talking about?"

"You have a whole fucking armed squad of men to protect you, Luna. Why the fuck do you even need us?"

I stand in shock, trying to understand the crap coming out of his mouth.

"You know, I spend as much time plotting your murder as I do loving you. It's fucking exhausting. I don't need you to protect me. I don't even need my men to protect me. I'm more than capable of taking care of myself. My guys are my family, we live together, joke together, and mourn together. It's what families do. You should get that better than most."

"You love me?" he asks.

I scoff, making him frown. "Why do you always ask me the most ridiculous questions? Of course, I fucking love you, you big giant pain in my ass. Why the hell do you think I'm here? Oh—" And now I get it.

"That's it, isn't it? It's not about my team or the fact I have my own ranch or truck or any of that shit. You want to know how I feel about you but you're too stubborn-headed to just come out and ask me."

He stalks toward me, his eyes looking black and feral as he pins me against the wall.

"One of these days that smart mouth of yours is going to get you into trouble, little girl," he tells me as a hand snakes its way up to grip my throat in a firm but gentle hold.

Feeding off his dominance, I pant out, "Well, then, maybe you should fill it for me."

"Are you mine?" he barks out, making my clit throb. "Answer me," he roars, stroking my desire into a frenzy.

"Yes, god, yes," I moan.

"You love me?" he questions, his voice sharp and lethal like the edge of a blade.

"Yes," I hiss out, needing something, anything.

"Well then, I think you deserve a reward, don't you, Cherub?"

I nod my head rapidly when he loosens his hold on me.

"On your knees, Luna." I sink to the floor, not needing any more instructions.

"Hands behind your back. This is about me, not you. This is for all the times you nearly gave me a fucking heart attack by putting yourself in harm's way." He unzips his pants and pulls his cock free.

"Show me what you've got, baby." He grunts as I open my mouth and welcome him inside.

He isn't gentle, which is good, because I'm not looking for gentle right now. I need raw and dirty and as he grips my hair hard with both hands and starts fucking my mouth, that's exactly what he gives me.

His pace picks up, each thrust bumping my head into the wall behind me, but I love every second of it. When I hum around him minutes later, he shouts his release as I swallow it down greedily.

"Good girl, Luna," he praises as he helps me to my feet.

"Let's get you out of these wet clothes." He doesn't wait for a reply, he just strips me bare right there in the kitchen before picking me up and lowering me down onto the kitchen table.

I gasp and arch up against the cold tabletop but one of his large hands holds me in place. Spreading my legs wide, he bends and feasts on my pussy like a starving man, making my head thrash about as I babble incoherently. His tongue flicks and slides, dips and retreats, and leaves me in a stupor before he plunges two fingers inside me.

"Ah, fuck," I yell as I come all over his hand, my pussy squeezing down against his fingers so tightly I'm surprised they don't break.

He trails his tongue up to my belly button, dipping inside briefly before making its way up between the valley of my breasts to my throat and finally my lips.

"I'm an asshole," he admits, remorse coating his words.

"I know, but I love you anyway. I'm not going anywhere, Gage, I promise. I know I left before but things are different now. I didn't want to get too attached just to have you snatch it all away from me. I'm sorry." He picks me up and carries me to the bathroom and places me on my feet as he flips on the shower, letting it warm up.

He kisses me softly before turning me to face the mirror. The steam is starting to obscure my view but I can still make out the blurry edges of us. The way he is looking at me causes a wave of arousal to rush through me. So much so that when he bends me over the counter, slides a condom on, and eases his way inside me, I moan and push back into him. He takes his time, worshiping my body until I'm spent and my legs refuse to hold me up any longer. Afterward, he lifts me into the shower before climbing in behind me, watching me clean myself before he does the same. We do it all in silence but, unlike before, there is comfort in the quiet. I can feel what he feels for me. It's in the stolen glances and barely-there touches as we dress.

When Orion and Halo arrive an hour later and find us once again wrapped up in each other's arms, they don't question it. They just strip and join us, loving me and letting me love them.

CHAPTER SIXTEEN

"So today it becomes official, huh?" I ask Halo as I smooth my hands down the front of his cut, tracing my fingers over the patch that proclaims him as enforcer.

"I guess so. In a way, it feels kind of weird. But if you think about it, Orion's been doing the job since that night, so nothing will change but his patch." He leans down and wraps his arms around my back dipping his head and sliding his lips over mine. Of course, with Halo, that's never enough. It takes seconds for one of his hands to grip my hair and the other to grab my ass.

I pull away reluctantly, knowing people are waiting for us and if we get started now, we might never leave this room.

"Have you seen Orion this morning?" he asks, watching me as I straighten my hair yet again. I'm at the point where I don't even know why I bother around these guys anymore.

"Yeah. Him and Diesel went over to see King." He freezes, looking up at my words.

"Not sure that was wise," he points out.

"I know, but they wanted to. I think they need some kind of closure. Like it or not, the man is dying. Anything they might want to say to him can't really wait."

"Diesel might kill him," he warns. Orion took the hit hard but Diesel, who is about to officially become vice president, well, he hasn't been the same since.

"I asked Gage to go too. He'll keep them in line," I explain.

"Thank you, sugar."

I reach up and peck his cheek before pulling back so he can't take it further. "I know you guys have a lot on your plate at the moment, but I really need to sit down and have a chat with you all," I tell him. The last week has been crazy and there has been no time to tell them about the baby.

"I'll try, sweetheart, but I can't make any promises at the moment."

"I know, I get it, Halo, but I wouldn't ask if it wasn't really important." He looks in my eyes, seeing I'm serious, before nodding.

"I'll figure something out."

A banging at the door breaks the moment. Halo walks over and yanks it open, revealing Inigo who winks at me.

"Priest and Bates are here," he tells Halo, who nods.

"Right boys, I'll run over to King's and let the guys know they're needed and then I'll catch up with you later for the cookout," I tell them, grabbing my gun, which Halo now insists I carry everywhere.

"Thanks, Cherub." He plants a quick one on me, which in Halo speak means he fucks my mouth with his tongue while squeezing my ass, completely unfazed that Inigo is standing there watching us with a smirk on his face.

"Christ, woman, you're killing me," Halo groans when he finally pulls away.

I breathe out, "You started it," and walk away with a smile on my face.

I make my way through the compound and out the back, heading up to the house on the hill at the back of the lot. It's mostly obscured by the trees, so much so I hadn't even noticed it until someone pointed it out to me. I wave at Gecko and Half-pint as they go about setting up the party for later and continue across the damp grass up to the house. I hear yelling and barking before I even get to the door and sigh, knowing I'm likely going to be walking into a shit show. I pull open the screen door and let myself in, knowing they won't hear me if I knock. Doggy King comes barreling toward me for a quick fuss before retreating.

I round the corner and see King sitting in an armchair that has been dragged to the window facing the woods. The man himself is staring out the window with unseeing eyes. I'm not sure if he can even hear the shit Diesel is spewing at him.

"That's enough, Diesel," I say sternly, making the three men standing turn toward me.

He bites out, "This has fuck-all to do with you, Luna, so back off."

"Diesel!" Orion snaps at him. "Watch how you fucking speak to my woman or, brother or no brother, I will put you down."

I watch as Diesel visibly deflates and shakes his head before looking at me with regret in his eyes.

"Sorry, Cherub. I'm a dick." I shrug it off and walk up to him, wrapping my arms around his waist and holding him tight. He hesitates for a second, probably checking to make sure Orion isn't going to rip his head off, before he wraps his arms around me and hugs me back.

"I get it, Diesel, I really do. But I don't think there is anything you can say or do that is going to make him feel any worse than he does right now. He fucked up, he fucked up huge, I'm not disputing that. But he didn't do it knowingly. He trusted his best friend, his partner—the one person who he thought had his back—and he's paying for it now dearly."

"It will never be enough, Luna. For what happened to my mother, it will never be enough." He squeezes me once more before letting go of me and walking out. Gage walks over and sighs. Kissing my brow softly he follows Diesel out, leaving me with Orion and his father.

"How you doing, Adonis?" I ask him quietly, stepping up to him so our toes are touching.

"I'll let you know when I figure it out." He leans down and rests his head on top of mine and is quiet for a moment.

"Halo's waiting for you. Priest and Bates are here. Go on

over. I'll be there in a little while." He leans back and watches me, turning to look at his father, who hasn't moved an inch, before turning back.

"You got your gun?" I nod.

"Okay, we will be in church for a while. Be good."

I salute him. "Yes, sir." Which earns me a slap to the ass. He turns to his father, opens his mouth to speak but shakes his head and leaves.

I look over at King and sigh. What a mess. I drag the footstool from the corner of the room and sit in front of him. I look out the window and try to imagine myself in his shoes.

"It's not your fault, King." He doesn't answer but I watch his hands tighten into fists.

"This is all on Joker and John. Sure, you made some piss-poor choices but if you had known what was going on, you would have stopped it. That's the difference between you and them."

"I don't think my boys feel the same way, Luna." His voice comes out scratchy and deep, but I can hear the sorrow in it.

"Cut them some slack. They just got dumped with a shitload of information at once. Give them time to process it."

"I don't have any time left, Luna. I'm so fucking done with this life I can't even convey to you right now how much I hope I close my eyes and never wake up again."

I swallow hard seeing a single tear roll from his eye. The mighty King has fallen.

"Well, that's just fucking unlucky for you then because

you aren't going anywhere just yet. I thought you were supposed to be the formidable King, ruler of Carnage, but you are nothing but a quitter."

"Luna..."

"The measure of a man is not by how many times he gets knocked down but by how many times he stands back up." His eyes blaze into mine as my words start to kindle a fire inside him.

"So you're gonna die. Deal with it. Are you going to go out like a pussy or are you going to man up and go out with a bang? Give those boys a reason to believe in you again."

"Nobody is gonna care—" I cut him off.

"I care." I place my hands on my still flat stomach. "We care. We want Gramps to leave behind a legacy filled with reverence, not shame."

His eyes stare at my hands over my stomach and widen.

"You're pregnant?" he asks in shock.

"It appears that way, yes. Now, are we going to the clubhouse or what?" Ball's in your court now, King, I muse to myself.

"They won't be happy," he says as he stands.

"Oh, well, they'll get over it. They might be assholes to you, hell, the whole club might, but you deserve a few jabs, old man. Aside from the Melinda shit, you let Joker run this club into the ground. They have a right to be pissed. You're just going to have to suck it up, buttercup. All you have to do is apologize. It's the right thing to do and sometimes that makes it the hardest thing to do too."

He looks down at me and nods, offering me his hand and helping me up.

"I'm thinking maybe you should be the president," he jokes.

"They couldn't afford me. Besides, I thought you had old-school rules about this kind of thing."

"Yeah, well, turns out I was wrong about that too. Seems like I was wrong about a lot of things lately."

"So you're human. Who knew? Get your ass up and take a shower. You stink. I'll make us something to eat. By then they should have finished with church and be back out in the common room for the celebrations to begin." I lose him for a second, his eyes glazing over at the mention of church. It must suck that he isn't there for it but they don't trust him enough anymore. That's going to take time to fix.

He heads up to the bedroom while I rummage around looking for something to make. I really need to drag his ass to the grocery store. I finally settle on grilled cheese sandwiches and soup as there isn't much else to pick from.

I'm just placing the food on the table when he comes back down. He smells better for sure but it's impossible not to see how much weight he's lost. The large handsome man I met a few months ago is gaunt and frail-looking now.

"Eat." He doesn't argue for once, eating in silence while I clean up the kitchen around him. When he's finished, I dump his stuff into the dishwasher and switch it on.

"Okay, we've procrastinated enough." I look up at the

clock and see it's been just over an hour since Orion left, which should have been plenty of time to figure shit out.

"Take your meds and let's do this." He does as I ask without argument, which is good, I guess, but to me, it's just another sign he's declining. Part of King's charm is how ornery he can be. This guy isn't the King I know. This is a man who has lost everything and is going through the motions. Well, I guess faking it is better than succumbing to it.

"Come on, let's go before you change your mind." I link my arm through his, making him give me a grateful smile as I half drag him back over to the compound.

It's quiet as we make our way to the main building. The guys have finished building up the fire pit. There are a bunch of folding chairs scattered about as well as a grill and a huge bucket, which I'm guessing will be filled with ice and beer in a little while. Heading inside, I see it's deserted still, which can only mean everyone is still in church. I figured they would be finished by now but then I guess there's a lot of ground to cover.

I can hear a couple of voices coming from the kitchen, probably just a couple of sweet butts, so I make my way over to the bar and park my butt on one of the high stools. King looks torn. He stares at the door that leads down to the room that holds church before turning back to me and sighing. He plops down on the seat beside me, resigned to the fact his reign has ended. Doesn't mean he has to be happy about it, though.

"I know it sucks now, King, but this is the way it has to be. Be proud of the men you raised and try to make today more about them and less about you."

"You're good for Orion, you know? It's why I wanted you to come back. He might hate me now but he's going to need you when I'm gone."

"He doesn't hate you, King. He's just pissed off and hurt. It happens."

Arguing filters in from the kitchen area, making me stand up with a huff. We have enough shit going on around here without more fucking in-house fighting too. I'm about to stomp off and shut the girls up before church finishes but King grabs my arm.

"Just leave them to it. Bitches will be bitches, Luna. You can't fix everything." I bite my tongue at his liberal use of the word bitch but let it go. I don't know what has me so on edge at the moment but it's almost as if my subconscious knows something I don't. Maybe things aren't going as planned in the meeting.

"I know. I'm just on edge, waiting to see what the Chaos Demons' next move will be. They won't care about the whys surrounding Weasel's death, only the fact I shot him in a property they ultimately considered theirs. To them, I'm the one who was trespassing."

"Trust your men to sort it out for you. They have Priest and Bates in there with them now too, wading through all this shit. They'll figure it out. It's been a long time coming and after everything that went down with Melly," he swallows hard as his guilt threatens to rip him apart, "they deserve to be eradicated like the infestation they are."

THE ARGUING SEEMS to have dipped in volume. The angry clipped voices are now harsh anger-filled whispers but as they seem to be approaching the bar area they're easy enough to hear.

"Fuck you." I recognize that voice. The lovely Stacey. Why am I not surprised?

"Not in this lifetime, bitch. I would rather lie with a dog; they have less fleas." Ouch. Talk about burn. Gecko turns the corner with Stacey, who looks like she is about to burst into flames as her anger spirals out of control.

"If I go down, Gecko, I'll take down everyone with me. You'd do well to remember that." She barely has her words out before she finds herself pinned to the wall with Gecko's hand wrapped around her throat.

"Gecko!" King barks out as I stare at a man I had come to like, who at this moment I hardly recognize.

He turns slowly to look at us, shame coating his features before he drops Stacey to the floor.

"Get out of here, girl. I think this club has had enough of your used up pussy," King tells her as she struggles to climb to her feet in her ridiculously high heels.

"You aren't the president here anymore, King, and both your boys love it when I suck their cocks. They won't be getting rid of me anytime soon." I think I just threw up in my mouth a little.

"Classy, Stacey, real classy. Orion hasn't been near you in months and we both know it, so stop trying to stir shit up."

"Oh, yeah? And how can you be so sure?" she taunts.

"Well, the fact that his cock's not gangrene and hanging off suggests it hasn't been within an inch of your penis flytrap. I think you should do as King says and fuck off. We have enough shit going on around here without you being, well, you." I turn to sit back down, dismissing Stacey as Gecko walks toward us but stop when I hear her angry screech.

"Stacey, no! What the fuck?" I turn and see Gecko with his hands up as Stacey points what looks like his own gun back at him.

"I say when I'm done. Not a pathetic dying man and his son's whore."

King and I stand still, not moving an inch, not wanting to antagonize her further. That sixth sense I felt before is screaming at me now. Not sure why I do what I do next but working on instinct, I pull my gun from the back of my jeans, making use of the fact half my body is obscured by King's. I slip the weapon into the back of his waistband next to his gun. I'll never get a clean shot from here without King or Gecko getting hit in the crossfire and that's a risk I won't take.

Stacey tears her eyes away from Gecko but keeps the gun trained on him while barking at us.

"King, toss your gun now or I'll put a bullet in Gecko's

head. That's one piercing he won't recover from." Looks like Stacey isn't as stupid as she looks. She steps in line with Gecko, blocking any shot King might have been willing to make. I watch as he pulls his gun and tosses it to the floor a couple of feet in front of him.

"There. What the fuck are you are hoping to achieve with this, Stacey? You have to know you're signing your own life away with this."

"You don't know what the fuck you're talking about, King, but then you seem to have no idea what's going on in your club anymore. You." She indicates me.

"Toss your gun too." I shake my head before I speak.

"I'm not armed. Funny enough, I didn't think I would need it today."

"Right and I'm supposed to believe that, huh? Gecko, get over there and search her."

Gecko doesn't move for a second before walking over to me. I step away from King so he can frisk me and offer him a small smile letting him know it's okay. His face looks pained as he runs his hands over my body and declares me clean.

"Lift her shirt and show me. I don't trust any of you fuckers."

Geckos large rough hands slide under my T-shirt, raising it to just under my bra. He lets Stacey run her eyes over me and turns me so she can see the back too.

"Fine. Gecko, get over here." He slides his hands down to my waist, hugging me lightly before letting go.

"I'm sorry," he whispers before turning back to Stacey,

leaving me wondering what the hell he could be sorry for. Two seconds later he charges her and I realize his intent too late. He's going to sacrifice himself for us. She fires a shot that goes wide before Gecko manages to punch her full force in the head. She goes down like a ton of bricks. I take a step forward to help but King stops me.

"Give him a second," King tells me as we watch Gecko take his gun from an unconscious Stacey. I look around, surprised everyone hasn't come flying out to investigate the gunshot. King must know what I'm thinking because he answers my unasked question.

"Church is held in a soundproof room. It wouldn't be wise to have the information discussed in there getting out."

"Makes sense, you know, unless the fire alarm goes off or, I don't know, someone gets attacked with a fucking gun," I snip at him. He smiles at me but frowns when he looks back to Gecko. I turn to look, expecting Stacey to have magically woken like they do in the movies but find something far more unbelievable instead. I find Gecko with a gun in his hand, pointing it straight at me.

"This isn't what I wanted, Luna. I like you, I really do, but I'm up to my neck in this. With you and King dead at the hands of Joker's favorite whore, it'll shift the focus enough for me to get everything sorted out. I just need more time." Seems that's everyone's line today.

Betrayal burns through me and yet I know it's a fraction of what my men will feel. Because despite what he says, they'll figure it out.

"Don't do this, Gecko," King tells him.

"I have no choice, old man." I see the exact moment he decides to pull the trigger but so does King. When the gun fires twice in quick succession, I brace myself for the impact. I don't realize King has stepped in front of me until it's too late. I suck in a sharp breath when King's body jerks back into mine as he takes the bullets meant for me. My brain goes on autopilot as I pull my gun from the back of King's jeans, lift it, and fire over his shoulder at Gecko, hitting him over and over in his chest, firing until I'm out of bullets. King turns slowly, wobbling and fighting for balance. I grab his shoulders, shocked he managed to remain standing. Maybe the bullets just caught his shoulder. As soon as he faces me, I know the only thing keeping him up is sheer will. He slides his hands down over my belly, over his grandchild, and crumples to the ground.

"No, no. Stay with me, King." I try to stem the flow of blood but with a bullet wound to his chest and his stomach, there is just too much. At this point, there is more of it outside his body than inside.

"Help us. Somebody, please help," I scream as I push my hands against his chest even as the blood continues to flow through my fingers.

I lean down over him and grip his head with both hands, my tears dripping onto his face and running into his beard.

"Why?"

He chokes out, "Redemption."

"Please hold on a little longer, let them say goodbye," I beg, knowing he can't.

"Tell them I love them and take care of my grandkid." He coughs and a stream of blood spills from his mouth and runs down the side of his cheek.

"Thank you." I press my forehead against his as the last of his breath rattles in his chest.

"Thank you for raising amazing sons and for protecting my baby. They will never know a day without you because I swear to you here and now I will shout about the hero their grandfather was until they are sick of hearing it."

A slight chuckle escapes with a hiss before silence rings out. I tuck my face into his neck, not giving a single fuck about the fact I'm covered from head to toe in blood, and I cry.

CHAPTER SEVENTEEN

"What the fuck?"
I lift my head, expecting to see a sea of leather, surprised I didn't hear them enter.

I don't recognize the face that spoke but I recognize the cut—he's one of two Chaos Demons in the room. I lift my gun and fire, forgetting I emptied the clip into Gecko. The loud click telegraphs there are no bullets left in the chamber. They are on me before I can make my next move. Despite every instinct telling me to fight, I will not risk my baby, especially after King just sacrificed his life to save it. They hustle me out the door and toward two chrome and black bikes. The fairer one climbs on one while the dark-haired one lifts me onto the seat behind him. I look around for the prospects that man the gate, for the first time wondering why the fuck they didn't come running at the sound of gunfire.

Prospects don't attend church and from what I can tell, the gates are never left unmanned. I find my answer lying on the ground in a pool of blood staring back at me with unseeing eyes.

I've never felt so helpless before, knowing there is a room full of people who would protect me with their last breath so close to me and yet they might as well be a million miles away. I wrap my arms tightly around the biker as he starts up the engine so I don't fall off and bury my head against his back. He stiffens for a second before revving the engine and driving through the still open gates. I let the loud noise of it mask my sobs, not wanting to give them the satisfaction of seeing me cry. I won't be another Melly and I won't subject my child to the horrors Megan endured. I need to calm the fuck down and figure out a plan. My nugget is depending on me.

I don't know how long we drive. I zoned out most of the way, stuck in a loop of watching Gecko turn a gun on us and King dying in my arms. When we pull up, I'm surprised to find it's at a small stained-wood cabin with a wraparound porch, not at their compound. Shit, I have no idea if this is a good thing or a bad thing. The plus side is it will be easier to get away from two bikers as opposed to twenty. The downside is it's doubtful the Kings of Carnage will have any clue where I am.

The bikes stop and the engines shut down but the silence that comes afterward is just as deafening. Hands on my hips lift me off the bike and set me to the ground. I look up and see the dark-haired guy looking down at me with an unreadable expression. He's a good-looking guy, I'll give him that. It's a shame he's a raving, fucking psycho.

The guy I was wrapped around climbs off the bike and stomps his way up the steps in his heavy boots before opening the door. The dark biker next to me puts his hand on the small of my back and pushes me forward. I swallow hard and place one foot in front of the other, taking in every detail, anything that might help me escape.

The inside has an open plan concept. The living room gives way to the dining room, which leads to the kitchen area. A large brick fireplace dominates the living room with a large flat-screen TV mounted on the wall above it. Two faded brown leather sofas face it and in front of them is a dark wood coffee table littered with beer bottles and pizza boxes.

"Sit," the dark-haired one barks at me. I move to the sofa closer to me and perch on the end of it. He follows me and sits on the corner of the coffee table, his long legs brushing mine. I lean back a little but halt when the blond sits beside me, far closer than necessary, and starts twirling a strand of my hair.

The dark-haired one snips out, "Start talking."

I look at him blankly. What the fuck is he expecting me to say?

"And here I thought club whores knew when to open their mouths," the blond says at my continued silence.

"I'm not a whore and you haven't told me what you want to know. Let's see, my first puppy was a mixed breed. I swear he had a little bit of everything in him. Cutest puppy you ever did see, though—" I'm cut off when blondie yanks a handful of my hair. Not enough to hurt but enough for me to have to tip my head up, bearing my neck to the guy in front of me.

"Don't piss me off, lady. I might not find any pleasure in hurting women but it doesn't mean I won't. Tell me why Zero and I just walked into a fucking bloodbath an hour after we were told to meet for peace talks," the dark-haired guy asks, his patience running low. I watch him speak and realize with shock he's telling the truth.

"Who called you?" I can't see Orion being down for talks with a club that hurt his sister and ultimately led to his mother's death.

"Gecko," he tells me, surprisingly. I didn't think he would reveal that. I close my eyes, my suspicion confirmed.

"Did you see the green-haired guy riddled with bullets bleeding out on the floor?" I ask him. He looks at the guy he called Zero and has a silent conversation before turning back to me and nodding.

"Well, that was Gecko. Before you arrived, he tried to kill me but King stepped in front of me." My voice breaks off at the end, my emotions still too raw to mask them. Zero loosens his hold on my hair and turns me into him. I struggle, shoving at him to move back, but he just holds me tighter until my shoulders slump and the dam breaks. Fuck being strong. Gecko's betrayal cuts me so deeply I'm surprised I'm not bleeding everywhere. I can't even begin to imagine what Orion, Gage, and Halo will be feeling. Except they don't know. The tears flow freely now as I realize they don't know King died a hero. Fuck. I pull away and this time he lets me. I swipe the last of my tears away, my face feeling tight and puffy.

"I think Gecko set you up to take the fall. If you came for peace, I'm guessing you didn't kill the prospect on the gate?"

Zero answers me with a head shake.

"We didn't even see him. The gates were open and I remember telling Viper it was a dumbass move to leave the gate unmanned and open just because we were coming for a meeting." He sighs, frustrated. "I should have realized we were walking into a trap."

"Orion and Diesel are going to lose their fucking shit. Their father is dead and Orion's old lady is gone. You need to make contact before they blow your clubhouse into tiny pieces."

"You the VP's old lady? Where the fuck is your cut?" They both look agitated now and even more pissed off than before.

"Today was supposed to be the patching in ceremony. I was getting my cut and they were getting theirs," I say softly.

"Getting theirs, they already have—fuck!" Viper runs his fingers through his hair.

"What? What am I missing?" Zero asks, looking between us.

"We just kidnapped the new president's old lady." He barks out a laugh and sits back.

"I knew I should have stayed in bed this morning," he tells me, looking at me intently.

"I'm not just Orion's. I'm Gage's and Halo's old lady too," I tell them both.

"Of course, even fucking better," Viper grumbles, glaring at me. "You know what's going on, don't you?" he asks me, never taking his eyes from mine.

I just stare at him. He is a sandwich short of a picnic if he thinks I'm giving up club business to him.

"Loyalty, I respect that."

I almost laugh out loud at the irony. How the fuck an enemy club can recognize my loyalty when my own have questioned it over and over is beyond me.

"But loyalty only works if people are alive to remember it. Dead men don't talk. Tell me what I need to know and I'll see if I can dig us out from under this pile of shit."

"I don't know who you are and what I know about your club is not exactly endearing me to it. I can't trust you." I think of Gecko. "I don't know who I can trust anymore."

They're both silent for a while before Zero speaks up. "I'm Zero. That's Viper. We're the new president and vice president of the Chaos Demons. We've been back stateside for less than a year, before that we were in the desert. We deployed just after we had patched in when we were eighteen and got out a year ago. Viper's uncles, John and Rock, were the president and vice president when we left but when we came back, John was dead and Rock was in charge. He stepped down so we could step up. A lot changed in the thirteen years we were gone and the club we thought of as home isn't the same place. We have plans to turn shit around but we can't do it if everyone keeps us in the dark."

I'm not sure what my options are here. I could be making a colossal mistake that could cost me everything based on nothing more than a gut feeling but something is telling me to go for it.

So I do. I tell them everything I know about King, Joker, John, and Melinda. I tell them about Megan but leave out everything personal and then, finally, I tell them about Weasel. I finish with what happened in the Kings of Carnage clubhouse before they arrived. They never interrupt me, letting me get it all out, perhaps worried that if I stopped I might never start again.

"Shit. What a clusterfuck," Viper states the obvious before looking at me again and coming to a decision. He pulls out his phone and hands it to me.

"Dial the number then hand it back. I'm gonna set up a meet to get you home and hopefully stop a lot of my brothers losing their lives unnecessarily."

I punch in Orion's number, hoping he can keep a level head, and hand it back to Viper.

He places the phone to his ear and waits. I know the second he answers as Viper looks at me and mouths "Luna" in question. I nod my head.

"If you shut the fuck up for two seconds and let me speak I might be able to let you know—" He's cut off again. I can hear yelling coming from the phone but I can't make out the words.

"For fuck's sake. Do you want your girl back or not?" He's quiet for a second before answering.

"Well, if that's how it's going to be then I guess we'll just keep her for ourselves. She sure is a pretty little thing." I frown at the idiot, wondering if he has a death wish. He pulls the phone from his ear and tosses it to me.

"Talk to that dickhead and tell him what went down. If I have to listen to him anymore, I might just put myself out of my misery."

I place it against my ear and wince, pulling it away slightly when Orion's thunderous voice vibrates down my ear.

"I swear to god if you cocksuckers hurt her, I will personally skin you alive and set you on fire."

"Adonis," I whisper, my throat clogged with emotion at hearing the underlying fear in his voice.

"Luna?" How he heard me, I don't know, but his voice drops to a comforting level, wrapping around me and offering reassurance.

"I'm here and I'm okay. I just want to come home," I tell him.

"I'm working on it, baby, I swear. I will gut them for what they've done. Gecko is—fuck, Luna, Gecko's dead and so is my father."

"I killed Gecko." There is silence on the other end of the line and for a brief second, I wonder if this is it, whether

I've finally crossed the line I've been so precariously straddling.

"He tried to shoot me but King protected me. I shot him until I ran out of bullets, then tried to stop King from bleeding but it was too late."

Zero twirls my hair and I realize it's his way of trying to comfort me, as opposed to freaking me out like I originally thought.

"How the fuck are the Chaos Demons tied to this?" he asks me.

"Gecko called them under the guise of peace talks." Orion snorts at that.

"They walked into Carnage and, well... found carnage. I think they realized pretty quickly they had been set up, so they took me with them."

"Have they hurt you, Luna? And don't lie to me." His voice leaves no room for argument.

"No, they've been fine. They were just trying to figure out what was going on."

"Hand the phone back over, okay? I'm bringing you home. Hold on just a little longer, okay? I love you." I blink back tears and swallow. My hormones really must be all over the place as I've never really been much of a crier before but damn it if I haven't cried a river today.

"I love you too." I never thought the first time we would say it to each other would be in a situation like this but if this all goes horribly wrong, I'd rather he knew how I felt then always question it.

I hand the phone back to Viper and watch as he walks away from me. I can hear him talking but his voice is too quiet for me to pick up what he's saying.

"Tell me about Megan," Zero tells me as he studies the strand of hair in his hand.

"No," I reply, wondering what his fascination is with it.

"She's not Carnage. She's a Chaos Demon," he points out. He has no idea what he's talking about.

"She's free." He stills for a moment, taking me in before his hand goes back to twirling my hair.

"Nobody in this life is ever really free. If she were, then none of the shit that went down at her shop would have happened."

I make my voice hard and cold. "She's the president's sister. She'll be protected at all costs."

Before he can speak again, Viper strolls back, a scowl firmly on his face.

"Considering I have their old lady, they sure went out of their way to piss me off. If I were a lesser man I would feel the need to take my anger out on you." For some reason, I can tell this isn't a threat but a warning for the future. Not everyone will treat me with as much caution as they have.

"Good thing you're not a lesser man," I tell him, making the corner of his mouth quirk up in a smile.

"We're heading back to your clubhouse in two hours," he says, trailing his eyes over my body with a frown marring his face.

"Let's get you cleaned up a bit first, okay?" He turns to

Zero and nods his head. Whatever signal that was, he understood it. He stands up and offers me his hand. I look at it warily. They have been cool with me so far but I would have to be an idiot to let my guard down now. Slowly I place my hand inside his and let him pull me from the room toward a hallway. He opens a dark wooden door on the left, revealing a bathroom, and nudges me inside. I expect him to leave. Instead, he turns the lock before turning on the shower.

"Get in before the water runs cold," he urges me with his arms crossed over his chest.

"I'm not showering in front of you. You can fuck right off."

"You will get in there and clean up or I will do it for you."

I fold my arms across my chest, acutely aware of my heart trying to beat its way out of my chest.

He sighs but turns around and gives me his back. "I'm not leaving and giving you a chance to escape or do something stupid. But you can't go back to them looking like that."

I look down at my clothes and skin and see King's blood smeared all over me. Orion, Gage, and Halo would be like bulls to a rag if they saw me like this.

"Fine, but stay facing the door or I'll punch you so hard in the dick you'll taste your own balls."

He laughs but doesn't answer me. I strip out of my clothes and toss them in the sink before climbing into the shower. I wash my hair and body with a masculine scented shampoo and soap before switching the shower off and snagging the towel from the rail. I step out and wrap it around myself just as I catch the reflection of Zero watching me in the mirror.

"You asshole!" I yell at him.

"Hey, I never claimed to be a monk. You can't put pussy as fine as yours in my face and not expect me to look."

I pull the towel tightly before reaching for a second one for my hair. I wrap it up, ignoring his eyes on me, praying to fuck we can get out of this bathroom sometime soon.

My prayers are answered when he leans over and opens the door, indicating for me to go through.

"Opening doors for me doesn't make you a gentleman when you just watched me shower naked, fucker."

"That's one smart mouth you've got there, Luna. I bet your guys have fun trying to fill it."

"Pervert!" I bite back.

He smiles at me. "Bitch."

"Stop antagonizing her, Zero, for fuck's sake," Viper calls from what I'm assuming is a bedroom. Zero's hand on the small of my back maneuvers me that way. When we get there, the door is open and Viper is holding up a pair of gray sweat pants.

"These should be okay." He tosses them to me. I reach out instinctively to catch them and nearly lose the towel in the process.

Zero closes the door and walks over to the bed. He sits with a smile on his face as he watches me, letting me know in no uncertain terms he won't be turning away this time.

I make sure the towel is secure before slipping the sweats up my legs. I pull the drawstring tight and put a knot in it to stop them from slipping down and leaving me bare. Viper walks over with a large black T-shirt and thick gray socks, offering them to me. I snag the T-shirt and turn my back on them both. I pull the turban towel from my hair before slipping the T-shirt over my head, pulling the towel from around my body and tossing it at Zero.

I snag the socks and move to the bed when the room tilts and I stumble.

"Woah. Steady, sweetheart." Viper's hands on my hips stop me from losing my balance but my head continues to spin. When my mouth starts to water, I know I'm going to be sick. I pull away and run back to the bathroom, emptying the meager amount of food in my stomach into the thankfully clean toilet. Fucking morning sickness. Why it's called that I have no idea. It's not that I get it often but it always comes on when I least expect it.

"Here." Zero thrusts a glass of water at me, a look of concern on his face.

"Pregnant?" he guesses. I don't know if I should continue to hide it but I am so fucking exhausted with all the goddamn subterfuge.

"Yeah, I'm pregnant," I admit. Saying the words out loud still sounds odd on my lips.

"How far along are you?"

"I'm not 100 percent sure but I would say I'm just over three months."

"Congrats. They know yet?"

I shake my head no.

"Probably for the best, given what's going on right now. They would forego any meeting and burn everything down if it meant getting you back."

"How do you know that?" I ask but I suspect that's true. Well, assuming they're happy about nugget in the first place.

"Because it's what I would do," he says softly.

"He's not wrong, we both would. That little baby is their legacy, the future of Carnage." Viper nods at my stomach as he leans against the doorframe. I don't dwell on their words. It's pointless right now and will only stress me out.

"Here." Zero hands me a toothbrush and helps me to my feet. I ignore them staring at me while I brush and try to get my thoughts in order. We're going to be walking into pandemonium. I have to hope they don't just shoot first and start asking questions later. It's a good thing my brothers aren't going to be there as well or—fuck! I really am off my game today. Maybe baby brain is real after all. I glance at my watch and turn, heading toward Viper who is still blocking the door. He doesn't move when I get close so we just stand, eyeing each other.

"Zero," Viper calls. I turn my head to face him but find my wrist snagged in his large hand. I try to grab him with my free hand but Zero snags that one before I can.

"What the fuck are you doing?" I struggle against them.

"Calm the fuck down," Viper barks as he slides my watch

off my wrist and tosses it into the bathroom garbage can. He drops my wrist and walks off.

I don't move for a second as I try to process what just happened. The GPS will work regardless but I wanted to send an SOS in case they were unaware of what had happened. There is no way these guys could have known there was an SOS function in that watch. Unless...

"You have someone inside Carnage," I whisper, feeling Zero's hands on my wrist tighten a little before he lets go.

"Now why would you think something like that?" He smirks at me but that smirk is anything but pleasant.

"Come on now, we have places to be." He nudges me out the door, urging me to follow Viper into the living room. I come to a halt when I catch sight of a second person in the room. I don't remember moving, I don't even remember pulling back my arm and throwing punch after punch until I find myself pinned within Vipers arms.

"Enough," he barks into my ear but the words don't stop me from struggling to get back to Kibble, who is standing in front of me wiping blood from his lip.

"You goddamn son of a bitch." I fight and kick until Viper roars.

"*Enough!*" I still in his arms, breathing heavy as the fight drains out of me.

"They trusted you," I whisper furiously, letting every ounce of my disappointment bleed into my voice. His jaw ticks, his only outward sign of reaction to my words.

"But not you?" he questions with a tilt of his head.

Viper lets go of my arms, sensing the threat to his friend is over.

"I don't trust men who hit women, full stop." I spit the words out and feel Viper tense beside me.

"Who'd you hit?" Viper asks him, his voice deceptively calm, too calm.

"Me. Like the fucking coward he is, he hit me on the back of the head with a gun and knocked me out." He glares at me when I call him a coward but his attention soon shifts to Zero who steps up beside me and Viper.

"And I suppose you had a good reason for this?" Zero asks, crossing his arms over his chest.

"Fucking Joker," Kibble spits out.

"Joker didn't know King asked you and Gage to bring me back to Carnage," I point out, remembering Joker and Gage's conversation when I was pretending to be unconscious.

"Oh, he knew and he was beyond pissed. He heard King telling us to go get you and grabbed me on the way out. He wanted you roughed up so you wouldn't agree to stay. He figured if you were scared of us, you would turn tail and leave no matter what Orion and Halo said to you. He just forgot to factor two things into that equation. Gage's feelings for you and your own lack of common sense," he explains, exasperated.

I flip him off.

"Knocking you out was the best I could do without raising suspicion. If I had done nothing, Joker would have questioned me and I couldn't afford to draw any more attention to myself."

"What were you doing at Carnage? Shouldn't you have left when Weasel did?" He looks to Viper before answering me.

"Joker patched me in as Weasel's replacement. Weasel brought me in as a prospect so he had someone to do his dirty work. Joker knew I was a Chaos Demon and needed me to fill Weasel's role as a go-between. It was working out well until that fucking dickhead went to Megan's shop and fucked us all up the ass." He sits down on one of the sofas with a sigh.

"So Stacey and Gecko were Chaos Demons too?"

He looks at me in confusion for a second before answering. "Stacey was Joker's whore. She had her sights set on becoming his old lady but that was never going to happen. Gecko isn't a Demon, we just have dirt on him that makes him look the other way when it comes to missing shipments."

I shake my head at him in disgust before his words register. He used present tense not past. He doesn't know about what went down today. I turn to look up at Viper in question but he's staring at Kibble with an odd look on his face.

"I'm pulling you out, now. Your cover's blown. Give the Carnage cut back to Luna and put your Chaos one back on," Viper tells him.

You would think he would be relieved at the news but if anything, he looks agitated.

"I'm not sure that's the best idea. I'm so close to finding out where these guns are coming from. If I can just get a lead back to Gemini, I'll be able to find my sister," Kibble tells him, making the plot thicken. I feel like I should be taking notes or something.

"You are never setting foot back in that clubhouse," I tell him emphatically.

He stands up and stalks toward me but Zero stands in front of me and shoves Kibble back.

"Back off, Grim. Luna's right. You will never be welcome back in that clubhouse. It's over," he tells him but if anything, this just pisses him off more.

"What, because of her? I'm sure we can keep her quiet for a little longer. I'm so close, guys, don't ask me to do this. Gecko has a meeting set up for tonight with one of Gemini's henchmen. I just need to put a tracker on their vehicle, then I'm out. Seriously, just a few more hours that's all." He's virtually begging now.

"Gecko's dead," I reveal emotionlessly.

"Shit," Viper bites out beside me.

"What?" Kibble or Grim or whatever the fuck his name is whispers, his voice filled with pain and regret.

"I filled him with bullets a little while ago so, you see, you're too late."

"What have you done?" He charges Zero to get to me but

Zero anticipated that and punches him. Grim stagers back, never breaking eye contact with me.

"I fucking survived, you fucking prick. Where were you today, huh? Tell me, where were you?" I scream at him.

"I was chasing a lead which means fuck-all now, thanks to you."

I walk around Zero, who grabs my wrist to stop me going any further but he doesn't pull me back.

"Whether it was an act or not, Carnage trusted you to have their backs. If you weren't in church, I'm guessing you had been given a job to do."

"Gecko and I were on guard duty while you and Megan were around but, with Megan at the shop with a couple of prospects on her, I knew Gecko could handle you," he spits out.

"Oh, really, and how did that work out for him, huh? Let me tell you what happened, shall I? Stacey pulled a gun on King, Gecko, and me. Gecko managed to get to Stacey before she could hurt anyone but then he turned the gun on me. Turns out he didn't trust you any more than I did and with Stacey becoming a loose cannon, he snapped. He was banking on my and King's deaths buying him enough time to sort his shit out. King saved me. He saved his grandchild," I explain with a hand on my stomach.

"King took a bullet to the chest and one to the stomach, both of which were meant for me. Gecko took King's life so I took his and fuck you, you piece of shit, for being so selfish and only seeing your own problems." My chest is heaving now as I stare at Grim but his eyes are firmly fixed on my stomach.

"You're pregnant?" he asks, looking as white as a ghost.

I don't get to answer before he collapses to the floor and roars, pulling at his hair and hitting himself in the head over and over. I turn to Viper in shock but he's already moving, trying to restrain a struggling Grim. I have no idea what's going on but Grim's anger and grief are palpable and at odds with everything I know about him. When Viper can't calm him down, I take a step closer. Zero's grip on my arm tightens.

"Luna?" he warns but I shake him off and step closer. I get on my knees in front of Grim, whose head is bowed and shoulders are jerking with the force of his rapid breathing. I place a shaky palm on his cheek and suck in a sharp breath when he freezes. Everything in him stills until he tips his head up and looks at me with anguish etched across his face.

I'm yanked against Grim's chest. I let out a shriek and hear Viper curse. Grim's arms band around me and grip me tightly as he buries his head against my shoulder.

"I'm sorry." The rest of his words tumble over each other until they become a tangled mess. I catch Viper's eyes, which look back into mine with a look of sadness of his own.

I don't say anything. I tentatively run my fingers through Grim's hair until his body starts getting heavier and heavier against my shoulder. I feel Zero's hands on my back as he slowly pulls me free of Grim's arms. Viper steps in before Grim topples forward. I realize belatedly he has fallen into some kind of trance, not quite awake, yet not asleep. Viper picks him up and tosses him over his shoulder before disappearing down the hallway to the bedroom. Zero helps me stand up and leads me to the sofa.

I open my mouth to ask a bazillion questions but Zero raises his hand to stop me.

"Not my story to tell." He sighs and sits next to me. "Fuck it."

"Grim, Viper, and I all served in the same unit. That unit had my back and after thirteen years, I consider them family. Viper and I were already patched members so when we left, we talked Grim into prospecting for the Chaos Demons. As soon as we got back, we knew something wasn't right. Viper's uncle John was dead and his uncle Rock had stepped up. It's wasn't a position Rock wanted and was more than happy to hand over the presidency and VP position to us. Perhaps we should have wondered why he was so willing but we just took it as a legacy thing. Viper's dad died when he was a kid, leaving him with just his mom, same for Grim. I never had one to begin with. My mother was a sweet butt and my father was nothing more than a cum shot at the end of a gangbang."

I make a face at that. I really could have done without that information.

"Anyway, long story short, Viper and I grew up in the MC and enlisted just after we got patched in which is where we met Grim. Grim came home from war to find his mother dead and his sister missing. The only lead we had was a name, Gemini, the guy who supplies Carnage with their guns. We found out that Joker had a deal with John and Rock had honored it after John died so we used that as a way to get Grim into Carnage and sniff around. He played the game but he's loyal to me and Viper. What you just saw is a man who hasn't slept more than two hours a night for almost a year realize he might never find out what happened to his sister. He doesn't hurt women and children. I think you made him realize just how far over the line he had crossed."

"I don't really know what to say to that. It's not okay. What he did to me and what happened after because he wasn't where he was supposed to be will never be okay but I have brothers. I get it, there isn't anything they wouldn't do for me."

He nods but before he can say anything else, Viper walks back into the room with my shoes.

"Showtime," he tells me, handing them to me to slip on.

CHAPTER EIGHTEEN

The ride to the compound feels longer than it did when we left. I can feel the adrenaline flooding my system in preparation for what's to come. When we pull up, I see MC members lining the gates, armed and ready. We wait, idling on the bikes as the gates swing open. We pull through and park, then Viper is off his bike and pulling me in front of him before Zero has even turned his engine off.

"Cherub." I look up when I see Orion barreling toward us.

Viper pulls his gun and points it at my side. "Not so fast."

I look down at the gun wedged into my ribs and notice it's mine. My empty one.

"You are not doing yourself any favors, Viper," I say quietly for only him to hear.

"I'm just trying to stop Zero and me getting taken out by a

fucking sniper. But just in case someone gets trigger happy, I don't want to accidentally take out you and the baby now, do I?"

If he wasn't a Chaos Demon, I think I could have really liked him. Zero too.

"Sugar?" I turn my attention back to Orion and see Halo and Gage standing beside him.

"I'm okay," I tell them with a wobbly smile.

Halo nods, then scowls at Zero and Viper.

"You know the chances of you walking out of here are looking increasingly unlikely, don't you?"

"Well, maybe we should just take Luna and go. I thought she meant more to you than your pride, but by all means, stand there swinging your dicks. I've got all the time in the world and I guarantee my dick's bigger."

"Not likely," I mutter.

"Something to say, Luna?" Zero asks from beside me, placing a hand on my hip and snapping the focus of all three of my men to it.

"I said not likely. If you have a bigger dick than Orion's, it would be classified as a trunk, trust me." At that, Zero starts laughing.

Although it wasn't my aim, the hostility of the moment seems to have ebbed a little. Orion rolls his eyes at me but I don't miss the quirk of his lips. I guess he's figured out if I can crack jokes, I really am all right.

"Let's take this inside," Gage barks out before turning on his heel and heading in.

I walk with Viper and Zero toward the clubhouse doors. I spot Rebel, Inigo, Half-pint, and Agro standing guard but nobody follows us inside. I guess they are there in case the rest of the Chaos Demons decide to descend on us.

Walking into the dimly-lit room, my eyes are drawn to the red smears on the floor. Someone has tried to clean up but they've done a piss-poor job. I freeze, staring at the stain. Replaying King's death over in my brain, I'm trying to figure out what I should have done differently when I feel a hand on my face. I look up into Viper's worried eyes before Gage yells from across the room.

"Get your fucking hands off my woman," his voice booms, vibrating over my skin.

Viper ignores him for a second, watching me. "You okay?" I just nod and swallow. He swings his head around to look at my guys, his face like thunder. "Are you fucking kidding me?" His voice is sharp and angry, surprising Gage. I look over at Halo and Orion who are watching us with a look of confusion. Behind them is Diesel and two guys I don't recognize but even from here I can sense the animosity pouring off them.

"You claim to love this woman so much you dragged her back in here without even cleaning up first. You're fucking lucky she's as strong as she is. Most bitches I know would have been a fucking wreck by now," Viper shouts at them.

"Well, we didn't have time for a fucking clean, you know, what with having to remove two corpses and all." I flinch at Gage's words, making him swear.

"Make fucking time," Zero states from beside me.

Gage looks at me with remorse in his eyes.

"Can we just get shit sorted out, please?" I ask quietly.

Halo indicates the large table in the back so we follow him over. Viper takes a seat and pulls me gently down onto his lap. Orion reaches out to grab me but Halo holds him back. Zero sits beside us, twirling a strand of my hair between his fingers again.

We wait for all the others to sit before Viper speaks. "I think Luna should go first," he says, his tone even.

Before anyone can protest, I recall what happened. "King and I came over to the compound thinking you guys might have been finished. Stacey and Gecko were arguing about something. The next thing you know, she's pulling a gun— Wait, where is Stacey?" I ask, remembering her for the first time.

"Well, here I am. Miss me?" We all turn at the sound of her nasal voice. Her nose and eyes are black and swollen. I might have been able to drag up a little bit of sympathy for her if she didn't have a gun pointed at Megan's head.

Every single person at the table, including Viper and Zero, pull out and point their guns at Stacey. I watch her face pale and see her swallow hard. At least the crazy bitch isn't too far gone to realize the danger she's in. Why the fuck she didn't just run when she had the chance, I don't know.

"What the fuck, Stacey?" Diesel asks.

"She's here to tell you everything that went down," she

bites out, eyes on me. "But she's a fucking liar. She's playing you all. You're just too blind to see it."

Huh? So this is her game plan. Okay, I'll bite.

"Everything started going to shit when she got here, not before." She carries on, making me snort. I remember Gecko telling me the same thing. Surprise, surprise.

I bait her. "Losing Orion, Halo, and Gage's cocks shouldn't really be enough to turn you into a homicidal maniac now, should it? I mean, they're good, but good enough to go on a killing spree? Seems a little extreme to me."

"Shut the fuck up, whore. You're no better than me, spreading your legs for everyone."

"I spread them for the three men I love. Count them with me, one, two, three. I'm thinking your number has a couple of zeros at the end of it. Even so, I actually wouldn't have had an issue with you if you hadn't made one. I didn't hold any ill will toward you because these three fucked around. That's on them, not you. Until you tried to hurt me, that is."

"It's not about them. They're nothing. Joker was my man. He loved me but you took him from me." The gun shakes against Megan's head, making her eyes go wide.

"This is about Joker claiming me as his old lady," I summarize. "Stacey, he never wanted me, he wanted to hurt me and hurt this club. That's all he wanted to do for a long time."

She turns her head to Orion, ignoring me as she plays her hand. "She's working with the Chaos Demons. Gecko and I found out about it. We were arguing about getting you out of church to tell you but Gecko said to wait. We didn't hear her and King come in but she heard us talking about her and so did King. He went to pull his gun but she was quicker. She shot King, then Gecko." She stands there giving a pretty convincing story as the tears run down her face.

"I was so scared, I froze, then she hit me in the face with the gun. When I woke up, King and Gecko were dead and I just knew it had been part of her plan all along. She was going to frame me, which is exactly what she was going to do now, when I walked in."

"That story would have been more believable if you weren't holding a gun to my sister's head," Diesel barks at her.

"I just needed you to hear me out before she had me declared guilty," she pleads. I see the two strangers at the table turn to face me suspiciously but I ignore them, focusing on my own men as I speak.

"Well, if that's true, you don't need Megan anymore, right? You've said your piece like you wanted so you can let Megan go."

She snorts. "What, so you can shoot me? I don't think so." I raise both hands in the air to show her they're empty and use my fingers to do a quick signal to Megan.

"I'm unarmed, see?"

"Right, like you were unarmed last time too, huh?" She freezes when she realizes what she said. Before she can react, I nod and Megan throws her elbow into Stacey's throat, making her drop to her knees gasping for air. Diesel stands to grab her but he didn't count on a pissed off Megan grabbing her by the hair and punching her over and over until Stacey is sobbing on the floor. Diesel pulls a still swinging Megan away and holds her tight while he waits for her to calm down.

"Is it always this exciting here?" Zero asks me, bringing everyone's attention back to us.

"Apparently so. Anyway, as I was saying, Stacey pulled a gun, Gecko charged her and knocked her out. We thought we were okay after that but then he turned the gun on me."

I take a breath and search out Diesel's eyes, needing him to hear this.

"King stepped in front of me, he saved me. I pulled my gun and shot Gecko until I ran out of bullets. I tried to stop King's bleeding but there was just so much. He... he told me to tell you both he loved you and he was sorry. I don't remember much else until these two showed up and kidnapped me. I'm getting really sick of getting kidnapped, by the way," I tell everyone, rubbing my temples.

"What the fuck were you doing here, anyway?" mysterious guy number one grates out.

"Who the fuck are you?" Zero asks him, looking him up and down.

The man stands up but the guy next to him grips his arm. "Bates," he warns.

Bates? Oh shit, he's the VP of the mother chapter, which means the other guy must be—

"I'm Priest, this is Bates. We are the president and VP of the mother chapter of Carnage."

Zero nods his head respectfully at that, making them, Halo, and Orion look at each other.

"We got a call from Gecko saying you guys had decided, with King getting sick, you wanted to initiate a peace treaty between the two clubs. Gecko was in our pocket. As much as he tried to be loyal to your club, he had a gambling problem that was out of control. He took payments from Chaos to look the other way when some of your gun shipments went missing. So, you see, we had no reason not to trust him. We knew he couldn't say shit about us without incriminating himself but when we got here, we realized he had set us up."

"That's the bit I don't get. How could he have known me and King were coming over in the first place?"

Stacey sits up, holding her ribs and wincing. "He didn't. He planned to take you out at King's place, figuring it would be safer in case church came out early. He cut the security feed, shot the prospect on the gate and we were making our way over to the cottage when we saw you here. It wasn't part of the plan. He fucked it all up. I didn't have anywhere else to go and he knew it but he refused to make me his old lady. Well, you know the rest."

I stare at her, surprised she spilled all that.

"If I tell you everything I know, will you let me go?" She looks at Diesel but he looks away.

"Sure," I tell her, ignoring the guys.

"That's not your call to make, Luna," Orion protests but I ignore him in favor of Stacey.

"You know I can get my brothers to relocate you anywhere you want but I never want to see your face again."

She nods rapidly.

"Gecko was going to do the drop-off tonight to collect the guns. He was going to shoot Kibble, take the guns, and sell them himself. He figured if he paid off his debts, he wouldn't have to accept the pay-outs from the Chaos Demons anymore. Everyone that knew about the deal would be dead and his secret would be safe."

"He didn't kill you," I point out

"I know but we both know he would have if you hadn't gotten him first." I nod, knowing she's right. Gecko couldn't afford to keep her alive after that, especially not when she had already threatened to take him down.

"Which brings us to you," Halo says, looking at Viper and Zero. "What do you think you're gonna get out of this? I have to say, taking our girl was the dumbest thing you could have done."

"Or the smartest," Zero answers. "Tell me, Halo, what would you have done if you walked out from that room and found me and Viper standing over a crying Luna and two dead MC members?"

Halo's jaw ticks but he doesn't answer. He doesn't need to —the answer is obvious. They would have slaughtered them before they had been given a chance to explain.

"Fine. I'll concede that point but what do you want now?

I can tell this is more about what you can gain from this situation than you dropping Luna off and explaining yourself. You want something," Orion tells him shrewdly.

"We want a truce," Zero tells him.

Diesel laughs out loud at that. "A truce with the club that killed my mother and maimed my sister? You must be out of your fucking minds."

"Nope. We're deadly serious. What happened with your mother had nothing to do with us. Fuck, we weren't even in the country the majority of the time she was there. We met her once but even then it was only in passing. She never really socialized."

"Yeah, I guess getting raped repeatedly will make you kind of anti-social," I translate Megan's rapid signing as she stands next to Diesel.

"What?" Viper looks to me in horror.

"How much time did you actually spend at the clubhouse?" I ask him.

"We lived with our mothers but came around for family shit. There was only a handful of kids in the MC back then and only a couple close to our age. We prospected early at sixteen, for two years. They allowed it, knowing we were enlisting. They wanted us fully patched when we came home. We just didn't expect to come back to the president's and VP's patch."

"Melinda was one of the club whores, right?" Zero asked, making the temperature of the room turn frigid.

Megan starts signing again so I tell them what she's saying.

"She was taken as a pawn in a game she never agreed to play. She was a weapon and a toy, used and abused and she took it all to keep me safe. She killed him, you know? Your uncle. She shot him in the face point-blank. I only wish he had suffered for longer, like she had." Her chest is rising and falling rapidly now. Diesel pulls her in for a hug, wrapping her up protectively like only a big brother can do.

"Melinda was Orion, Diesel, and Megan's mom. King, Orion, and Diesel's father was under the impression she left to be with John when, in fact, he took her while she was shopping."

"What?" Viper appears shocked. He turns to look at Zero who seems just as surprised as he is.

"She was locked up until she had Megan. Then they used threats against Megan's safety to keep her in line."

"And your father never came for her?" Viper looks incredulous

"Yes, well, apparently Joker was very convincing. He had my father believing she ran away and was happy with the Chaos Demons. It's one of the many reasons our clubs stayed away from each other," Orion tells him, a slight mocking tone to his voice.

"Joker! That man was a fucking waste of space," Zero spits out. "He didn't do anything he couldn't gain something from. So what was in it for him?"

"With the double-crossing? Access to more money

through the drugs your club runs. With regards to Melinda? It was nothing but spite that motivated him. He was given free rein to use Melinda's body and there wasn't a damn thing she could do about it," Gage explains.

Viper looks up at Megan and shakes his head. "I'm sorry, I didn't know. I have a vague memory of a little girl with dark curls but you must have been about eight. I think it was the day we were leaving for boot camp. Like I said, we didn't really interact with the kids much but most of them were familiar. You, I couldn't place, but I didn't think much of it at the time." I can see her reading his lips so I don't bother to sign.

"So we're cousins?" he asks looking, dare I say it, disappointed. I guess having family in a rival club will put a monkey wrench in the works.

"No, thankfully. John wasn't my father, Joker was," I tell them for her, watching her fingers shake a little as she signs.

Zero breathes out beside me. "Thank fuck for that."

"Okay, here it is. Viper and I are new to this. I'm not gonna lie, this has turned into a bigger clusterfuck than either of us predicted but the truth remains the same. We want a truce. I have enough rot within my own club to sort out by the sound of things without having to worry about retaliation from outside the MC too."

"How the fuck do you expect us to call a truce with the Chaos Demons after all the shit they've pulled?" Diesel barks out, understandably pissed.

"I expect you to figure it out from a president and VP

point of view and not as grieving sons. I get it, I do, but we didn't wrong your club, John and Joker did. They're gone and you can't hold us accountable for our families' sins without holding yourselves accountable to yours," Viper points out, and I hate to say it but he's right.

Everyone is silent. Even Stacey has stopped crying, clearly anticipating the gravity of the moment.

Orion, Diesel, Priest, and Bates turn their backs on us for a second while they discuss but Halo and Gage never take their eyes away from me. I can't make out their words but I can hear Diesel's angry, harsh whispering.

Finally, they turn back to face us, their faces grim but resigned that this is the best thing for both clubs' futures.

"Fine. You have your truce." Orion leans over the table to shake but Viper shakes his head, making me frown. Isn't this what he wanted?

"It's not going to be quite that easy, I'm afraid. You see, as much as I want this, I don't trust a single one of you to keep your word." The table erupts into growls of anger.

"You can bitch all you want but don't lie to me and pretend you trust me either. It needs to be earned on both sides and that shit takes time."

"Well, what the fuck are you proposing then?" Bates finally finds his voice, clearly reaching the end of his rope.

"We want Megan," he tells them softly, only to find every gun in the room aimed at him. Well, except the one now pointed back at me. Fucking hell.

"*No.* My sister is not for sale and she'll never set foot back in that hell hole," Diesel grinds out adamantly.

"If your sister is there, I know you won't do anything stupid like burn my compound to the ground," Viper replies, unfazed by the guns cocked and ready to kill him.

Diesel grins evilly at him. "It won't stop me from slitting your throat while you sleep."

"Then I guess she'll have to sleep beside me now, huh?" Viper antagonizes him.

"Enough. Megan's not going anywhere so ask for something else," I demand.

"I'll go," Stacey pipes up from the floor.

"We are trying to get them to *not* bomb the compound. You get that, right?" Zero tells her sarcastically.

"It's Megan or Luna. They are the only things you guys give a shit about. I'm not sure about anything other than how much you care for them. Until the allegiance can be trusted, I would like one of them to be my guest. I'm asking nicely but this isn't a request. This is a requirement," Viper says coolly. Orion and Diesel stand and I can see this spinning wildly out of control. I stare at Megan who has tears in her eyes.

"We'll take our chances. Get the fuck out of my clubhouse. We don't use our women as bargaining chips," Orion tells him, his face hard and unyielding.

I swallow down the wave of love I feel for him, for all of them, and for the first time I feel truly protected by Carnage. It's just not going to be enough. These guys are right, the Chaos Demons will never trust a treaty on the words of the two new Kings of Carnage. My baby deserves to grow up safe. I don't want to have to keep worrying about kidnapping attempts and shoot-outs. But I will never ask this of Megan, not after everything she has endured at their hands.

"I'll go," I say in a quiet voice. Viper's body goes solid beneath me at my words.

His voice is soft and tinged with remorse when he says, "No, Luna, you know you can't."

"I'll go." I ignore Viper and say it louder for the others to hear me.

"Like fuck, you will!" Halo roars, standing up and leaning over the table. Ignoring all the guns and all the men, he snags my lips, pouring his love into every movement.

"I told you, I won't let you go, Luna, and I won't, even if it makes you hate me. You are mine," he murmurs against my lips. I can feel the tears running down my face. There's no other way.

Movement catches my eye, drawing my attention from Halo and up toward Megan, waving to get my attention.

It has to be me, she signs, a mix of fear and determination clear in her eyes.

"No." I shake my head at her. Never.

She looks down to where my stomach is hidden by the table and swallows before standing taller, the fear replaced by resolve.

It has to be me. That's my niece or nephew in there. They need to be here with their fathers. I'll never be able to look at myself in the mirror if you go.

"I don't fucking care!" I shout at her.

"What the fuck is she saying, Luna?" Diesel shouts at me, watching backward and forward as our fingers communicate with each other.

I refuse to answer. I'm not handing her over. I won't do it. I look away from her so I can't see her words, which is a fucking bitch move when the person you're arguing with can't yell at you for being a bitch.

"Woah, feisty," Zero comments before my hair is snagged and yanked.

"Megan," Gage warns but she can't hear him. She's standing between Zero's legs, seemingly oblivious to his presence as all her anger is focused on me. She lets go of my hair so she can sign, her movements sharp with her anger.

"Don't do that. Not you. Don't use my deafness to your fucking advantage. You want to argue about this shit, then fucking argue, but don't turn away like that," I repeat her words with a wobble in my voice.

Not everything is about you, Luna, so stop being a fucking martyr. You're staying, I'm going, end of conversation. Don't fight me, you won't win, not with this.

I cup her face with both of my hands, letting the tears run freely now.

"I love you," I tell her, watching her swallow, knowing she never heard those words from anyone but her mother.

She pulls me up off Viper's lap before wrapping both her arms around me and squeezing tight.

"Well, this is touching and all but do you think we can move this shit along?" Bates calls.

I pull away and glare at him.

"Fuck you. What a shame they can't take you instead." I don't give a shit who he is. He moves to stand but Gage beats him to it, standing and facing him down, his black-looking eyes making him look like the devil himself.

Bates throws his hands up, muttering under his breath, but stays seated. Megan takes the opportunity to twist us around before gently nudging me out from this side of the table. Viper reaches up and snags Megan by the hips, pulling her down onto his lap, letting her take my place. Zero reaches over and snags a piece of her hair and starts twirling it. She gives him a weird look before turning back to me.

I don't see anything else, finding myself wrapped up in Halo's arms, his smell enveloping me as I hold on for dear life.

"So we have a deal then?" Zero's voice rings out.

"No, we don't have a fucking deal. Haven't you heard anything we said? We don't bargain with our women," Diesel shouts.

"Fucking hell, I really need to learn to sign," Orion grumbles. "Cherub?" I turn at his voice and see Megan signing at her pissed off brothers. I pull away from Halo and Orion wraps his arms around me for a second before turning me to face Megan.

"What is my sister yelling about?" he asks, making me smile for the first time since this fiasco started.

It's not up to you, Diesel. You're thinking as my brother and I adore you for it but Viper is right, you have to think about this from a VP's perspective. You won't hurt the Chaos Demons if it means putting me in danger and they won't hurt me knowing they will have not just you guys but the mother chapter after them. She nods, indicating Priest and Bates who are watching her with interest.

"You don't know they won't hurt you. How the fuck could you possibly know until it's too late?" Diesel barks at her.

They won't hurt me, she signs, tensing when Viper pulls her back onto his lap more fully.

"Don't be so fucking naïve, Megan!" Diesel grits out.

Her face hardens at his words. "I know this because they just sat here for the last half-an-hour pointing an empty gun at Luna. When Stacey brought me out, Zero leaned forward so he was obstructing Stacey's view of her. He was keeping Luna safe." All the men look at Viper and Zero in surprise.

"How do you know the gun is empty?" Diesel asks. I'd like to know that too.

"I saw him switch out the one he had pointed at you for the one at his back. There was no reason to do that unless there were no bullets to fire."

"Well, fuck!" Halo says from beside me. He walks forward, holding out his hand for the gun, my gun, and surprisingly, Viper hands it over without a fight. Halo opens it up and shows the men it is indeed empty.

"Why in the hell would you come here and point an empty weapon? You had to know if things turned to shit, you wouldn't have time to draw your other one," Priest asks him, looking genuinely curious.

Megan answers for him and I translate without thinking.

"Because they didn't want Luna or the baby getting hurt accidentally if something happened to them."

Everyone freezes, making me realize what I just said. I'm spun back around in Orion's arms to face him. He's now flanked by Halo and Gage, all of them staring down at my stomach, looking at it like an alien might pop out any second.

"You're pregnant?" Orion asks, his voice full of emotion.

I nod, choked up.

He drops to his knees in front of me, in front of his club brothers and the Chaos Demons and lifts my T-shirt before placing a kiss just above my belly button. Gage shoves him aside, making me laugh through my tears as Orion topples backward and Gage takes his place. His large scarred hands almost wrap around my waist completely.

"Hey, little one." He doesn't get anything else out before Halo sends him flying. I can't help the laughter that erupts from me when Halo presses a kiss to my belly.

"Are you guys happy?" I choke out, making them all stop ribbing each other and take in my face. They must realize this is something I had been worrying about.

"This is what you wanted to talk about, huh?" Halo kisses me long and hard before I can answer. "We're happy, sugar, how could we not be?"

"Well, congrats. We'll just leave you to this love fest," Zero jokes from behind us, breaking the moment.

We all turn to face them as they stand. No one is happy about this, despite knowing it's the right thing to do for the protection of both clubs.

"Orion?" Diesel calls out to his brother, looking for any hint from him that he can tell them to fuck off but Orion's eyes are only for his sister.

"You don't have to do this," he says, making sure she can see him clearly enough to read his lips.

"Yeah, I do. It's okay, Orion, Diesel. I'm stronger than I look," she insists, putting on a brave face.

He stomps toward her, making Viper and Zero reach for their guns again, but all he does is wrap his arms tightly around her before pulling back and brushing his lips over her forehead.

"She checks in daily," he tells Viper and Zero who look at each other before nodding.

"If she gets hurt, I'll kill every last Chaos Demon and anyone they have ever had any kind of connection to. There will be no escape and I won't ever stop hunting you," he warns them as Diesel steps in for a hug of his own.

"If she gets hurt, I will hold them down for you to shoot before shooting myself," Viper vows, making me take a relieved breath. I believe him and I can tell by the faces of those around me, they do too.

"I'll pack up some of your stuff and get it sent over to you. If you need me, I'm there," I sign for her. She nods and offers me a small smile.

Viper and Zero each grab one of her hands and walk her

toward the entrance. I follow behind with my guys at my back and stand on the steps, watching her walk away. The rest of the MC looks up at Orion for confirmation before parting to let them through. Viper climbs onto his bike and Zero lifts Megan on behind him. She rests her hands loosely on his waist before seeking me out through the crowd.

I can see the fear in her eyes she hid from me before. I stop myself from running over and ripping her off the bike but it's not what she needs right now. What she needs is faith.

I lift my hands and sign.

You've got this. You are so fucking strong that I'm humbled by you. I have a feeling you're going to bring that club and those men to their knees. She looks at me with confusion, clearly oblivious to the way Viper and Zero have been looking at her.

Time to take back that crown, sweetheart.

She rolls her eyes at me but at least the fear is gone.

Oh, and Megan, I have eyes on you. Take care. Her eyes bug out at that.

What did you do? She signs back as Zero climbs on his bike and revs his engine.

Say hi to my brothers for me. I smile at her as Viper pulls away, making her grip his cut. Without being able to sign, she winks at me before both bikes pull away in a cloud of dust and smoke. I turn and walk back inside, ignoring everyone else as they follow.

I head back to the table. Priest and Bates have Stacey on a

chair between them. If she had read them correctly, she'd have shit her pants but instead, she attempts to flirt with them despite looking like a raccoon. When that gets her no reaction, she slides her hand over Priest's cock. He doesn't acknowledge her but he lifts his head and his blazing eyes meet mine.

"Stacey, get your shit. You're leaving in ten whether you're ready or not," I tell her. She turns to me with a smirk.

"But what if I don't want to? Maybe these boys want to take me back with them." She starts to unbutton Priest's jeans but yelps when he grips her wrist and squeezes it hard.

"Nine minutes," I tell her.

"Oh, come on. Stop acting so high and mighty. You just sold out Pres and VP's sister. You think they're going to want to keep you around after that? And as for that baby—" She throws her head back and laughs. "That could be fucking anybody's. You were gone for two months. No way a girl like you kept her legs together for that long. It's okay, girl, I get it. Sometimes you just need a hard cock, am I right?"

Now, I have to be honest, not much shocks me but seriously, the stuff coming out of her mouth right now is insane.

"How the fuck you hid from us all that you're batshit crazy is beyond me but I've got to admit, I feel like a chump right now." Diesel looks at her like he hardly recognizes her.

"Diesel, can I borrow your phone please?" I ask him sweetly. He doesn't question why, he just pulls it from his pocket and hands it over.

I dial a number from memory and put it on speaker, placing it on the table in front of us.

"Oz's diner. You kill 'em we grill 'em." I look to the ceiling, praying for strength as Halo snorts beside me.

"Oz, can you just try to be normal for five minutes?" I ask him, exasperated.

"Gee I don't know, sis, can you try to not get kidnapped for like five minutes?" he asks in an exaggerated girly voice.

"Give the phone to Zig."

He mumbles something but passes the phone. "Luna?" Ziggy's soothing voice calls over the phone. Thank goodness one of my brothers is sane.

"Can you do me a favor real quick and punch Oz in the fucking face for me?" He doesn't answer but a second later we hear the sound of skin hitting skin and Oz cursing.

"Thanks, Ziggy. Love you. Can you pass me back to the fucktard for a minute?"

There's shuffling before Oz's voice comes back through the phone.

"Was that necessary? For fuck's sake, Luna, I just had that tooth capped."

"Oz." My tone shuts him up straight away.

"Tell me what you need," he asks me, switching from dumbass brother to the soldier he trained to be.

"You have a perimeter set up around the club and house?" I ask, feeling the guys around me stir. I might not have been able to get an SOS out but the GPS will lead them right to that ranch if it hasn't already.

"I'm hurt you even need to ask," he replies. See? Fucktard.

"They have Megan," I say softly, knowing my brothers have grown close to her in a sisterly way.

"Extraction?" he asks, all business.

"No, not yet at least. Just watch and report. If you can find a way to let her know you're there without alerting anyone else, I would be eternally grateful. If you can get her a weapon, I'll get you that date with my friend Cally you so desperately want."

"On it. Timeframe?" he asks. I look at the guys around me. Some look at me in awe, some look at me with nothing but love. I shrug.

"For as long as it takes. Megan is priority number one. Pull in as many guys as you need."

"Done. Anything else?" I look at the guys who all shake their heads but then my look falls on Stacey and the calculated gleam in her eyes.

"Yeah, I need someone relocated. Completely off the grid. Carla still looking for another girl?"

"She'll take her for you. I'll send Greg round to collect her. He'll be there in twenty." He hangs up the phone without saying goodbye, like the tool he is. He's so freaking lucky I love him.

"I said it before but I'm saying it again, Orion, I'm stealing your girl," Diesel tells him, pulling me into his arms.

"Thank you, sweetheart," he whispers. I kiss his cheek before finding myself up in Orion's arms with his hand on my ass and his tongue in my mouth. There really are no PDA rules in an MC. I don't pull away, knowing he needs this. I soak him in, glad to be home and in his arms.

"Does someone want to tell me what the fuck just happened?" Priest shouts.

Reluctantly, Orion slides me to my feet and pulls away, making me groan. Can't a girl make out with her man for five fucking minutes without being clam jammed?

"Luna here has protection on Megan. She'll be safe for sure. There isn't a chance Oz and Zig will let anything happen to her," Halo explains, making me feel warm and fuzzy.

"What about me? Where am I going?" Stacey whines when she realizes nobody is paying her any attention.

"My friend Carla will be taking you in," I inform her, being deliberately vague. I see the calculating look behind her eyes again. I'm not the only one.

"Luna—" Gage speaks but I interrupt him.

I scan the room and see Half-pint leaning against the wall.

"Half-pint, will you take Stacey to get her shit?" I've seen the way he looks at her, he's really not a fan, which means she wouldn't be able to twist him up with the promise of a blow job.

She shuffles over to him. Sore, I'm sure, from the ass-kicking Megan gave her but she goes without protest.

"Luna, after the shit she pulled we can't just let her leave. You can't seriously think she can be trusted," Gage tells me.

I snort. "Not in this lifetime. Carla is a housekeeper. She runs a tight ship. She'll keep her in line."

"A housekeeper? Well, why didn't you say so?" Bates chimes in sarcastically.

"Oh, I'm sorry, did I forget to mention the house Stacey will be living and working in is owned by Pablo Flores? If she tries to leave or better yet, stir up trouble, she'll find herself very dead, very quickly."

"You want to tell me how you know a Columbian drug lord?" Gage stares down at me.

"We recovered his daughter when a rival took her as leverage." I shrug, not willing to go into it anymore. It's none of their business.

"Who the fuck are you?" Priest looks me up and down. I wish I was wearing a bra and dressed in something other than borrowed sweats but it is what it is.

Halo is the first one to answer, a smile on his face filled with pride, love, and respect.

"She's the Queen of Carnage."

The End... for now.

ACKNOWLEDGMENTS

Jodie-Leigh Plowman – Designer extraordinaire. Thank you for my beautiful cover.
Tanya Oemig – My incredible editor - AKA miracle worker, who goes above and beyond.
Missy Stewart - Proofreader and lifesaver.
Gina Wynn - Formatting Queen.
Sosha Ann – My amazing PA and friend. You are one of the strongest people I know, and I adore you.
Aspen Marks - My sister from another mister. You have more heart and courage packed into that tiny body than anyone else I know. Your strength is inspiring, I love you.
AC Wilds - My voice of reason in a world of crazy. No, wait, my voice of crazy in a world of….you know what, never mind. All that matters is that my world is a better place because you are in it. #rideordie #butletsstopforfoodfirst

Isobelle Carmichael - my gorgeous friend, who has no idea just how beautiful she is both inside and out. One day you will see what I see, then look out world.

I am truly blessed to have such amazing best friends. Thank you for all the love and support you give me. I cherish each and every one of you.

Julie Melton, Rachel Bowen, Sue Ryan - My Beta Angels. You ladies are the bee's knees. I will never be able to tell you how much I love and appreciate everything you do for me. I couldn't imagine doing this without you.

Thais Neves – I'm getting choked up just thinking about how much you have come to mean to me. For someone who writes, I oddly can't find enough words to express how much I love and adore you. You have been my shoulder to cry on, the reason why my stomach has hurt from laughing, and the voice in my head that refuses to let me quit. Your unwavering belief in me is humbling. I promise I won't let you down.

My readers – You guys are everything to me. I am in awe of the love and support I have received. You guys are the reason I keep going even on my darkest days.

Thank you for taking a chance on my book. If you enjoy it, please leave a review.

ABOUT THE AUTHOR

Candice is a contemporary romance writer who lives in the UK with her long-suffering partner and her three slightly unhinged children. As an avid reader herself, you will often find her curled up with a book from one of her favourite authors, drinking her body weight in coffee. If you would like to find out more, here are her stalker links:

FB Group https://www.facebook.com/groups/949889858546168/

Amazon amazon.com/author/candicewrightauthor
Instagram https://www.instagram.com/authorcandicewright/?hl=en

FB Page https://www.facebook.com/candicewrightauthor/

MeWe https://mewe.com/join/thecandishop

Twitter https://twitter.com/Candice47749980

BookBub https://www.bookbub.com/profile/candice-wright

Goodreads https://www.goodreads.com/author/show/18582893.Candice_M_Wright

Printed in Great Britain
by Amazon